Praise for *Shadow of a Life*

"Tifani Clark brings an old maritime mystery to life in this haunting, paranormal tale of love, loss, regret, and unfinished business. I'm so glad I read it! It's one of my better reads this year and I highly recommend it. If you are on the fence about reading Shadow of a Life, just jump over that fence and do it. You won't be disappointed!"

Holly Kelly, author of *Rising*

"Tifani Clark has re-imagined ghosts and made them her own. I am excited to see what more she can do."

Nathan Huffaker, author of *Stranded*

Shadow

of a

Life

Shadow

of a

Life

by
Tifani Clark

Shadow of a Life by Tifani Clark

Dedicated to the real Sophia Briggs and her family, wherever you are.

Table of Contents

Shadow

of a

Life

My eyes popped open and I stared wide-eyed at the ceiling, heart pounding. Something had pulled me out of a deep sleep. A noise. I'd definitely heard a noise. I lay motionless, listening for any sign of movement, but the only sounds I heard were the faint tick-tick-tick of my watch and my own heart thumping in my ears. The room was dark except for a thin stream of light extending from the crescent moon outside my open window. *What made that noise? Is someone in my room?*

"Come on, Jamie. Don't be a baby," I whispered to myself. My heart raced faster and faster as I forced myself to turn my head and look into the shadowy corners of my bedroom.

Nothing.

My alarm clock flashed 12:00 a.m. I'd fallen asleep during a spring rain shower, and the storm must have knocked the power out at some point during the night. I fumbled for my cell phone on the nightstand and checked the time. 3:48 a.m. I sighed and sat up, turning on my lamp as I did so. The sudden burst of light blinded me for a few seconds, and I rubbed my eyes to relieve the blurriness before reaching to reset my clock.

And then I smelled it. A floral scent—rose, with a hint of lavender—and it was strong. My heart began to pound again. Something wasn't right. I swung my legs over the side of the bed and stood on trembling legs. Cautiously, I stepped toward my window just as a gust of wind blew my pale green curtains, whipping them against my dresser.

"*Ouch.*" Something hard mangled my foot. I looked down and saw the metal lid of a perfume bottle.

Ahh . . . it all made sense. The wind blew my curtains into the bottle and knocked it off the top of my dresser. That would explain the noise *and* the smell. I bent down and grabbed the overturned bottle, hoping to save some of the contents before it all leaked onto my antique hardwood floors. No such luck. I sighed again. The smell would be in my room forever, or at least until I was well into my college years. I slammed my window shut and climbed back into bed.

It wasn't the first time something like that had happened. In the previous few weeks I'd had more experiences than I cared to admit where I found myself feeling like something wasn't right—or that I was being watched—when I knew for sure that I was the only one home.

I worried that I might be developing anxiety problems. Or worse, that I'd lost my mind. I was Jamie Peters—the tough one. The one that let bad things roll off her back without thinking twice. The one that nothing exciting ever happened to. I didn't want to tell my dad about my problem. He had enough on his mind without me adding childish fears to it.

I knew myself well enough to know that I wasn't going to fall asleep again. I reached for the latest novel I was working my way through and began to read, hoping to lose myself in another world— a world where people *aren't* losing their minds.

"Hey," I yelled after crashing headfirst into someone in front of me.

"Maybe you should try looking up once in a while," the figure responded gently.

I did look up—and saw a stunningly beautiful girl.

"Sorry," I mumbled.

As if my morning hadn't already been off to a bad enough start, the textbooks and papers I'd been so carefully holding as I walked to the bus stop were now scattered haphazardly across the sidewalk. I guess it served me right for not taking the time to stuff everything into my backpack. I bent to retrieve my things and the girl I'd just barreled into stooped to help.

"Thanks," I said, looking up again.

The blonde-haired, blue-eyed girl didn't say anything, but she gave me a fleeting smile before continuing on her way. I watched her retreating figure as she disappeared around the corner and wondered how my life would be different if I looked like her. I wasn't ugly—at least, I didn't *think* I was—but I definitely wasn't gorgeous like the blonde girl. With plain brown hair that fell just below my shoulders, brown eyes, and average height, there was nothing to make me stand out from the crowd. Sometimes I would attempt to style my hair or wear a little makeup, but I always felt like someone trying to cover up a botched plastic surgery. I'm sure most of the problem was that I had no clue what to do when it came to makeup and hairstyles. My dad was raising me alone and it wasn't like *he* could give me beauty tips.

I zipped my quilted jacket as high as it could go, pulled its hood over my hair, and tucked my free hand into my pocket as I trudged the rest of the way to the bus stop. I could see my breath and I lowered my head—this time with my eyes facing forward— to block some of the bitter cold wind from my already reddened face. The weather was frustratingly cold considering it was late May. I'd lived in Massachusetts all my life and was used to crazy weather, but that was just ridiculous.

The school bus was already at the curb when I arrived and I got in line with the rest of the students waiting for a ride to Old

Rochester Regional High School. "I wish I was still in bed," I muttered under my breath.

"Huh?" the boy in front of me, Peter Ashby, asked as he pulled buds from his ears and looked at me expectantly.

"Nothing." I blushed. I hoped my face was already too red from the wind for anyone to notice.

"Jamie, there you are." My best friend, Camille Spencer, waved from the back of the bus. I pushed my way through students and backpacks and climbed over mountains of feet in the aisle as I worked my way to the seat next to her.

"What took you so long? You're usually first in line at the bus stop," she pointed out.

"I couldn't sleep last night and I had a hard time dragging myself out of bed this morning." I sighed. "And, to top it all off, I ran into an Aphrodite."

Camille raised her eyebrows. "A what?"

"An Aphrodite. You know, a girl that's really pretty and . . . never mind."

Camille didn't question me any further and I wasn't surprised. I didn't usually have anything interesting to talk about. She, on the other hand, had a mind that worked a mile a minute and could change subjects faster than I could think.

"Jamie, did you hear about Anthony Dewitt? He got caught smoking pot behind the school and now they aren't going to let him graduate. Everybody's talking about it this morning. You didn't notice my new shoes, by the way. Mom got them for me yesterday. Want a bite?"

I glanced at Camille's outstretched hand clutching a half-eaten Pop-Tart. "No thanks."

Camille and I had been best friends since elementary school and lived only a few blocks apart. Her looks more than made up for my plainness. Her green eyes had actual sparkles in them. Of course, she sometimes wore glitter on her eyelids—that probably helped the effect. And did I mention that she was a flirt?

I'd always been the sidekick. The number two. The tagalong. The "other one." Maybe I wouldn't be the "other one" and maybe I wouldn't blend into the background if my best friend wasn't so pretty. *I should find ugly friends.*

"Heads up," a voice called from somewhere in front of us.

My reaction time was slow and I didn't look up until it was too late to do anything about the football arcing its way toward me. It landed in my lap. For the second time that morning I was yanked from my thoughts by my pile of books scattering—that time all over the nasty bus floor. I jerked my head up to glare at the culprit, but Camille smiled and batted her eyelashes, emitting a giggle that I couldn't replicate even if I wanted to.

I should have known. The football belonged to Travis Andrews. Football season ended months before, but he still carried that stupid thing around all the time. Heaven forbid anyone forget that he was one of our school's star players. Travis was also Camille's date for Saturday's prom. And no, I was *not* going to the dance with anyone. I gathered my books once more, waving away help from Travis who just shrugged his shoulders and continued flirting with Camille, apparently feeling the need to constantly be near her.

It was Friday and, after the weekend, we only had one week of school left before summer break. My countdown had begun. I both longed for and dreaded summer vacation. It was nice having a three-month reprieve from homework and tests, but I always grew bored long before the hot month of August came to a close, heralding the start of another school year. When I was a little kid, I would spend my summer breaks at Smiley's Summer Camp. Basically, it was a glorified day care for kids whose parents worked and couldn't be home to babysit when school wasn't in session. Needless to say, I was glad those days were behind me.

Chapter 2

J amie Peters?" Mr. Hanover called.

"Here," I yelled.

It was dissection day in our freshman biology class—the last period of the day. I have a strong stomach and seeing the insides of something that used to be alive doesn't bother me. Camille, on the other hand, refuses to watch horror movies and turns pale at the sight of gore and blood. One time when we were in second grade she fell off a swing and skinned her knee. When she saw that she was bleeding, she totally passed out. I thought she'd died. It was kind of traumatic for a seven-year-old.

Camille skipped lunch that day in anticipation of the upcoming science experiment. For some reason she didn't want a full stomach hindering her best efforts at a frog autopsy. We had all but one class together, and since we were pretty much inseparable, it was only natural that we were lab partners in our science class. It's not a secret that I'm a better student than she. I try to help her out when I can, but that day I wasn't in the mood to do all the work on a project.

We both donned the unflattering smocks—stained with the remains of countless science experiments gone awry—and goggles that would undoubtedly leave circular impressions around our eyes for the rest of the day. Needless to say, we didn't need to worry we'd be solicited by any modeling agencies in those outfits. Camille hung back as I opened the canister containing the frog. The smell of formaldehyde engulfed us instantaneously and I could feel the little hairs in my nose burn.

"Jamie, I think maybe this would be easier if I take notes while you do the cutting. It'll still be a team effort," Camille pleaded.

"No way, Cam. You'll never get over your squeamishness if I always jump in to rescue you. I did all the cutting when we dissected grasshoppers *and* owl pellets. Owl pellets aren't even alive. It's your turn to cut today," I responded, growing more annoyed by the minute. Call it PMS or lack of sleep, but for some reason I wanted to lash out at her and everyone else that day.

"Maybe owl pellets aren't alive, but the stuff mushed up inside them used to be alive. Who wants to touch stuff that some bird puked up?" Camille whined as she pulled latex gloves over her purple-nailed fingers.

She gingerly inched the tray closer and asked for a scalpel. I obliged, feeling like a nurse in an operating room.

"Just cut it. I'm sure that once you dive in it will be easier than you think," I reassured.

She took a deep breath, gave me one last imploring look, and plunged the knife into the belly of her victim. Frog juice spurted onto the tray and into the air. Camille screamed, threw her hands over her mouth, and ran from the classroom. Everyone in the room laughed. I tried to ignore all of them in defense of Cam, but inside I struggled to hold back my own giggles. What a drama queen.

I sighed and finished mutilating the frog, taking notes as I went. Five minutes after Camille made her spectacular exit from the room, Mr. Hanover approached my lab table.

"Ms. Peters, will you go check on Ms. Spencer? I'm sure she's gone into the ladies room or I'd do it myself. Let me know if she's okay, will you?" he asked as he pushed his thick-rimmed glasses back over the bridge of his nose.

I felt guilty. I knew how much Camille had been dreading the day, but in my bad attitude I made her do it anyway. I went in search of her, heading straight for the nearest girls' bathroom. I stopped in surprise when I stepped through the door. The blond Aphrodite that I'd literally run into at the bus stop earlier that day was perched on top of the counter by the sink, swinging her long slender legs. I'd never seen the girl before in my life and now I'd seen her twice in one day. Aphrodite looked at me sympathetically and pointed toward a graffiti-covered stall. I stepped to the door and tapped on it softly.

"Cam? Are you okay? Do you need anything?" I whispered.

I'm not sure what I planned to do to help. Maybe hold her hair out of the toilet? I hadn't yet added mothering skills to my repertoire. The stall door opened slowly and Camille stepped out, wiping her mouth with a wad of toilet paper and looking as pale as a ghost. I felt bad. Aphrodite must have left while I was trying to talk to Camille through the door because she was nowhere to be found when I turned around. I hadn't even heard the door shut. Weird. Camille shuffled over to a sink and splashed cold water on her face. I offered her a drink from a water bottle I'd grabbed out of my backpack before I left the classroom. She took a sip and attempted to hand it back.

"That's okay." I shuddered and waved it away. "You keep it."

We hurried back to the classroom and finished cleaning up our lab table just as the final bell of the day rang. Noisy students ready to begin their weekend jammed the halls as we hurried to our lockers to retrieve our homework and jackets—blissfully unaware that our lives were about to be turned upside down.

On Saturday morning I woke up way earlier than intended, just as the sun rose over the ocean outside my bedroom window. I slept much better than I had the night before. Thankfully, no creepy feelings or sounds woke me up again. After spending at least an hour trying unsuccessfully to fall back asleep, I got out of bed and crossed the hall to my bathroom. Dad had a bathroom in his bedroom, and since I didn't have any siblings I got the other bathroom all to myself. I guess that's one perk of being an only child.

I took a long, hot shower and only came out when my skin was beet red and shriveled and the water had started to run cold. After pulling my still-wet hair into a ponytail, I shuffled down the stairs. Dad sat at the kitchen table reading the newspaper.

"Good morning. How was your night? I came in to see you when I got home, but you were already asleep," he said.

"I was tired so I went to bed kind of early." I poured myself a bowl of cereal.

"What are you doing this weekend? Any grand adventures planned?" he joked.

"Not really. Cam and I might get together Sunday, but tonight is the prom. She's going. I'm not."

"Oh. I see." Dad twisted uncomfortably in his seat before changing the subject. "Jamie, I know I've been working a lot lately, but we're trying really hard to straighten out some budget issues for next year and I'll probably be working most of the weekend. Do you have any books to read or something else to keep you occupied?"

"Not right now. I've finished everything I checked out during my last trip to the library," I said between bites. Dad hated it when I talked with food in my mouth. "I planned on biking over there this morning. I still need to finish an English report, too. I'm sure I can keep myself busy."

He folded his newspaper and gave me a look mixed with both love and pity. Leaning down, he kissed me on the forehead before grabbing his car keys and briefcase and hurrying out the door to the garage.

Dad, or Randall Peters to his colleagues, was the Dean of Academic Affairs at Newton University in nearby New Bedford. He was a good father and he tried hard, but I think he sometimes hid at work so he wasn't reminded of his loneliness. My mom left us when I was only six. I had a few happy memories from when she was still around, but mostly I just remembered her fighting with Dad all the time. When she left they didn't get divorced—they separated. It only made matters worse. Dad wouldn't even consider dating anyone else since he was technically still married. I think he secretly hoped she'd return for good someday. Anyway, Dad was an economics professor at Newton University, but shortly after Mom left he was promoted to Dean of Academic Affairs and left me with the task of raising myself.

I carried my empty cereal bowl to the sink, rinsed it, and put it in the dishwasher along with the dishes Dad left. Gazing out the kitchen window, I let out a deep sigh. I felt dull. It was as if life was passing me by and I just watched, waiting for something to happen, but nothing ever did.

While in junior high, I read all the Nancy Drew mysteries. I used to think of myself as Nancy Drew. She was raised by her father like me, but Dad and I don't have the luxury of a full-time housekeeper like Nancy did. In our home, I was the housekeeper. I wished that there would be some mystery that would fall into my lap so I could go on fact-finding journeys with my friends George and Bess. In my case, it would be Camille and whichever other friends we could persuade to come along. I wouldn't even mind having a hot boyfriend like Nancy did. I really did live in a fantasy world.

I wandered back upstairs to my room and plopped onto my bed, sitting cross-legged with my laptop in front of me. If I started right then, I knew I could finish my English report before the library even opened for the day. I was writing a report on the John Steinbeck novel, *Of Mice and Men*. We'd been given two weeks to read the book and then another week to write a three-page paper about it. I finished the book in two days. I was pretty sure Camille was still somewhere in the first half.

At eleven o'clock I hit save on my computer and printed the final copy of my report. Probably not my best work, but I was confident it would get an 'A' anyway. I stretched my arms over my head and twisted in my chair in an effort to straighten my back, stiff from being hunched over the computer for an hour. I emptied the contents of my backpack onto my bed, refilled it with library books ready to return, and headed for the garage. At least Dad had gotten me a nice bike a couple of years before. I would have hated to ride the same purple bike with a basket and a bell that I had when I was a child. Talk about a reputation killer. I got plenty of exercise riding my bike everywhere. If there were frequent flyer miles for library addicts, I'd be traveling free for the rest of my life. I think there's even a rut on the sidewalk—thanks to me and my Schwinn— between my house and the library in town. It's not that I didn't like to do anything else but read, I just got bored by myself. A lot. And books could take me to places I couldn't go in reality.

I let myself out through the garage using the keyless entry and headed down the driveway. That morning felt much more like spring than the previous day and my light jacket was more than enough to keep me warm. I even heard birds chirping in the trees. I could feel my mood getting better with every turn of my wheels.

The Elizabeth Taber Library is an older multi-story building with mature trees shading the front of the structure. Its white and gray exterior welcomed me as it always did. I chained my bike to a rack on the rear side of the building and went inside. I browsed through the young adult section, looking for any good mysteries that I hadn't already read a million times. Since nothing jumped off the shelf at me, I made my way to the adult section in hopes of finding something more intriguing.

As I moved up and down the aisles, pulling out books and reading their covers, the familiar creepy feeling returned. I felt like I was being watched. The hair on my arms stood up and I shivered unexpectedly. Slowly, I lifted my head and turned my gaze toward the end of the aisle. I gasped and dropped the book I'd been holding when I saw who was standing there. Aphrodite.

Okay, things were getting a little weird. Other than Dad and kids from school, I didn't usually see people I knew three times in two days, let alone complete strangers. Our town was small so it was odd that I didn't know who the new girl was. Aphrodite disappeared around a shelf as quickly as she'd appeared and I went back to making my book selections, shrugging off the incident. I finally chose three that sounded promising from the descriptions on their book jackets and weaved my way to the circulation desk. You know you're a library freak when *all* the librarians can greet you by name before you even pull out your library card.

There's a cushiony chair near a window in the back of the building that I usually sat in while reading. It had a permanent butt imprint and I was almost certain it was made entirely by my rear end. I could always go home and read, but there I would be alone. At the library, I could read and watch as the world moved by around me. Occasionally I'd even see someone from school and get invited to "hang out." Hey, I wasn't a complete book nerd.

I was pulled from a story of sabotage and blackmail by the sound and feel of my stomach growling. Smells from Grandma's Café and Bakery across the street drifted in through one of the open windows of the library. I glanced at my watch, shocked to see that it was almost one o'clock. It occurred to me that I could read at the café just as easily as I could at the library, except at Grandma's I could eat a grilled cheese and greasy fries while I read. And, who was I kidding? I was definitely getting a milkshake, too.

Chapter *3*

Dad said that Grandma's Café and Bakery already existed when he was a kid growing up in Marion, Massachusetts. Of course, back then "Grandma" was actually alive and running the joint. The café had changed hands many times over the years, but it was still a favorite local hangout. After placing my order I chose a table in the back where I could spread out and not be in the way. There were a few families finishing up lunch and a couple of older classmen from my school polishing off burgers at the counter. I didn't recall their names, but I'd seen them around many times before.

When my order number was called I meandered through the maze of tables and booths to claim my food. As I turned away from the counter, the bell above the door signaling someone entering chimed. Instinctively, I looked up and again found myself staring at Aphrodite. At that point I was determined to find out her real name so that I didn't slip and call her by the imaginary name I'd given her. I didn't have to wait long for my opportunity.

After scanning the restaurant, her eyes stopped on me and she headed straight for where I stood at the counter. "Hi," she said upon arrival.

I turned to make sure there wasn't someone behind me she was greeting before I quizzically responded, "Uhh . . . Hi?"

"I've never been here before. What do you recommend?" she asked with a sunny grin.

"Everything's great," I mumbled.

"Your milkshake looks delicious. What flavor is it?"

I looked down at my tray. Apparently the pink color wasn't a dead giveaway.

"It's strawberry," I answered. "And you are?"

"Oh. Sorry. I'm Sophia. I've seen you around. I think we go to the same school. You always have a lot of books with you."

The words coming from Aphrodite's mouth sounded rehearsed. I stared at her for a minute, trying to figure out why she was talking to me, before I responded.

"Yeah. I've seen you, too. There *is* only one high school in the area so I guess it's not surprising." I didn't count the snobs at the prep school across town.

"Do you mind if I sit with you?"

I finally caught on to what I assumed was her motive for talking to me. I'd dealt with the blonde-cheerleader-type before.

"Look," I said. "I'm flattered that you think because I carry a lot of books that I'm smart and that I want to do everyone's homework, but I don't. I know it's the end of the year and that you've probably been told you won't graduate unless you finish a bajillion assignments before next week, but that isn't *my* problem." The whole thing bubbled out of my mouth before I had a chance to stop it. Again, I wasn't in the world's best frame of mind.

The look on Sophia's face was one of confusion and then it quickly changed from realization to pure enjoyment. She laughed, a beautiful, lyrical laugh. *Of course her laugh is perfect, too.*

"I think you've misunderstood me. I do want a favor, but it doesn't involve school work." Sophia paused, trying to put something into words. She looked up and proclaimed, "I think you might be my soul saver."

My face burned red as I began to back away from her, slipping over my words as I muttered, "Umm . . . I . . . uh . . . think you got the wrong impression from me. I didn't know I gave off that kind of vibe, but I'm not really into those weird super hero role-playing games."

Sophia looked stunned and then burst out laughing. "That's not what it means. *Believe* me. I don't know how to explain it, but I just feel drawn to you. I think maybe you can help me. Can we sit down so that I can try to explain it to you?"

"Sure—I guess. I have a table in the back." My face color returned to its normal shade, but I was still apprehensive. I sat down and dug into my burger and fries while I waited for Sophia to join me with a shake of her own.

"Sooo . . . you think I'm your soul saver. What exactly is that supposed to mean?" I asked rudely. *Geesh, what is my problem?*

"Sometimes people have predicaments that they can't necessarily fix on their own. They need a little push from someone else. That someone else is called a soul saver. I didn't think I had one, but then a few weeks ago I saw you and your dad on the subway in New York and I felt compelled to follow you. I've been watching you and the feeling hasn't gone away so I decided it was time to talk to you."

Dad and I *had* been in New York a few weekends ago. He was speaking at an educator's conference so I tagged along and hung out at a second-hand bookstore until he was finished with his work commitments. He surprised me and took me to a Broadway show afterwards.

"Wait . . . are you *stalking* me?" I asked in horror as Sophia's words sunk in. "That is *really* creepy." Apparently I'd found the source of my so-called anxiety.

"Listen. I'm going to tell you something and you're going to flip out, but you can't. Okay? I mean, you really need to just hear me out. It's hard for normal people to understand all of this."

"Understand *what?*" I was getting frustrated.

Sophia leaned in over our trays and whispered seriously, "I'm a ghost."

It was my turn to burst out laughing. "A ghost? That's the best excuse for stalking that you can come up with? Come on, tell me something believable. How about 'I'm a princess from the planet Jupiter,' or how about 'I raise pink elephants in my garden.'"

Sophia just sat there without smiling. "Are you through?"

I thought about it. I couldn't think of any more good comebacks so I told her she could continue.

"Believe me, when I was alive I thought that ghost stories were strictly to scare little kids . . . and then I became one."

"And when exactly was this?" I asked.

"When was what?"

"When did you become a ghost?"

"After I died."

I rolled my eyes. "When were you *living?*"

"Oh. I was born in 1870. On Halloween, actually. Pretty funny that I became a ghost, isn't it? Of course, back then people didn't celebrate Halloween like they do now. I certainly never did anything for it."

"So if you were born in 1870, when did you die?"

"In 1888, a few days after my 18th birthday."

"Okay, but if you're a ghost, why can I see you?" I asked skeptically.

"Have you ever heard the saying that behind every myth or legend there's some truth? Well, that *is* true, but legends rarely have *all* the facts straight."

Sophia reached across the table and rested the palm of her hand on my face. My body tensed. I wasn't a fan of being touched by people I didn't know.

"Is something supposed to be happening?" I asked as I pulled my face away.

"I was trying to show you that even though I'm a ghost you can still feel me."

"Oh wow. That's impressive," I mocked, "but I have news for you. I could *feel* any one of the other people in this restaurant right now. That doesn't prove anything. Look, I'm not sure why you decided to follow me, but this is all just a little weird, don't you think? You should probably be careful what you walk around blabbing to people or you're going to end up in an institution. I need to leave." I grabbed my tray and stood to go, but Sophia reached out one of her perfectly formed hands and gently laid it on my arm.

"*Please*," she pleaded softly, a desperate look in her bright eyes. "That's why more ghosts aren't known. We don't like to be rejected. Everyone threatens to put us in institutions—as if they could actually hold us there. Very few people really believe in ghosts and even fewer take the time to actually listen. I know it sounds dramatic and cliché, but you really are my only hope. I've been waiting around for more than a hundred and twenty years to find my soul saver and I don't want to lose the only chance I might have. Is there somewhere we can go where I can prove to you that I am what I say I am? Somewhere that is void of people? If you still don't believe me, I promise I'll stop following you and you'll never see me again."

I sighed. "Fine, but I can only talk for a few minutes. I have plans later."

She looked at me doubtfully. "No you don't. Tonight is the school prom and no one asked you. Your dad is working all weekend and the only plans you have involve those library books you just stuffed in your bag."

Wow. That was blunt. Most people who knew me even a little could probably figure out that I didn't date much. It wasn't for lack of desire; it just all boiled down to supply and demand. Why date the friend when they could date Camille? I had guy friends, but that's all they were . . . friends. When we were in elementary school I often played sports with the boys at recess. Sometimes I was even better than they were at whatever game we were playing. I think they still thought of me as one of them even though many years had passed and I hadn't played baseball or soccer in years. I'd been on exactly two dates in my life. One with a nephew of one of Dad's coworkers whom he owed a favor. The kid was so vain that he spent the entire date talking about himself. The other date was when Camille set me up with a friend of the guy she was dating. Again, I was the sidekick. He was weird and kept picking at the bottoms of his shoes and then chewing on his nails. It was really gross.

"Alright." I gave in. "I know a place where we won't be seen. Come on."

As we exited the building I wondered if I'd made a huge mistake. I felt for my cell phone in the pocket of my jacket. Dad had given me pepper spray to carry, but that was safely zipped away in an inside pouch of my backpack. If Sophia turned on me, I didn't think I'd be able to get it out fast enough. Like I mentioned before, I was pretty tough, but Sophia was a good three or four inches taller than me, and obviously a little psychotic. I wouldn't have gone with her except I thought that it might be a way to pull myself out of the doldrums. I *had* hoped for adventure. Besides, odd as it may sound, I felt strangely drawn to her, too.

I took Sophia to a favorite spot of mine by the Sippican River. There's a small grove of sycamores that I used to hide in while I lost myself in a book. I went there often during the warm summer months.

I led Sophia underneath the branches of the tall trees to my "secret hideout." Inside the cluster of trees the ground was still moist from melted winter snow, the air musty and damp. The branches of the trees shaded the area from the view of outsiders and made it an ideal place to pass a few hours on a long summer day. I removed my backpack and sat on it so that I wouldn't have a muddy butt when I stood up. Sophia looked around expectantly and then awkwardly sat on her hands.

After taking a deep breath and exhaling it loudly she plunged forward with the story she'd started back at Grandma's Café.

"Jamie, I know this is odd and it's a lot to take in, but I really want you to hear me out. I'm thinking the only way to convince you is to just show you. I've never shown anyone that I was a ghost before so don't freak out, okay?"

I didn't respond.

She stood up again, breathed in and out a couple of times, and said in a sing-song voice, "Now you see me . . ."

With her words she vanished before my eyes and the world around me was completely silent, except for the sound of my heart that pounded so hard it threatened to burst through my chest. I sat motionless, not knowing what to do, until I heard a whisper in my ear, " . . . now you don't."

I cried out and half jumped, half rolled across the ground turning my head in every direction trying desperately to see where Sophia had gone. A ghostly cry of pain and misery erupted from the branches above me. It encircled the entire grove of trees, echoing in all directions. As quickly as the cry had begun, it ended, followed by the soft laugh I recognized as Sophia's. I looked up to see her perched on the edge of a tree branch twenty feet off the ground, swinging her legs just as she'd been doing while sitting on the counter the day I saw her in the girls' restroom at school.

"How did you do that?" I yelled up at her.

"Do I really need to say it again?" she yelled back.

I sat in stunned silence as she let go of the branch and floated down to where I was sprawled across the muddy ground.

Is this really happening to me? I didn't know if I believed in ghosts or not. It was something I'd never given much thought to. My friends and I would tell ghost stories to scare each other—okay, it was usually Camille we were trying to scare—at slumber parties back in junior high, but it had never occurred to me that I might actually *meet* one.

"So if I can see and feel you, can everyone else? Or is that just a privilege for me since I'm supposedly your . . . your . . ."

"Soul saver."

"Right, your soul saver." I *really* hoped I hadn't made a giant fool of myself in front of everyone back at the restaurant. The last thing I needed was for people to think that I talked to myself.

"Don't worry. Everyone sees me as you do. Well, except other ghosts, that is."

"Other ghosts can't see you?"

"Oh, they can definitely see me, and I can see them, but I see them as if they are surrounded by an aura. A ghost can't hide their true identity from other ghosts."

"I thought ghosts are supposed to be invisible and hide in attics rattling chains and moaning?"

"We can do that, but most of us choose not to. We're left on the earth when we die because we have unfinished business. We refer to the process of finishing our business as extrication. When we finish up whatever we need to, we move on. Just don't ask me where we go next, because I have failed to ever get that far. Some ghosts remain on the earth for a very short time while others are here for hundreds of years. Have you ever heard of little kids insisting that their dead grandma came to say good-bye when they were sleeping?"

"Umm . . . yeah. I've heard stories like that."

"Sometimes the key to a ghost's extrication is something as simple as saying goodbye to someone and then they move on."

"So how long after you die do you become a ghost? Is it immediate?" I asked, my curiosity overcoming the remnants of fear.

"Becoming a ghost is an instantaneous occurrence, but it takes a person a while to figure out what happened to them. I couldn't always be seen or heard by people, either. You have to train yourself to be able to take on the human form. For a lot of us, we can't train ourselves to be physically touched until after everyone who knew us on earth has moved beyond this life, too. Some ghosts can't even figure out how to make themselves be seen in *any* form for decades."

"This is so overwhelming. I feel like my head is on overload right now." I paused before asking, "People say that ghosts can't actually hurt a human. Can you hurt me?"

Sophia smiled and then reached over and pinched my arm. It hurt.

"Oww," I hissed.

"Yes. I can hurt you."

I reached over and pinched her arm. She just stared at me.

"So you can hurt me, but I can't hurt you?"

"Yeah, that pretty much sums it up."

When she saw my worried look she continued, "Don't worry. I have no reason to harm you. *Most* ghosts are good people who just didn't have enough time on earth to finish up what they needed to. Evil people are usually sent straight to wherever it is they go. It's rare that they remain on earth after they pass on. The evil ones who do remain are usually attracted to evil people who are still living, so you shouldn't ever have anything to worry about." She patted my shoulder in an attempt to reassure me. I tensed again.

"I can't even begin to describe how I'm feeling right now." I sighed. "If I'm your soul saver, what do I have to do?"

"I'm not sure. A soul saver helps a ghost to figure out and finalize everything for their extrication. Not every ghost has a soul saver and not every soul saver even knows that they are one. Sometimes they help a ghost without even knowing they did anything. A person is usually dead for a really long time before they find someone that can help them. More often than not, a soul saver is related to the deceased person, although I don't think that's the case in our situation. I really feel like you're supposed to help me, Jamie."

I stood up. "Fine. I'll make you a deal. My head is seriously swimming right now and I want nothing more than to go home and take a nap. I'm still not convinced that I won't wake up tomorrow and realize that you and everything you've told me weren't anything but a crazy dream. If I wake up and you still exist, I'll try to help you."

"I knew you would." Sophia jumped up and threw her arms around me. I tensed and pulled away.

"So . . . do you have any guesses as to what your unfinished business might be?" I asked. "Have you ever heard of the ghost ship known as the *Mary Celeste*? It was found floating in the Atlantic Ocean a hundred and forty years ago without any of its crew or passengers."

"Of course I've heard of it. That's one of the greatest mysteries in all of American history. The *Mary Celeste's* captain lived here in Marion. I'm pretty sure we've studied about it in school every year since Kindergarten. Legend says that everyone on board disappeared including Captain Briggs and his wife and daughter . . ." My words trailed off as realization struck. My heart pounded again and my throat was suddenly so dry I could barely swallow.

Sophia started to nod her head before the words were even out of my mouth.

"You're Sophia Briggs. You're the daughter of Captain Benjamin Briggs. You were on board the *Mary Celeste*."

Chapter 4

I dreamed all night. Only they weren't happy dreams with fluffy bunnies and hot fudge sundaes. At first the dreams were normal, but then people would mysteriously vanish into thin air or turn into creatures I'd never seen before. Other times I dreamed of ships being tossed around on towering waves while the passengers on deck screamed and prayed, pleading for their lives. I'd left Sophia's side in shock the day before. I'm not sure if I even said goodbye to her. I hoped to wake up laughing about the bizarre ghost incident and find that it was just something my imagination had concocted, but everything still felt incredibly real.

I sat up and rubbed my bleary eyes while I yawned. Reluctantly, I swung my legs over the side of my bed and slid my feet into fuzzy slippers. Grabbing my bathrobe off its hook on my door, I trudged across the hall to the bathroom where I splashed cold water on my face.

I entered the kitchen to find Dad studying his newspaper again. It was kind of our morning ritual. Dad was so proper that even at home he rarely wore anything but a suit and he always sat perfectly erect in his chair. I, on the other hand, plopped down on a chair at the table and pulled my knees up into my chest, wrapping my arms around my legs. My posture—or lack thereof—was a constant worry of his.

Dad looked up from his paper with concern. "Are you feeling okay? You don't look so good this morning."

"Thanks, Dad. I love you, too," I said sarcastically. "I'm fine. I didn't sleep very well. I kept having weird dreams."

"I thought I heard you cry out a couple of times, but when I peeked into your room you were sound asleep."

"Sorry. I didn't mean to keep you up."

"Don't worry about it, honey. I feel bad that I've been so busy lately. Try to get some more sleep while I'm gone today. I should be able to make it home by early evening and maybe we can go to dinner together."

"I'd like that." I gave him the best smile I could get out at that time of the morning. It wasn't big.

He left for work and I shuffled back upstairs to get dressed. My eyes were so bloodshot that I figured it hopeless to even attempt makeup. Instead, I grabbed the book I'd started reading the day before, pulled the down comforter off my bed, and trudged downstairs to the living room where I promptly curled up on the couch.

Much of my time not in school or doing homework is spent just like that—huddled under a warm blanket with a book. Apparently seeing me like that annoys my dad because he constantly tells me I need to get up and move around more. These comments are usually accompanied by a lecture on how getting my blood circulating would warm me up and blah, blah, blah . . . *Does he expect me to run laps around the house or something?*

I must have dozed off at some point because I awoke to someone shaking my shoulder. I opened my eyes to find a smiling Sophia peering back at me. I jumped. And then I screamed.

24

"How did you get in here?" I yelled. The words were out of my mouth before I realized how dumb they sounded.

"Sorry. I didn't mean to scare you. I thought I was done having to pretend I was normal around you. Next time I'll knock on the door. I promise."

I sat up, but kept the comforter wrapped around me. "I guess yesterday wasn't all a bad dream, huh?"

"Nope."

"Fine." I sighed reluctantly. "Where do we start? What 'unfinished business' do I need to help you with?"

"I have no idea. That's why I need *you*, remember? I've spent years trying to answer that question."

"It's got to have something to do with the boat you were on when you died, doesn't it?"

"I didn't die on the *Mary Celeste*. I was two when I sailed with my parents for Italy all those years ago, but I died when I was eighteen. Didn't I mention that already?"

"I don't understand. The way I always heard the story was that something happened on the ship so everyone piled into a lifeboat, but you were all washed away in a storm. The *Mary Celeste* was found abandoned by another boat days later and hauled to someplace in Europe without any of the original crew on board."

"Remember how I said that behind every myth or legend there's some truth?" Sophia asked.

"I guess so."

"Well, that's the case in my situation. When someone becomes a ghost they can distinctly picture every memory of their entire life, even the moments when they were just babies. No two-year-old is going to remember anything for very long in real life, so it wasn't until after I'd died that I knew who I was and that there was a mystery surrounding my life."

"Maybe you should just tell me the story from the beginning. I'll try not to interrupt."

Sophia sat on the couch next to me and pulled some of my blanket over to her. Her face took on a somber look as she spoke.

"My dad was a seaman all his life. It was something that was in his blood. When he was in his mid-twenties he married my mother, Sarah Cobb. They were cousins."

"Ewww," I grimaced, forgetting my promise not to interrupt.

"Don't worry; it was completely normal back then. Anyway, my mother's father—my grandfather—was a preacher, so my parents were religious. They were good people, Jamie."

I nodded.

"I have an older brother. His name was Arthur, and he was born here in Marion a few years before me. I graced the world with my presence on October 31, 1870. Arthur adored me. He was always willing to entertain me when Mother needed a break. My only memories of him are truly happy ones."

"Why didn't Arthur go with your family on the *Mary Celeste*?"

"Because Mother insisted he stay home so that he wouldn't miss school." Sophia's countenance suddenly brightened. "Speaking of my mother, she was absolutely enchanting. I wish you could have met her, Jamie. I wish *I* could have spent more time with her for that matter. She had such a sweet personality that everyone who met her loved her instantly. She loved music. Father said she could sing like a bird." Sophia laughed.

There was so much sadness behind the sparkle in Sophia's eyes that I felt myself feeling even more drawn to her than I had the day before. It felt as if we'd already known each other for a lifetime.

"Anyway, about the time of my second birthday, we set sail for Staten Island where Father was to receive a load of alcohol and sail with it to Italy. The night before we left, my parents met with Captain Morehouse for dinner. He was the captain of a ship by the name of *Dei Gratia* and a friend of my father. Captain Morehouse was sailing to somewhere in Europe, too. I don't recall where exactly and it's not important. They all expected to see each other in Italy in the weeks ahead."

"Isn't Captain Morehouse the one who found the *Mary Celeste* sailing by itself?"

Sophia nodded. "Yep. Good memory. I take it you've heard the story before?"

"Many times. It's fascinating."

"We spent the first two and a half weeks of the crossing trying to keep ourselves entertained. Mother emptied out our large sea chest and I would sit inside it and play. She would pretend she didn't know where I was and I would sit in the bottom of the case giggling. It was a very peaceful time. Unfortunately, the morning of November 25th brought choppier seas and a little bit of rain."

"So there *was* a big storm? Is that what happened to your family?" I had a hard time waiting for Sophia to get to the part of her story where they all "disappeared."

"Well, as you seem to know, one theory about the mystery of the *Mary Celeste* was that we were caught in a big storm. Yes it was stormy, but it wasn't anything that concerned my father much. He'd sailed in seas and storms like that many times before. The rain stopped and the fog was starting to clear so my mother took me to the upper deck to get some fresh air. About midday, one of my father's crewmen started yelling. Apparently, when the mist cleared they realized we were headed right into the path of another ship. As we sailed closer the crew noticed that this ship had its sails down and was flying a white flag."

"A white flag? What does that mean?" I interrupted again.

"It means the same thing on a ship as it does on land. If someone's waving a white flag it means they surrender, or that they're peaceful," she answered.

"Oh. Gotcha. You can continue now."

"Yes, ma'am." Sophia winked at me. "We stopped a short distance from the ship and were then able to read its name—*The*

Aurabelle. None of the crew recognized it, but it appeared to be a merchant ship of some sort. A lifeboat was lowered into the water from the *Aurabelle* and some of their crew paddled toward us. They stopped and yelled to my father, saying that the storm had damaged their ship and they were taking on water. Father, being the good man that he was, graciously welcomed them aboard the *Mary Celeste*. They had a woman with them and Mother quickly took care of her, offering a blanket and tea. The captain of the *Aurabelle* introduced himself as Jeremiah Goodwin. He told father they were sailing from Portugal to the Caribbean. There was no reason to suspect anything to be amiss so his story wasn't questioned further, and soon all the crew of the *Mary Celeste* had gathered to hear the tales of this seemingly jovial man."

Here, Sophia paused and took a deep breath. Her countenance darkened as she continued with her story. "It wasn't long before Jeremiah revealed that their ship was actually in fine shape. He and all of his crew—including the woman—pulled out guns and announced that they were taking command of the Mary Celeste and her cargo."

I gasped. "You mean they were pirates?"

Having studied the mystery of the *Mary Celeste* for most of my life, I knew there were many theories as to what happened to her crew. Some thought there'd been a great storm, others believed there to be an undersea earthquake of sorts. Some crackpots insisted the crew had all been abducted by aliens. Even Sir Arthur Conan Doyle wrote a story about his own theory before he became famous for writing stories about Sherlock Holmes. Piracy had been suggested at the time, of course, but it was quickly disregarded. Apparently that was a bad idea.

Sophia continued. "I doubt the word pirate ever even crossed my father's mind when he let Captain Goodwin and his crew on board the *Mary Celeste*. After all, pirates did most of their dirty work hundreds of years before I was even born. They were definitely a rarity at that time and in that area."

"What happened after they pulled out guns?" The tone of my voice was rising. By that point in the story I was on the edge of the couch hanging on every word coming out of Sophia's mouth. *Could all the crew of the* Mary Celeste *have survived? If Sophia lived to be eighteen, what happened to everyone else on board?*

"Everyone was stunned. No one knew what to do or what was going to happen. I remember my mother clinging to me, but I think at the time I was oblivious to what was going on around me. My father's crew was made up of loyal men, and when Captain Goodwin tried to tie up my father they retaliated and attacked him. Shots were fired. My mother screamed, and I cried inconsolably. When the smoke cleared, two of Father's crewmen were lying dead on the deck. Captain Goodwin's entire demeanor changed. He was enraged. He forced my family and the rest of Father's crew onto his lifeboat. Just before they began lowering the boat with all of us into the water, the woman yelled for him to stop. Turns out she was Elsa Goodwin—Jeremiah's wife. She and her husband whispered to each other for a minute and then he came over and . . . and . . . ripped me from my mother's arms."

Sophia's voice cracked, but she continued on, not looking up from her hands as she spoke.

"I was still crying hysterically, but Elsa held me close and watched over the edge of the *Mary Celeste* as the lifeboat was lowered to the water. I could hear my parents crying. The sound of mourning filled the sea. My father was yelling and pleading with Jeremiah. I think he even tried to climb back up the ropes, but Captain Goodwin just looked over the edge of the ship's deck, aimed his pistol, and fired. Father was instantly silent, but my mother's screams have haunted me ever since I died and my childhood memories returned. There was another shot fired, and then she too was silent. It was the last time I saw my parents, swallowed up by the unforgiving ocean."

I glanced at Sophia when she stopped talking. There were silent tears streaming down her face and suddenly she didn't look so perfect anymore. Instead of feeling jealous of her as I had the first few times I saw her, I pitied her, and something inside me ached for the pain she'd been forced to endure.

I stood up, surprised at how stiff my body was. My muscles were so tense from anxiety that I could hardly move. I took a couple of tissues from a box on a side table and offered them to her. The revelation that Sophia was a ghost was nothing compared to how my mind felt just then. I couldn't believe I'd heard the true story of the *Mary Celeste*.

I convinced Sophia that we should take a break from the living room and head outside to the patio. After what I'd just heard, I needed some fresh air. I grabbed a bag of chips and a couple of sodas as we passed through the kitchen on our way to the patio door. I offered the bag of chips to Sophia first, but she politely turned them down.

She smiled slyly. "Actually, ghosts don't really need to eat. Sometimes we do just to keep up appearances, but it isn't necessary and we don't really taste the difference between one food and another. It gets kind of old chewing on stuff that tastes like paper when it isn't doing you any good."

"Really? If you don't need to eat, do you need to sleep?"

"No, but we can . . . sort of. We have a way of temporarily turning our minds off and falling into a trance-like state, but it's not really sleeping. I do it just to help pass the time, though. I try to live as human of a life as I can, but I never actually change."

Suddenly, a crazy thought entered my mind. I really hoped it wasn't true. "If ghosts are real, what other mythical beings exist? Please tell me there aren't vampires or werewolves or zombies roaming around out there."

Sophia laughed. I could tell she was feeling better. "Honestly, I don't know. I've never met one of those characters, but that doesn't mean they don't exist. It's highly doubtful, Jamie."

I got up and moved to the patio swing, rocking back and forth slowly. "So why did what's her name, Captain Goodwin's wife, want to save you if they got rid of everyone else? It obviously wasn't for ransom."

"Elsa. Her name was Elsa. Although for most of my life I called *her* Mother."

"They . . . *kept* you?"

"Apparently she wanted a child, but they hadn't been very successful in their attempts to conceive. When she realized that a perfectly healthy child was about to be sacrificed, she stepped in."

"You were raised by the couple who killed your family?" I asked incredulously.

Sophia nodded.

"I'm still confused. If Captain Goodwin wanted the cargo and ship, why did he just leave it out in the ocean for the *Dei Gratia* to find days later?"

"Captain Goodwin had more crew members hidden below the decks of the *Aurabelle*. The plan was to divide the crew between the two ships and sail west to the Azores Islands. They would secretly change the name and paperwork of the boat and then sail both of them into the Caribbean, which was much more familiar territory to Jeremiah. This is the part of the story where the modern explanation of what happened to the *Mary Celeste* most closely resembles what *really* happened.

"The crew of the *Aurabelle* began exploring the rooms and cargo area of the *Mary Celeste*. They of course had to sample the alcohol in the barrels below deck even though I don't think it was the kind of alcohol that was meant to be ingested. Somehow they unknowingly caused some of the barrels to leak or something, because the next day fumes were coming from below deck. Some of the crew got sick and everyone was nervous and scared. Seamen tend to be overly superstitious and they thought they were being poisoned and cursed for their piracy. No one wanted to remain on board. The crew went down in the lifeboat of the *Mary Celeste* and kept themselves tied to her to see if they could wait it out, thinking the fumes would dissipate. While they were in the lifeboat something made a loud noise from the ship and they were so scared that they didn't dare board her again. Everyone returned to the *Aurabelle* and continued on their way, leaving the *Mary Celeste* to drift around on her own. I'm not positive, but I'm pretty sure that was Captain Goodwin's first—and last—try at piracy."

"What made the loud noise?"

"I don't know. My memories are only of things that I actually witnessed or heard. No one was on the boat at the time so no one knows what the noise was."

"This is by far the craziest story I've ever heard. You must have been terrified."

"Remember, I didn't have any recollection of any of this until my childhood memories returned. When I found out, I was so angry with Jeremiah and Elsa that I spent years haunting them. I couldn't ever show myself to them since I'd known them when I was alive, but I definitely gave them a lot of sleepless nights," Sophia said proudly. "After six or seven years I finally got bored and left. I took myself on a tour of the United States and I've been all over the world. No one can say that Sophia Briggs doesn't know how to party. But I finally decided it was time to figure out what I needed to do to be extricated. I thought if I retraced the steps in my life it would all make sense. Here we are years later and I'm *still* trying to figure it out."

I thought for a minute. "Okay, the best thing for me when I'm trying to figure something out is to make a trip to the library. I guarantee they have every book, paper, and pamphlet ever published about the *Mary Celeste* and your family. I think I should read up on the history of it all and see if I can come up with any more unanswered questions or—" We were interrupted by the ringing of my doorbell. I slipped back through the sliding glass door, walked hurriedly into the living room, and opened the door to find Camille standing on my porch. *Crap.*

Chapter 5

"Hey, look at that. You *are* alive. Would it hurt you to answer a call or a text once in a while?" Camille said as she strolled by me into the house and plopped down on the sofa.

I felt my pockets and realized I hadn't grabbed my cell phone off my dresser when I'd gotten dressed that morning. I'd been so preoccupied with Sophia all day that I hadn't even noticed it was missing.

"Sorry. I left my cell upstairs, I guess. I've been hanging out down here all morning. How was the dance last night?" I knew that if I redirected the conversation towards Camille, she would do most of the talking and forget that she was supposed to be mad.

"The dance was a-maze-ing."

"Tell me about it."

"Well, first let me say that I looked stunning in the red dress you helped me pick out. You were right about the color. It definitely made me stand out in the crowd. And, I'm not going to lie—Travis looked pretty darn good in his tux."

Camille handed me her phone so that I could see a picture of the smiling couple standing on her parent's front porch. The pair wore matching white roses pinned to their chests. She *did* look amazing and I was happy for her. Maybe someday I would go to a dance . . .

"Trav picked me up at six and took me to dinner before the dance. We went to a place that had candles on every table and those fancy cloth napkins. I felt so mature." Camille giggled.

"Anyway, we got to the dance around 8:30. Trav's a pretty good dancer—for a football player. I could totally tell that some of the other girls were jealous because they kept watching us *all* night. I think their own dates were starting to get mad."

"If I know you, Cam, you loved that part of it."

"Of course. That goes without saying. The best part of the night, though, was when he took me home." Camille blushed.

"Let me guess, he kissed you?"

"Well, duh."

I rolled my eyes and laughed.

"I think we're going to be seeing a lot more of each . . ." Camille's words trailed off as she stared past me toward the kitchen with an odd expression.

I turned to see Sophia standing in the doorway.

"Oh. Umm . . . Camille, this is my . . . uh . . . my . . . umm . . ." I didn't know what to call her.

"Hi. I'm Sophia. I'm Jamie's friend." Sophia walked into the room and stuck her hand out to Camille.

"Uh, nice to meet you," Camille said slowly as she shot me a quizzical look.

I didn't know what to say. I couldn't exactly give up Sophia's secret to Camille on their first meeting.

Sophia saved me again. "I'm new in town and I met Jamie at the library yesterday. We started talking and I invited myself over today."

This appeased Camille who I think chose to just ignore Sophia for the time being. She turned back to me. "If you would have been answering your texts, you'd know that I was trying to invite you to go to a late lunch this afternoon."

"You know that normally I would, but I kind of already made plans with Sophia. I'm sorry. Maybe we can go for ice cream after school tomorrow?"

"Sure. Whatever. I guess I better be getting back home. You guys have fun." Camille began walking to the door. I could tell her feelings were hurt.

I felt bad, but I didn't think she would enjoy an afternoon spent at the library researching one random subject. If I told her of Sophia's true identity, she would probably freak out and stop talking to me anyway.

"Goodbye. I'm glad you had fun last night," I yelled after her. She didn't respond as she quietly shut the door behind herself.

"Have you always let her run your life?" Sophia asked.

"What?"

"Camille. She always decides what the two of you will be doing. In all the weeks I was watching you, I don't think I ever saw the two of you do something because *you* wanted to."

It gave me the creeps to think of Sophia watching me for weeks, but I was even more stunned that she'd picked up on the inner workings of our relationship so quickly. Truthfully, Camille *did* usually make all the major choices in our friendship, but it was also true that I didn't really care. When something really mattered to me, I stepped in and said something. Camille was good enough to let me get my way on those rare occasions, but I didn't know how to explain all of this to Sophia who hadn't been with us since the first grade. I probably should have defended Camille, but I didn't.

"Let's get going if we're going to get any work done today. The library opens late and closes early on Sundays. I'm going to have to ride my bike since not all of us can fly." I paused. "*Can* you fly?"

Sophia didn't say anything, but rose up and slowly floated across the room. I rolled my eyes. "Show off."

Just as I expected, the library was a treasure trove of information about the *Mary Celeste*, the Briggs family, and their tragic ending. After spending a couple of hours searching through material, we checked out a bag full of books at the circulation desk and headed back to my house. I opened the garage door and saw that my dad's car was back in its place. Great. What would I tell *him*?

"Dad," I called as we entered through the kitchen.

We found him in the living room watching a Sunday afternoon political news program. He actually had his tie loosened.

Dad stood and reached his hand out to Sophia immediately. "Hello. I'm Jamie's father. And you are . . .?"

Sophia responded just as easily as she had with Camille earlier in the day. I guess situations like those make decades of practicing to be 'normal' come in handy. I felt like everyone was looking at Sophia and I wherever we went, wondering what was wrong with her, but in reality she was as 'normal' as any other teenage girl in town.

"My name is Sophia. I'm visiting Marion with my parents for the summer. They're thinking of buying a second home here. Jamie and I met at the library yesterday and she graciously offered to introduce me to the town." Sophia beamed.

"Did she? Well, my daughter has lived here her entire life and I don't think you could find a better tour guide."

"I'm sure we'll have fun together, Mr. Peters."

Dad turned to me. "Are you still interested in going to dinner tonight? I made sure I left the office early enough to go for Chinese if you wanted."

"Mmm. That sounds perfect. Sophia needs to be getting back home anyway. Right, Sophia?" I hinted.

Sophia nodded and headed for the door. "I'll call you tomorrow after you get out of school, okay?"

"Sounds great. Have a good evening."

It dawned on me that I didn't know where Sophia went at night. Did she have an actual home? I had a feeling that she was probably still lurking somewhere in the shadows and I hoped she wouldn't follow my dad and me wherever we went that night. The thought gave me the heebie jeebies and I shivered as cold tendrils crawled up my spine.

There was a quaint little Chinese restaurant called Dragon Star near the waterfront that Dad and I frequented. The food was authentic because the owners were actually from China. Sometimes we had a hard time understanding them when they spoke to us since English wasn't their first language. I ordered my favorite sesame chicken with sides of steamed rice and an egg roll, and Dad opted for a couple of the spicier options on the menu. We lingered over our dinner that night and Dad made a sincere effort to talk to me. He'd probably clued-in to the mood I'd been stuck in, but I didn't want him to worry about me. Things were definitely changing in my life and the summer was starting to look up. My mind continuously wandered during our meal and I think that made Dad worry more. I wondered how open he was to the idea of spirits floating around our town.

"Dad," I finally asked. "Do you believe in ghosts?"

It's hard to surprise my calm and proper father, but I could tell he was taken aback by my comment. He set his chopsticks down and cleared his throat. He stretched out his hands and looked at them before refolding them in his lap and answering my question.

"Well, I don't know that I believe in ghosts of the sort you see in movies and such, but I think there's a good chance that a type of spirit can linger when people pass on. I don't think the spirits can actually do anything that would affect the living, but I believe they are sometimes there." He creased his brow and looked at me. "Why the sudden interest in the occult?"

"No special reason. I just read a book about ghosts recently and it made me wonder what I believed."

We sat in an uncomfortable silence for a few moments before I cleared my throat and changed the subject. "It sure is gorgeous weather today. I think I'm finally ready to put my winter clothes in storage for a few months."

"The forecast says it will be sunny all week. I think we're done with the cold weather for the season." Dad played along. "Sophia seemed nice. Do you have any plans of getting together with her again?"

"I think so. We did hit it off. Her parents plan on staying here for the entire summer before they decide to buy or not."

"Maybe we can invite her family over for a summer barbecue sometime to welcome them to town. Does she have any siblings?"

I was starting to get nervous with the subject and before I could think I blurted out, "She had an older brother, but he's dead now."

"Oh. That's really unfortunate. Was it recent?"

"No. I think it was a long time ago. She doesn't really remember him much. I don't know if her parents would want to come over, though. She says they're pretty private people." The lies continued to march out of my mouth.

"Huh . . . well, we'll have to see as the summer progresses."

Dad knew I was hiding something, but he let the subject drop. He left a tip on the table and we went for a walk near the water, looking out at Buzzards Bay, before returning to our car. It was nice to spend time with Dad. The older I got, the fewer opportunities I had to do it.

By the time we got home the sun had set and I was safely able to excuse myself to my room without causing any suspicion. I *really* wanted to get started on my research. As I reached the top of the stairs, I could see a faint glow coming from under my door. I didn't remember leaving my lights on. I slowly opened the door and peered inside.

"Hey. You're back," Sophia sang out.

I jumped. For the umpteenth time in the last two days it felt like my heart would stop.

"I thought you said you'd knock the next time you came over," I whispered while looking behind me down the hallway. The last thing I needed was for Dad to find out that Sophia was in my room.

"I told you I'd knock the next time I came over, but technically I never left."

"I saw you go out the door."

"Noooo. You saw me *disappear* at the door. I've been up here sorting through all this stuff we got at the library."

I shrugged my shoulders and entered the room, shutting and locking the door behind me.

"Where do you want to start?" Sophia asked. "I've been marking pages that I thought were fairly accurate."

"Let's start with those pages then, I guess." I sat down next to her on my bed and we began to quietly read. Sometimes we would comment on something or jot down a note. Other times we would burst out laughing when we came across particularly funny explanations for the disappearance of the *Mary Celeste's* crew. We read until my neck was so stiff and my shoulders so hunched that I could barely move. I looked at the clock and was shocked to see that it was almost 1:00 a.m. I'd been so engrossed in my reading that I hadn't even heard Dad come up for bed. If I knew my dad, he'd walked up the stairs promptly at 10:00 p.m.

I sighed and tossed the book in my hand to the foot of my bed. "I think I'm going to call it quits for tonight. I can barely see straight anymore and it might not mean much to you, but I've still got another week of school left. I don't want to be a zombie all day tomorrow."

"I really do appreciate your help," Sophia said. "I'll leave. And I promise I won't sneak in while you're sleeping."

Somehow her words weren't all that reassuring. We quickly organized the books so that we could return to them later and I fell deeply into a much needed sleep as soon as my head hit the pillow.

Chapter 6

I felt like I had an extra spring in my step the next day. All of a sudden my life had purpose and meaning. For the first time in a long time I looked forward to summer break.

Camille immediately noticed the change in me. "What's with you today? You seem bouncy."

"I dunno. I guess I'm just happy that we're almost through with school."

"Yeah, but we have tests today."

"Some of us have actually been studying for the tests. I'm not concerned about any of them."

Camille rolled her eyes and slammed her locker door shut. We walked side by side to our first period class. She'd been particularly quiet on the bus that morning and I guessed that she was still angry about being rejected on Sunday.

First period was English and I handed in the assignment I'd finished writing on Saturday. Thankfully I'd finished it during the first part of the weekend. If I'd met Sophia first, I don't think I would have gotten around to it.

The rest of the day dragged on without anything eventful happening. I found myself continuously looking over my shoulder and peering into the middle of crowds, expecting Sophia to pop up at any moment, but she stayed away. In fact, I didn't see her until Camille and I were heading out the school door at the end of the day. We planned to ditch the school bus and grab a ride on a city bus to Grandma's Café so that I could make good on my promise to hang out with her. Sophia suddenly appeared, carrying a backpack and looking like any one of the other hundreds of kids spilling out of the school.

"Hey, you two. Where are you headed this beautiful afternoon?" She wore the sunniest smile I'd ever seen.

I could feel Camille tense next to me. She said nothing and just kept walking.

I shrugged. "We're heading over to Grandma's Café for some ice cream. Want to come?" I probably shouldn't have invited her, but I thought that if Camille got to know Sophia it would help.

"Sure, that sounds fun. You don't mind, do you, Camille?"

Camille turned to Sophia and half-smiled, but the look in her eyes screamed, 'Go away'.

Apparently half the school decided that ice cream sounded good because Grandma's was packed when we got there. We finally managed to snag a table made for two and an extra chair from a nearby table. It wasn't a secret that a lot of the eyes in the room were on our little group—especially those belonging to the opposite gender. I'm sure they were all wondering who Sophia was and how they could possibly find out so they could try to hit on her. Sophia acted oblivious to the attention we were getting, but Camille kept flashing her own famous smile and tossing her hair over her shoulder with a flip of her head. I wondered if I should try the hair flip thing. With my luck I'd pull a neck muscle and end up embarrassing myself horribly.

The three of us made small talk and I kept looking at my watch. I wanted to get back to our research, but I didn't know how to nicely get rid of Camille. Sophia tried to include her in the conversation as much as she could, but for the most part Camille ignored her and spoke only to me.

Finally, unable to stand it any longer, I pushed back from the table. "It's getting really late. I should probably go home." Camille looked at her watch. "What are you talking about? School's only been out for forty-five minutes."

"I have homework to do," I lied.

"What homework?" Camille quizzed. She didn't believe me.

"It's for my math class." The answer seemed safe since it was the only class we didn't have together. I was in an advanced math class and Cam wasn't.

"Whatever. Let's go then," Camille said dejectedly.

The three of us barely spoke as we walked home. When we got to my street, Sophia and I turned off together. Camille stopped walking.

"Are you following her home?" she asked Sophia in an accusatory tone.

"What? Oh, no. Well, sort of. I left something at her house when I was over there yesterday and I'm just going to grab it quickly," Sophia answered.

Camille nodded slowly before quickly turning and continuing toward her house. I'd gained a spring in my step, but it seemed as if she'd lost one.

The rest of the week actually flew by and before I knew it, Friday was upon us. The last day of school was always a half day and, in my opinion, a waste of time. It wasn't like we actually did any work. We spent time signing yearbooks and goofing off. The teachers didn't even try to quiet us or discipline anyone because they were just as excited as we were for the end of the year.

Sophia had gone to school with me every day that week . . . sort of. She never actually came to any classes, but she showed up between them and ate lunch with Cam and I every day. I wondered what she carried around in her backpack. I doubted it was textbooks. On Wednesday I asked her where she went when she wasn't with me. It turned out there's a whole network of ghosts that work together when needed. Who knew? Ghosts who were adults when they died could easily get a home and a job if they desired and live somewhere until people started to notice that they weren't aging, and then they would just move on. Teenagers and children had it a little harder because the non-aging issue was a lot more noticeable. So, the younger looking ghosts would adopt friends who would claim to be parents when needed and sometimes they would even stay together. That was Sophia's case. When she got to town, she met ghosts by the name of Jack and Rita and hung out at their home most of the time she wasn't with me. She offered to introduce me to them, but I thought one ghost was enough for me to deal with right then.

On my way to Mr. Hanover's biology class, Peter Ashby stopped and asked if I could sign his yearbook. He was at least six inches taller than me with dirty blonde hair and a skinny build. He was one of those guys that had no trouble making friends and knew everyone. And I was madly in love with him. Too bad he had no idea and I had no intention of ever telling him. I signed his book with a shaky hand. Sophia started laughing before he'd even walked away.

"What?" I glared.

"You like him."

"I do not. He's just someone from the neighborhood. I'm surprised he even knows my name."

"Ha," she guffawed. "In the few weeks since I've been watching you, Peter has said 'Hi' six times, talked to you twice, and smiled at you in the hall nine times. Every single time you had contact with him you blushed, just like you did when he asked you to sign his yearbook just now. You didn't blush with any others guys."

Stunned, I didn't know what to say. My crush on Peter dated all the way back to the fourth grade when he first moved to Marion, and no one—especially Peter—had ever picked up on it. Even Camille, who knew me better than anyone, had never caught on. When we were kids I thought we were destined to be together because his first name was Peter and my last name was Peters. The childhood fantasy had never faded.

"Whatever." It was the best I could come up with in that short amount of time.

"It's true." Camille giggled. "I've wondered about it for years. You do blush every time you talk to Peter."

Of course, now *she decides to side with Sophia.*

"Can we *please* just go to class? I'd like to end this school year so I can get on with my life." I really hoped no one in the hallway heard our conversation. I would be mortified if someone told Peter that I liked him. I doubted I was his type and he'd probably never consider asking me out. And I definitely didn't want him to do it out of pity.

At the end of the day, after much cheering and rejoicing from the entire student body when the last bell rang, Camille and I climbed on the bus. Jubilation filled the air and everyone squirmed in their seats. Yearbooks passed up and down the rows and paper airplanes flew through the air. I got nailed in the head by the airplanes and a couple of books. The bus driver ignored everyone and pulled his visor down farther so that he didn't have to look at us.

Camille glowed in her seat. "So, what are we doing tomorrow for our first day of summer break? We could go to the swimming pool, the beach, go on a picnic, or shop for summer clothes at the mall, but please don't suggest we go to the library. I know. Maybe we could—"

"Actually," I cut her off, "I promised Sophia that I'd take her to visit some historical sites in Marion."

Camille waited expectantly. I knew she wanted an invitation to go along, but I just couldn't give it. That time I *really* felt bad. I didn't want to hurt Camille, but I couldn't exactly bring her along without her questioning what we were doing.

"You know, just forget it. I can see when I'm not wanted. You and Sophia have a spectacular summer together and maybe I'll see you around school next year . . . or maybe not." Camille spat the words out, jumped off the bus, and quickly began walking down the road to her home.

"Camille," I called, trying to push through the dispersing crowd to run after her, but she just kept walking. I shook my head and stood on the sidewalk watching her go. Surprisingly, it was the first time we'd ever had a fight and I didn't know how to react.

"Everything okay?"

Startled out of my thoughts I whipped my head around to see Peter Ashby standing next to me. I could feel the blush creep out immediately.

"It's fine. Just a little disagreement."

"Wow. And all these years I thought you two were attached at the hip. Who knew?" Peter laughed.

I tried to fake a smile, but it wasn't very convincing.

"So . . . what are your plans for the summer?"

I shrugged.

"I was thinking that it might be fun if, you know, we umm . . . hung out sometime this summer." Peter stumbled over his words and stared at his feet.

I was stunned. My throat felt as if it was closing off, but I managed to blurt out, "I'd like that—text me sometime," before I turned and jogged the remaining block to my house. It should have been one of the happiest moments of my life, but the pain I felt from knowing that I might have just lost my best friend ruined that.

"What took you so long today, slow poke?" Sophia asked when I arrived at my house. She sat on my front steps with her legs stretched out in front of her. "Let's get to work."

I didn't respond. I just walked past her and unlocked my front door. On that afternoon's agenda was a trip to the site where Sophia's family lived before they all died. Her grandparents, Nathan and Sophia Briggs, built a home in Marion long before she was born. They planted so many rose bushes that it became known as Rose Cottage. Eventually Sophia's parents, Benjamin and Sarah Briggs, built their own little home next to Rose Cottage. When they set sail on the *Mary Celeste,* Arthur stayed behind at Rose Cottage with Grandma Briggs. Little did he know that his family would never return for him. Grandma Briggs and her son James sold the home not long after the incident with the *Mary Celeste,* probably to escape the memories of the tragedy in their lives.

I put my things in the house and grabbed a snack. I didn't bother to offer Sophia anything. "So," I said finally, "how do you propose we get around this summer? I can't drive yet nor can I fly around or creep through walls like you. I only have one bike and I'm sure as heck not pumping you around all over town."

"Wow. You're kind of touchy today."

I rolled my eyes.

"Don't worry about it. You might not be old enough for a license, but I am. Remember?"

I looked up to see Sophia jingling a ring of keys in front of me. Attached to the ring was a small ship keychain. I knew immediately that it was a replica of the *Mary Celeste*. It was the exact kind of keychain I'd seen in souvenir shops my whole life. Tourists loved them.

"What do you drive? Wait, let me think . . . A little red, sporty, two-door something or other?" I guessed.

"Ha! I try to blend in, remember?"

I peeked out my front window to see a non-descript, white, four-door sedan parked across the street. It was the kind of car you could walk right by after you got off the school bus and not even notice.

I grabbed a notebook and we jumped in the car.

"So how long have you been driving?" I'll admit I was a little anxious. It wasn't often that teenagers drove me around.

Sophia put a pair of sparkly pink sunglasses on and looked at me. "Honey, I've been driving since Henry Ford rolled his first Model T off the assembly line."

"Yay. I'm sure that would be the perfect story to tell my father when he finds out that you're old enough to drive and proceeds to question your driving ability."

Sophia was right—she was actually a great driver. In fact, probably better than a lot of the adults on the road. She'd been around for almost a hundred and fifty years, and I guess it was good that she had something to brag about. The site where Rose Cottage used to stand was on the other side of town. The cottage itself had burned down back in the early sixties. We didn't know what we were looking for or what we were supposed to do. We hoped there might be other ghosts hanging around that could shed some light on the subject for us. We didn't want to be caught trespassing so we sat on a grassy area across the street and watched the site where Sophia's family used to live.

"My grandfather was killed at Rose Cottage, you know," Sophia said after we sat in silence for a while.

"Killed? You mean he was murdered? Maybe that's a clue to something."

"No. He wasn't murdered. He opened the front door to look outside during a big storm and was struck by lightning. He died immediately. Grandma Briggs cradled his body until the storm ended and she was able to get help."

"That's crazy. The chances of being struck by lightning are rare. Combine that with what happened to your immediate family and you could say that your family had a bit of bad luck."

"Ha!" Sophia scoffed. "You don't know the half of it. We had so much tragedy in our family that the townspeople began to talk about the Briggs family curse. All but one of my father's brothers sailed as well. My Uncle Nathan died of yellow fever while at sea. Father's sister and her husband, Maria and Joseph Gibbs, died when they were washed overboard when their ship collided with a steamer near North Carolina. They hadn't been married very long and they left behind a son who stayed with Grandmother Briggs at Rose Cottage. Their son died a short time later, too. Then, the month I was born, my Uncle Zenus died of yellow fever while on my Uncle Oliver's ship. The list just keeps going."

I was astounded. I grew up with the story of the Mary Celeste, but I didn't remember hearing anything about all the other tragic events. My heart ached for the strange ghost and her lost family.

"I'm really sorry, Sophia. No family should have to go through that much pain." It sounded lame, but I didn't know what else I *could* say.

"It *is* a really sad series of stories, isn't it? But keep in mind that I was so young when I was kidnapped that I never knew any of my real family members. I didn't learn about most of it until I started trying to extricate. And some of it I didn't discover until this week when I was reading books in your bedroom. I know all of it happened to my family, but I'm having a hard time feeling any connection to them or this place where Rose Cottage used to be."

Eventually, Sophia decided to invisibly poke around in a couple of the nearby homes. We didn't find any ghosts that we could talk to. Our first mission was a complete failure.

Sophia dropped me off just before six, and I ran up the porch stairs and into the house where I found Dad making dinner.

"Dad? You're home earlier than I thought. Sorry I was gone so long. I *did* plan on making dinner."

Since Dad was gone so much, he gave me access to a household expense account. I usually did the grocery shopping and made dinner more often than not. Because I was typically a responsible child, he always kept money in the account that I could use to hang out with friends or shop for myself. It was a pretty good arrangement in my opinion.

"Don't worry about it. I'm just glad I get to see you on the first day of your summer break." He paused to stir some soup in a pan on the stove. "Jamie, Camille stopped by a little while ago."

"She did?" I didn't mean to sound surprised, but it totally came out that way.

"I think she was upset about something, honey. Were you out with Sophia again?" he asked gently.

"Yes. We thought it would be fun to visit the site where Rose Cottage used to stand."

It was Dad's turn to look surprised.

"Remember? I'm showing her all our town has to offer this summer. She's got to learn the story of some of Marion's most famous people."

"I vaguely remember when the cottage burned down. I was pretty young, maybe five or six, but there were rumors of it being haunted. Kids in town would dare each other to go onto the property at night," Dad reminisced before changing the subject. "Can we talk about something that's been bothering me, honey?"

"Sure. What's up?"

"Jamie, I'm worried about you. I don't want you to throw away friendships that you've had your entire life to hang out with someone who might only be here temporarily."

51

He didn't know how right he was about the temporary thing. "I know, Dad. Sophia and I try to include Camille when we can, but she doesn't get as excited about some of our suggestions as we do." It was only a partial lie.

"Just be careful, sweetie. Remember to think before you act. How old is Sophia anyway?"

Now came the moment of truth. I wanted Dad to know that she was old enough to legally drive, but not that she was old enough to have graduated from high school already. What eighteen-year-old would willingly hang out with someone three years younger? I decided to go somewhere in the middle. It seemed safe.

"She just barely turned seventeen, Dad. She has her own car and she's a really safe driver. Her parents totally trust her. I promise."

Dad raised his eyebrows. "Just stay off your phones when you're in the car, okay?"

"Of course," I promised.

After eating dinner and helping Dad with the dishes, I retreated upstairs to my bedroom. A short time later there was a quiet tap on the door. I opened it to find Sophia standing in the hall. I grabbed her arm and yanked her into the room.

"Are you trying to get me into trouble?" I hissed.

"I didn't know if your Dad wanted you to have friends over this late and I promised not to sneak up on you, remember?" she hissed back.

Sophia looked at me in my pajamas and registered a look of surprise. "Are you going to bed already?"

"I don't know. I guess. I usually put my pajamas on after dinner and then read until I fall asleep."

"We should go someplace. Ghosts tend to feel more comfortable going out at night. Maybe we can go find some. Come on, put some clothes on." Sophia snapped her fingers.

I couldn't take it anymore. "You know, I'm doing you a favor and it wouldn't hurt you to be a little more appreciative and a lot less demanding. I didn't *ask* to be your soul saver. I've spent every extra moment with you in the last week. Have you even noticed that I'm losing the people I care about most? I understand your predicament and I feel sorry for you. Really, I do. But the fact is that sooner or later you're going to be gone and I will still be here. What if I have no one left to stay with me when you're gone?"

Sophia appeared shocked as I fiercely whispered at her. I know I was shocked. Outbursts were not common coming from me.

I took a deep breath and continued. "I think you should leave for tonight. I have a lot of thinking to do."

"Ok. Sorry, Jamie. I'll see you later." Sophia stepped back toward my closet and vanished.

I threw myself onto my bed and sobbed. Camille didn't want to hang out with me anymore. I was disappointing Dad who I knew loved me dearly. If I didn't help Sophia I would disappoint someone who had been lost for decades. I didn't know what to do so I opted for Plan C. I cried myself to sleep.

Chapter 7

I felt much better the next morning. I still didn't know what I was going to do, but I felt like everything would work out okay. I took a quick shower and dressed by 8 o'clock. Considering that it was the first full day of summer break, as well as the fact that it was a Saturday, I was willing to bet that I was the only teenager in all of Marion up at that hour. I felt so good that I even took time to put a little makeup on and ditched my usual weekend ponytail for an attempt at a hairstyle. Dad was reading his newspaper, of course, in the living room that morning. He offered to make me pancakes and I took him up on his offer. It was a rare occurrence and I couldn't help but question his motives.

"Jamie, I know your break is just starting, but I got a call this morning and I need to go to Chicago for a conference on Tuesday. I'll be gone for 4 or 5 days. I'm really sorry. You know I try to keep my summer travel to a minimum, but I *have* to go on this trip."

"Don't worry about it. I can find something to do to stay busy. I'm not a little girl anymore." I kissed him on his cheek for added emphasis.

When Dad traveled without me, he usually notified a neighbor, but I was ultimately left on my own. To some people the arrangement might seem odd, but Dad checked in often and there was never a problem. Dad's trip to Chicago was actually a blessing in disguise. If he were out of town, I wouldn't have to be so cautious with Sophia in the house.

"I'm glad you aren't upset, honey. I'll make sure there's plenty of money for you in your household account before I leave. And no wild parties." He laughed.

Dad knew me well enough to know that it would never even occur to me to throw a party while he was gone. I really wasn't a typical teenager.

I spent the rest of the morning helping Dad catch up on the household to-do list. I cleaned my bathroom, vacuumed the living room, and washed some laundry. I even mopped the kitchen floor.

Our home was nothing fancy, but it worked perfectly for us. We once had the American dream: a modern three bedroom, two bathroom home on a quarter of an acre in the same family-oriented subdivision as Camille and many of the other students at my school. We moved out shortly after Mom left us. Our first home was only a couple of blocks south of our new home and was similar in square footage, but memories of Mom were in every room and Dad couldn't stand being there. It was as if the walls still breathed her scent in and out, in and out. The new home was an old two and a half story home built sometime in the 1890's, which meant it was well over 100 years old.

My room and its impressive ocean view was the best part of our house. In one corner of the room a small circular staircase that led to the attic. From the attic you could step out through a tall window to a miniature widow's walk. History says that widow's walks were built on coastal homes so women could watch the ocean while waiting for their seafaring men to come home. The idea of ladies in long flowing dresses pacing the floor above me as I slept sometimes gave me the creeps. Dad wasn't a big fan of me going out on the roof so we rarely even went into the attic. The staircase leading to it had become an extension of my closet and I often threw my clothes there when I was too lazy to hang them up or toss them into the hamper.

Previous owners had done an amazing job of keeping the home in good condition, but when dealing with an old home there are always little maintenance jobs to do. It had become a project for me and Dad and we genuinely enjoyed working on it together. Sometimes we spent his rare days off going to antique stores. Our goal was to eventually have the entire home furnished in Victorian era décor. Our pièce de résistance was a beautiful bedroom set Dad bought on one of our antiquing trips to Boston. I couldn't stop admiring it so Dad splurged and got it for my birthday present when I was thirteen. I especially loved the intricate four-poster bed.

The doorbell rang shortly after Dad and I returned to our projects after stopping for lunch. I opened the door to find a very subdued Sophia.

"Hi," she said cautiously.

"Hi."

"Do you mind if I come in?"

I stepped aside and she entered the living room. Dad was outside in the yard working on his summer vegetable garden. It only consisted of tomatoes and a few herbs, but he was proud of it nonetheless.

"I'm sorry about last night," Sophia began. "You were right to be angry. I've been alone for so long that I've forgotten how to act around true friends. Yes, I have ghost friends, but they come and go. You never know when someone is going to extricate and disappear for good without so much as a goodbye. I've been waiting for so long to finish *my* business so that I can go be with my real family that I haven't been very nice. I'm sorry."

"Apology accepted. I'm sorry I yelled at you."

"I did a lot of thinking last night . . . and . . . I decided we should tell Camille about my true identity."

"Really? Are you serious?"

"Yes."

"You don't get struck down or something if you share your secret with too many people, do you?"

Sophia laughed. "No. Ghosts can tell whoever they want, but most people don't believe them and it's much easier to live a normal life if people don't think you're crazy. I was able to convince you so I thought maybe we'd be able to convince Camille as well. Are you okay with her knowing?"

"Absolutely. Let's do it." I felt a huge weight lifting off my shoulders. "I will warn you, though—Camille will absolutely flip out. I don't think her reaction will be what mine was."

"You weren't exactly a picture of calm yourself," she reminded me.

I grabbed my cell phone and texted Camille, asking if we could come over to talk. Her response was only one word. "Fine." At least it wasn't "No."

Dad came into the house just then, raising his eyebrows when he saw Sophia standing next to me.

"Hello, Sophia," he said in his always polite voice.

"It's nice to see you again, Mr. Peters."

"Dad, Sophia and I are going over to Camille's house. I think the three of us will go do something after that so I might be kind of late." I hoped he knew we were making an effort with Cam.

"That's fine. Enjoy yourselves, but be safe."

"Don't wait up," I said as I grabbed a jacket and we hurried out the door.

As "old-fashioned" as my home was, Camille's home was modern. Her mother, an interior designer, continually changed the decor. I never knew what to expect when the door opened. Sophia and I rang the doorbell and Camille's older sister, Allison, answered it. She would be a senior the next year and was a total snob. She rarely gave Cam or me the time of day. That time was no exception.

"Camille," she screamed up the stairs without even greeting us. "Your friends are here."

Allison turned back around and gave Sophia a second glance and a nod of approval before disappearing into the kitchen. I looked around the living room from our position near the front door. It *had* been changed again. There were new throw pillows in yellow and blue on the cream-colored leather couches and a new bowl filled with yellow and blue glass beads on the coffee table. It was a simple look that complemented the sky blue walls. I was sure that by autumn the decor would be changed again.

I looked up to see Camille slowly walking down the stairs. She looked disheveled. I didn't remember ever seeing her that way before. Apparently she had a rough night, too.

"I stopped by last night," she said flatly when she reached the bottom of the staircase.

"I know. Dad told me."

"I'm sorry," Camille and I said at the same time and then laughed.

"I haven't been trying to ignore you or push you away. I promise. There were just some things that I couldn't talk about before," I said.

"I guess I shouldn't expect you to be at my beck and call all the time."

Camille glanced at the entrance to her home and gave a nod and a half-smile to Sophia.

"Hi, Camille. I'm sorry I caused a rift between the two of you. I didn't mean to and I'd really like to start over. Jamie's been helping me with a project and I made her keep it a secret, but I want to let you in on the secret now."

"A secret? What kind of a secret?" she said with a hint of distrust in her voice.

"I think we should go somewhere where we won't be interrupted." Sophia nodded toward the kitchen doorway where Allison had just disappeared.

"Let's go to the tree house, Cam."

When we were younger, Camille and I spent all our time outside in her tree house. We would play house, or school, or dolls, or a million other things out there. As we started to get a little older, that's where we would go to gossip and talk about boys. We slept there on occasion and even hid there when we'd done something we shouldn't have—like pranks aimed at Allison. The walls held many of our secrets. I knew Allison would never in a million years come out into the backyard. Camille's parents tended to ignore her, too. In some ways it was good—she could pretty much come and go as she pleased.

"I haven't been out there in years, Jamie. There better not be animals living in it."

The three of us retreated to the backyard where we climbed an aging ladder and disappeared into the floor of the tree house about twelve feet up. The entrance felt much smaller since I was bigger. The inside didn't feel nearly as expansive as I remembered, either. Dust and old leaves covered every surface.

"Okay, you have me thoroughly curious. What's going on?" Camille asked after the three of us settled on the old rug lining the wooden floor.

Sophia cleared her throat. "I think you should explain it to her, Jamie."

"Are you sure?"

"Yeah. Go ahead."

"Umm . . . okay. Cam, you know I'd never try to hurt you or lead you astray, right?"

Camille frowned. "What's going on, Jamie?"

"The truth is that Sophia and I didn't meet each other at the library the other day. She first saw me when my dad and I went to New York a couple of weeks ago. Do you remember that?"

She nodded, not taking her eyes off Sophia.

"I didn't know she'd seen me, but she felt like we had a connection and she followed me. She's been following me ever since."

"*What*? That's sooo creepy." Camille glared at Sophia.

"That's what I thought at first too, but it turns out I'm her soul saver."

"Am I supposed to know what the crap that is?" Camille was getting annoyed. I wasn't sure how to proceed. It wasn't like I'd ever told anyone about ghosts before and it wasn't going the way I intended.

"Cam, do you remember the story of the *Mary Celeste*?"

"Duh. I may not be as smart as you, but I haven't exactly been living under a rock in this town."

"I know. Sorry. Do you remember the name of the little girl on the boat?"

"Yeah, Sophia Briggs."

I continued on. "Camille, that little girl didn't actually die on the ship. She survived. And when she eventually did die, she became a ghost."

Camille gave a little start and looked Sophia's way. The color slowly drained from her face. I could tell she was confused—and a little bit angry.

"Are you trying to tell me that Sophia here is the ghost of the two-year-old Sophia Briggs?"

"Yes."

"Jamie, that's the stupidest thing I've ever heard. Why are you guys doing this to me?" Her voice betrayed her hurt and her eyes glistened as tears threatened to spill out onto her cheeks.

I looked to Sophia for help, but she just sat there staring at her hands. I tried to tell the story of the pirates who had attempted to take over the *Mary Celeste,* hoping that I wasn't leaving out any important details, but I think I only made matters worse.

Frustrated, I said, "Sophia I think you should show her. When you told me, I didn't believe you at all until you showed me what you could do."

"Fine, but Camille, please don't scream. I promise I'm not going to hurt you."

Camille scooted across the rug until her butt hit the back wall of the playhouse and had nowhere else to go. She tucked her legs up under her chin and wrapped her arms around them.

Sophia decided to employ the same method she used with me. "Now you see me," she said as she disappeared, "now you don't."

I couldn't see her, but judging by the sound of the last statement, she was hovering somewhere at the top of the tree house.

Camille let out a blood-curdling scream, the likes of which I'd never heard before. At first she was frozen in place and then she jumped up and began to run in circles around the floor of the tree house, screaming and flailing her arms all the while. I finally managed to grab her and pull her into my arms where she began to sob. She shook uncontrollably and I was concerned that we'd permanently scarred my best friend.

Sophia reappeared near us and Camille screamed again.

"Stay away from us, you . . . you . . . *demon.* Get away from me."

"Camille, look at me." I forced her head up and held her hands in mine as I spoke. "She's not going to hurt you. *Please* let her explain her story. I've promised to help her and I intend to keep that promise. I really want you with us, too."

Camille slowly nodded her head, but she wouldn't look at Sophia and she wouldn't stop clutching me. And so, Sophia retold the story that she'd already told me. Her voice so gentle and reassuring that by the time she finished Camille had relaxed a little and only held onto me with one hand instead of two.

"Can you hurt me?" she asked. Apparently we were more alike than I realized because that had been one of the first questions that came to my mind, too.

"Honestly? Yes. But I won't. I have no reason to. I really just want to move on," Sophia answered.

Camille asked a few more questions and then with a raspy voice asked, "Where do we start?"

I smiled and put my arm around her. "How do you feel about going to a graveyard . . . in the dark?"

"I'm starting to regret this already," she groaned.

One theory Sophia and I had come up with about her unfinished business was that maybe she was left behind because of something to do with her brother Arthur since he had, in a way, been left behind by the rest of his family. He'd been taken in by his mother's brother after his parent's disappearance back in 1872 and had younger cousins to grow up with. Sophia told us that in the early 1900's she came back to Marion in hopes of meeting Arthur. When she saw that he had his own little family and was trying to move beyond the tragedy, she quietly left town. It's very difficult—almost impossible—for a ghost to show themselves to someone who knew them on earth. Arthur looked so happy with his family that she didn't want to try something that would only freak them out and bring back sad memories.

Arthur was buried in the Evergreen Cemetery in Marion. We wanted to see if he was permanently gone or if by some miracle he remained as a ghost. According to Sophia, ghosts tend to hang out near their bodies when possible. Apparently it was comforting to most of them. It had taken Sophia a long time before she dared venture very far from her own grave. Living people are often scared to visit cemeteries at night because they're afraid of ghosts and spirits. I realized that there was a lot of truth behind people's fears. Since cemeteries aren't often visited at night, it's a place that ghosts could gather to "be themselves." Sophia insisted we were going to the cemetery at night. I'll admit it—I was more than a little bit nervous. Camille was terrified. Sophia was giddy with excitement and couldn't stop smiling.

We packed backpacks with jackets, snacks, and flashlights. I texted Dad and told him I would be spending the night with Camille. I really needed to stop telling him half-truths. As Sophia pulled into the parking lot of the Evergreen Cemetery, the sun started its descent from the azure sky and there was a cool breeze in the air, bringing the smell of new spring foliage with it. Marion received a ton of rain earlier in the week and the earth was still damp. We slowly weaved through the rows of headstones, reading names and dates as we went. Sophia walked slightly ahead of Camille and me, appearing to know exactly where to go. She stopped to look at a stone monument, her fingers gently tracing the names on the stone. I caught up to her and read the names, too. It was a cenotaph erected in honor of Benjamin Spooner Briggs, Sarah Elizabeth Cobb Briggs, and Sophia Matilda Briggs. Camille and I didn't say anything and Sophia soon continued walking. Eventually we made it to the grave of Arthur Stanley Briggs. It was a small stone covered with white lichen. We had to brush away dead and overgrown grass to read the inscription.

I read his headstone aloud. "Briggs. Arthur H., 1865-1931, and Margaret H., 1871-1939."

"He died on my birthday—October 31, 1931," Sophia said sadly.

"He died on your birthday?" I said incredulously.

She nodded. "I didn't find out about his death until many years later, but when I heard the date, I thought maybe it was his subconscious way of showing he was still connected to me. Silly girlish dream, I guess."

"Wait," Camille said. "If you die on Halloween, do you automatically become a ghost?"

"Not necessarily. That's just an old wives tale. You *can* become a ghost if you die on Halloween, but it isn't assured."

"Sophia, this really could mean something. There has to be some sort of connection between you and Arthur that wasn't completed." I was starting to get excited.

"I'm starving." Camille announced as she spread a blanket on the ground in front of Arthur's grave, sat down, and pulled out a granola bar. She was doing a lot better with Sophia's news than I expected and in only a couple of hours she'd gone from hating Sophia to acting like an adoring fan.

"Ouch." I rubbed a spot on my head where an acorn had just landed. "Aaggh!" I was hit again. "I think the squirrels in these trees don't want us hanging out here."

"Who are you calling a squirrel?"

Startled by a male voice, I whipped around to see Peter Ashby appear from behind a tall monument a few yards away.

"Peter. Hi. What are you doing here?" I felt my voice go up an octave and I squeaked like a mouse. I could hear Camille snickering on the blanket behind me and I turned around and glared.

"I came to put flowers on my grandparents' graves."

"That's mighty . . . uhh . . . noble . . . of you." *Why do I always sound like such a dork around him?*

"My parents usually come on Memorial Day, but they're on a cruise right now and they made me promise that I'd come out here for them this weekend and leave some flowers. I think they're afraid my grandparents will haunt them if they don't make their presence known." He laughed at his own joke. Camille and I involuntarily glanced at Sophia.

"How about you guys? What are you doing here?" He spied the blanket and basket of food. "Are you having a picnic in a *cemetery*? Cool."

Sophia was the first to respond. "Why not picnic in a cemetery? Want to join us?"

Peter seemed to notice Sophia for the first time and he smiled at her before answering. "Sure. I'm Peter, by the way. I've seen you around, but I don't think we've been introduced."

"My name's Sophia. I'm a ghost."

Camille began choking on her granola bar and had to spit it out on the ground. I was still standing a few feet away and I'm convinced that my heart stopped beating for a short time. I felt the blood drain from my face and I had to sit down on the ground and put my head between my knees so I wouldn't faint. *How could she? She knows I like him. Now he's going to think I—we—are crazy.*

"A ghost, huh?" Peter chuckled, taking the pronouncement in stride. "Well, it's nice to meet you. My name's Peter. I'm a werewolf." He bowed mockingly and stuck out his hand for Sophia to shake.

I finally got control of myself and caught Sophia's eye. I glared.

"Sophia? Can I please talk to you for a second—over here?" I asked as nonchalantly as I could.

She dutifully obeyed and followed me behind a nearby tree.

"What are you doing?" I hissed angrily. "He was *finally* starting to show interest in me and now he's going to think I'm a lunatic."

"Calm down, Jamie. You're helping me so I'm going to help you," she whispered.

"How could you *possibly* think this is *helping*?" I was squeaking again.

"If Peter helps you and me on our little quest, think how much time you're going to get to spend hanging out with him."

She had a point. There was a chance he would believe us—after all, Camille did. Of course, Camille could be kind of gullible . . .

"Fine," I huffed. "But *please* don't be obvious about my liking him."

She winked and returned to the blanket. I followed, probably looking like a lost puppy, and sat next to her. The blanket wasn't huge and with four people sitting on it we were pretty cozy.

"So, do you picnic here often or is this a new form of entertainment?" Peter was completely oblivious to the elephant in the room.

I cleared my throat loudly. If I was going to make a fool out of myself by telling Peter about Sophia's secret, I didn't want to do it sounding like a mouse. "Peter, do you believe in ghosts?"

"Oh . . . I get it. There's a full moon tonight and you guys came out here to tell ghost stories. This is awesome. No offense, but I didn't think girls liked to do stuff like this."

"Peter, I'm serious. Do you believe in ghosts?" I asked sincerely.

He looked at me and then glanced away, picking at the blanket as he answered. "I think so. I don't claim to have ever seen a ghost, but I'm open to the possibility that they might exist."

I turned to Sophia. "Now would be a good time to do your thing."

She smiled and rose to her feet. "This is starting to get kind of fun. I should have started doing it decades ago."

She turned and addressed Peter. "Now you see me . . ." she disappeared into the night just as the sun sank below the horizon ". . . now you don't." I heard her whisper the last part of the sentence into Peter's ear, but I couldn't see her. His reaction was priceless.

"Holy—" he screamed, covering his mouth before the entire expletive made its way out. He dove across the blanket and grabbed Camille and I, cradling both of us between his arms at the same time. If it hadn't been so funny I would have liked to stay there with his arm wrapped around me the entire night, but as it was I let a giggle escape and he relaxed and let go.

"Wait . . . is this a joke? Are you guys pranking me? That's what Sophia and you were whispering about a minute ago." I couldn't tell if Peter was angry as he was yelling or if he thought it was funny. I think he was still in shock.

"It's true, Peter. Sophia's a ghost. I found out just a few hours ago. Apparently Jamie here has known for a week and didn't bother to tell anyone," Camille said.

Peter looked at me. His mouth was moving slightly, trying to form words for questions he didn't know how to ask.

"I don't get it," he finally said. "Is this *really* real?"

"Why don't you ask her yourself?" I pointed behind him to where Sophia hovered lazily above Arthur's headstone.

"Oh geez," he breathed. "This is crazy. Either I'm dreaming or I've completely lost it. Someone wake me up. *Please.*"

Sophia came back to the blanket, curling her long legs under herself as she sat down gracefully and began to tell her story for the second time that day. By the time she got to the part where she, Camille, and I decided to go to the cemetery, it was completely dark except for the light coming from the full moon Peter had mentioned. We'd eaten most of the snacks we brought and put on our jackets. The nights were bearable, but still cool at that time of year. A breeze rolled in from the ocean and we huddled closer together. The telling of ghost stories while sitting in a cemetery didn't exactly help to warm us, either.

"Are you overwhelmed?" I asked Peter.

"A little. I kind of feel euphoric, too. Questions that have been asked for hundreds of years can actually be answered. That's amazing. I wonder how many times I've passed a ghost on a sidewalk or in a crowded mall and didn't even know it."

"For all you know, there are ghosts that have been following *you* around for weeks, watching *your* every move." I playfully punched Sophia in the arm.

"There is one thing in the story I missed, though. Sophia, you said you died in 1888 after you were taken to live as the daughter of Jeremiah and Elsa, right?" Peter asked.

She nodded.

"How did you actually die, then? You were so young."

I couldn't believe it. I'd been reading and studying and researching everything I could about the disappearance of the *Mary Celeste* and the Briggs family in the previous week and I had never bothered to ask Sophia how she actually died. My curiosity was piqued.

Sophia didn't answer Peter immediately, but sat in silence for a while. Judging by the look on her face, her death was a sensitive subject. Finally she spoke. "I guess I better start where I left off before. The beginning of my death sentence actually started about a year and a half before I died."

Chapter 8

Spring and Fall of 1887
Virginia

Sophia Goodwin was a good girl, but those who knew her often felt sorry for her. She was a girl trapped by life's circumstances—an honest girl born to parents who devoted their lives to trickery and deceit. They treated her as a servant rather than their own flesh and blood. People who knew—or knew of—the family would often ignore the parents and only greet Sophia. She never had nice clothes to wear, but she kept herself clean and always wore the most radiant of smiles. Her polite, gentle way of speaking endeared her to everyone.

Just like she did every morning, Sophia trudged along the path to the well at the back of their parcel of land. It was her duty to collect the day's water. She was a strong girl, but it was quite a task even for her. She filled the two large buckets, hauling the water up from the hole in the ground like she'd done hundreds of times before. Then she attached the buckets to a yoke which she carried across the back of her shoulders. It was always a long walk back to the house as she strained under the weight.

On that particular morning, Sophia was in an especially pleasant mood. The sun was shining, birds were chirping, and the wildflowers were beginning to blossom in an array of colors throughout the meadows. She stopped to pick a bouquet of those flowers and tucked them into the front pocket of her apron before she headed back with the water. She would most likely be lectured for taking too long, but she didn't care. Spring was her favorite time of year. It held the promise of new beginnings and new possibilities.

Just as she stooped to again pick up the heavy yoke, a young male voice called out. "Let me get that for you, miss."

Startled, she jumped back, almost knocking one of the buckets over in the process. She looked up and found herself staring into the most beautiful cobalt blue eyes she'd ever seen. The eyes were set into the handsome, chiseled face of a boy who was hovering on the verge of manhood. His beautiful face was attached to a body that was strong and toned, probably from years of hard work.

Sophia's heart fluttered and her hand involuntarily went to her cheek. She knew she was blushing.

"You startled me, sir," she said.

He reached up and took his hat off, running his hand through his dark brown hair. "I do apologize, miss. I thought it was better to make my presence known than to continue to lurk in the trees. I didn't want to interrupt your beautiful singing."

Sophia hadn't even realized that she was singing.

"My name's Nicholas Trenton," he said, extending a hand to Sophia.

Her hand trembled as she reached out and shook his. She could feel her entire body tingle as soon as their palms touched.

"Sophia Goodwin," she finally managed to say.

"Are you by any chance related to Jeremiah Goodwin? I was hired as his new apprentice."

Sophia rolled her eyes before she could stop herself. "He's my father."

If there was one thing Sophia knew about her father, it was that he was always in the middle of some elaborate scheme to con someone. It was out of his realm of possibility to try to make an honest living. For as long as she could remember they had moved from place to place, and he had moved from trade to trade, always claiming to be an expert at whatever new thing he started. At first meeting, he was fun and jubilant—a man that people felt they could trust fully. They never saw the con coming until they were slapped in the face by it and Jeremiah and his family were long gone. Two years ago he had purchased a plot of land on the coast of the James River near Newport News, Virginia. The James River led to the Chesapeake Bay and out into the open Atlantic Ocean. Sophia loved it. She had hoped that the purchase by her father meant he had changed his ways and wanted to put down permanent roots. What could he possibly need an apprentice for? The man was a jack-of-all-trades, master of none.

"What will you be doing for my father, Mr. Trenton?" she asked curiously.

"He'll be teaching me everything he knows about ship building, of course."

Sophia laughed out loud. The poor young man had no idea what he was getting into. Her father was delusional if he honestly thought he could build a ship. Her father's father and his father and his father had all been seafaring men. For generations they had been integral in the slave trade industry. By the time Sophia's great grandfather took over the family business, they owned an entire fleet of ships and would sail them from Africa to the southern United States and all over the Caribbean. The products being shipped had changed in the last century, but the business was still hanging in there when Jeremiah's father took over. However, within a few years of taking the helm of the business, Jeremiah had completely run it into the ground. The man had no idea what he was doing and wasn't willing to spend the time it took to properly get anything done correctly. He was selfish and only wanted to participate in activities that would directly benefit him. He lived for instant gratification.

When Sophia was just a little girl, maybe five or six, he lost his last ship, the *Aurabelle,* when it was taken to pay off old debts. A huge shipyard was under construction in Newport News and the railroad had recently been completed in the area so it was a prime location for an attempt at returning to his old "career." The sea was in the Goodwin blood and Sophia knew that her father itched to get back into the shipping business, but building his own was ludicrous. *Ship building? Really, Pa?*

"Follow me and I will take you to my father." Every fiber of Sophia's being prodded her to tell Nicholas to run and never look back, but the thought of not getting to look at his beautiful face again made her keep her mouth shut.

"I'll make you a deal," he said, smiling. "You lead my horse and I will carry this load of water for you."

He was a gentleman, too? He couldn't be more perfect. "I will take that deal," Sophia said, smiling back at him.

As they approached the house at the top of the gentle slope, the back door opened and Sophia's mother came out, yelling about Sophia being lazy and slow before she even looked up. When she finally realized Sophia was not alone, her countenance abruptly changed and she slapped on a phony smile.

In her sickeningly sweet voice she cooed, "Aww . . . you brought company for breakfast, my sweet Sophia."

"Mother, this is Nicholas Trenton, Father's new apprentice. He's here to help Father build his ship." The words came out roughly and her eyes bored into her mother, asking a million silent questions.

"Oh. Of course. Come on in. I'm Jeremiah's wife, Elsa. I'm sure he will be delighted to know that you've arrived."

Jeremiah rose from the breakfast table when they entered the room and quickly shook hands with Nicholas. He wasted no time turning on the charm and his new apprentice was soon laughing as Jeremiah recounted tales of life at sea. Sophia didn't know whether there was even a semblance of truth in any of the stories, but she loved the sound of Nicholas's laughter so for once she wasn't embarrassed by her father's lies. Even Nicholas's beautiful blue eyes sparkled when he laughed.

Nicholas told of his family and how he came to be looking for an apprenticeship. His father had lost his legs while fighting for the Confederacy during the war. After living as a bedridden invalid for many years, he finally succumbed to his injuries and died when Nicholas was just a baby. Nicholas's Mother and older sister had recently contracted tuberculosis and had both passed on. He found himself orphaned and alone at the age of seventeen and badly in need of steady work.

At length, Jeremiah pushed his chair away from the table. Sophia knew that it was her cue to begin gathering the breakfast dishes and to get on with the morning chores.

"Come on, Nicholas, my boy, I'll show you to your living quarters and then we can get in an honest day's work," Jeremiah said.

Sophia laughed to herself at that remark. Father didn't know the meaning of honest, but the part that stood out most was the part about Nicholas staying with them indefinitely. That spring was full of all kinds of possibilities.

Much to Sophia's relief, it turned out that her father wasn't intending to build a ship from the ground up. He had somehow managed to buy a small, salvaged ship after it ran aground during a storm. It was in poor condition and her father intended to restore it to its original beauty so that he could return to the sea as a merchant, ferrying cargo up and down the Atlantic Coast. Sophia hadn't yet figured out what her father's con was going to be, but she was sure there would be one at some point that involved the new—er, old—ship. Her father, two of the crewmen from his earlier sailing days, and Nicholas made up the team that would attempt to renovate the boat and would eventually sail her.

The boat was anchored not far offshore from where their little home sat near the coast. Sometimes, on the rare day when Sophia would finish her chores early, she would walk down to the rocky beach and stand as close to the water as she could. She would stand there until the afternoon breeze carried the voices of the men working back to her waiting ears. There were the rough voices of her father's crewmen and her father's deep, hearty voice. Sometimes she even heard the young voice of Nicholas drifting back toward her. That is what she waited for. Besides, she didn't know why, but there was something about the sea that pulled at her. Even when the men weren't hard at work on the ship, she would sometimes go to the beach and watch the horizon. Nothing felt better than letting her golden hair loose to blow in the breeze while water lapped at her bare toes. She felt as if she was waiting for something . . . or looking for something . . . but she could never be sure of what it was.

Evening had become her favorite time of the day. The men would paddle their little boat in just before dusk and the crewmen would head for their shack farther down the road, but Nicholas and her father would come into the house for dinner. She did her best to help her mother without complaining and tried to make every meal a feast. Was it true that the way to a man's heart was through his stomach? Before Nicholas's arrival, Sophia had been biding her time, waiting until she was just a little older and could marry a decent man and leave her parents for good. She felt horrible for feeling that way, but she had never felt close to them and she honestly didn't think they would miss her much when she was gone. But then, with Nicholas around, her life wasn't so bleak and she wasn't in such a hurry to find someone to whisk her away. She could only wait and dream and hope that Nicholas felt the same way about her as she did about him.

After the evening meal had been served and cleaned up each night, they would gather around the fire and her father would tell tales or read aloud while she worked on the basket of clothes to mend. It was *almost* as if they were a happy family.

Sometimes Nicholas joined in the storytelling. Sophia loved it when he participated because his stories were always sincere and from the heart. His tales didn't need to be embellished like her father's did. Nicholas would tell stories of his childhood and the antics he would get into. He had been quite a mischievous child in his younger years, but by the time he was eight or nine his father had been gone for long enough that Nicholas himself had become the man of the house. His mother worked as a maid for a wealthy family in town and was gone from sun up until sun down. He and his older sister, Elizabeth, were left at home to cook and clean and make any needed repairs to their home. Apparently Elizabeth, who was just two-years older than him, had always been sickly and would tire easily while doing the simplest of chores. This put a great burden on Nicholas's shoulders.

"Elizabeth was the first to come down with tuberculosis. That was just over four months ago," Nicholas explained one night. "My mother tried desperately to care for her and help her to recover, but it was of no use. She passed away two weeks after she started coughing up blood. I tried to take care of my mother when she too started showing signs of the terrible disease, but there was nothing that could be done. She was so heartbroken from losing Elizabeth that she lost the will to live. We buried her next to Elizabeth only eighteen days later." The mood in the room was somber. In the space of less than a month, Nicholas had lost everyone he cared about and his whole purpose in life. Sophia couldn't imagine being in his shoes.

Not long after his mother's death, Nicholas sold his family's few belongings and ventured out with his beloved horse, Mabel, to look for steady work and greener pastures. He made his way from North Carolina to Virginia where he met Jeremiah Goodwin, looking for a hard-working apprentice. The circumstances that had brought

Nicholas to the Goodwin's door were tragic, but Sophia felt that fate had somehow put her hand in it.

Days turned into months and before anyone could believe it, summer had come to a close. The summer days had been unusually warm that year and everyone was a little relieved when the autumn breezes began to blow, and the leaves on the trees changed from green to vibrant shades of yellow, brown, and red. At the same time, Sophia felt melancholy, as if something good was about to come to an end. In reality, the ship her father had spent his summer repairing was finished, and he and his little crew—Nicholas included—were preparing to set sail on their first voyage in the newly christened *Mist Seeker*. She was much smaller than Jeremiah's previous ship, the *Aurabelle*, and could easily be managed by a four man crew. The plan was to sail her to destinations along the eastern coast of the United States, taking small loads of merchandise to coastal towns along the way. Sophia had no doubt that her father would be carrying illegal cargo at times—that's just how he was—and she hoped that he would not involve Nicholas in anything that would corrupt his gentle nature.

A few days before the men were set to leave, Jeremiah sent Nicholas on an errand into town to pick up a few last-minute supplies for the ship. Sophia was asked to accompany him to get some items that Elsa would need at home. Other than their first meeting many months before, Sophia had not been alone with Nicholas, though she longed to sit and talk with him. She could hardly contain her excitement as they made their way down the rutted lane in her father's creaky old wagon.

"Are you excited for your trip? Have you ever sailed before?" she asked Nicholas.

"Never. This voyage will be the first of many things for me. I've dreamed about seeing the world and traveling to places completely different than anything I'm used to, but I honestly never thought my dreams would come true," he answered.

"Are you nervous at all, Mr. Trenton? The sea can be a dangerous place."

"The only thing I am nervous about is that I might find my stomach can't tolerate the sea and I will spend many miserable days being seasick over the side of the *Mist Seeker's* rail. And, Sophia, please call me Nick. Surely we are friends enough to drop the formalities. Besides, I'm not that much older than you."

Sophia's heart soared. Not only did the person she couldn't stop thinking about consider her a friend, but he also went out of his way to point out that they weren't so different in age. Surely that had to mean something.

"I'm sure you will find the sea to be soothing rather than sickening, Nick," Sophia replied with a smile in his direction.

Nick returned the smile and kept his eyes on her for more than just a glance.

"And what of you, Miss Sophia? What plans do you have to while away the time until your father and I make our grand return?"

She wished she could answer that she planned to lie in bed and do nothing but dream, but that would only embarrass her, and it wasn't as if her mother would let her become lazy anyway. No, she was sure that things would return to how they'd been before Nicholas arrived in the spring and Sophia would find herself being forced to do most of the work around the house while Elsa lazed about. But she couldn't tell Nick that.

"Winter is almost upon us. I plan to spend most days inside with my sewing and handwork and helping my mother keep the house. Perhaps it will snow and I can make a snowman for my birthday at the end of the month," she beamed.

"Your birthday, huh? And when might that be?"

"The last day of the month. I'll be seventeen, you know." She didn't know exactly when Nicholas's birthday was, but she was fairly sure it fell sometime in the early spring. For at least a few months they would be the same age in number.

They arrived in town and Nicholas, ever the gentleman, helped with Sophia's errands before proceeding to buy the things on Jeremiah's list at the local general store. A few people in town greeted Sophia, and many more turned to have a second look at Nicholas. The most playful greetings came from the local bachelorettes. He had been handsome when he first arrived in Newport News in the spring, but the hard work in the summer sun had turned Nicholas from boy to man, and his physical appearance was not one to go unnoticed. She knew a few of the girls her age because she had attended almost a year of school at the little red brick schoolhouse after her family moved to town. Jealousy crept in when these same girls looked at Nick. It was all she could do to stop herself from putting a possessive hand on his arm. He must have sensed something was amiss because he reached down and took her hand, placing it on his arm just below the elbow as any gentleman would do when escorting a lady through town. Her heart fluttered and she sincerely hoped that her palm wouldn't start sweating through the sleeve of his shirt. That would be mortifying.

The young pair finished their errands and returned to the wagon. The journey back to the Goodwin home was filled with pleasant conversation about nothing of great importance, but something had changed in the air, and there was longing in every word they spoke to each other. The trip came to a close too quickly in both of their minds. Nick reached up to help Sophia down from the wagon and let her hand linger in his longer than necessary, giving it a little squeeze before he released it. From that moment on she knew that her heart could never belong to anyone else as long as she lived.

Chapter 9

Winter of 1887-1888

Virginia

The day of the *Mist Seeker's* departure was upon them and Sophia held back tears as they prepared to say their goodbyes. It would be at least a few months before she saw Nick or her father again. Even though the goodbyes were imminent, the morning chores still had to be done and Sophia found herself down at the family well once again filling the water buckets. The air was crisp and she could see her breath as she worked to haul the buckets up from the icy trough, trying desperately to keep her shawl from falling off her shoulders as she did so.

"You really should let me do that for you."

Surprised, she turned to find Nick standing behind her at the well. Even though she was used to his startling beauty, the sight of him there made her breath catch in her throat. He took a step toward her and took her hand in his. Her legs wobbled and she didn't know if she would be able to remain standing.

"Sophia," he said in the gentlest of ways. "I wanted you to have something. I know your birthday will be next week after we are gone, so I have no choice but to give you your present early."

He reached into his pocket and pulled out a beautiful gold chain with a small rose-shaped pendant. Her heart fluttered as his fingers slowly glided around her neck to fasten the necklace in back.

"This was my mother's and I want you to have it, Sophia."

"Oh, Nick. I can't accept this. You should keep it. I'm sure you don't have many mementos of your mother left."

"Maybe, but I want to give you something that will assure you will still be here when I get back."

Sophia couldn't believe her ears. Even in her wildest dreams she hadn't dared to believe that Nick might feel the way about her that she did about him. He cupped his hands around her face, caressing her cheeks, and slowly lowered his head nearer to hers. She could feel his warm breath on her and just when she thought she couldn't stand it any longer, he softly touched his lips to hers for the briefest of seconds. Then he turned, picked up the water yoke, and quickly walked away. It was a long time before Sophia could compose herself. She couldn't seem to stop the silent tears of joy from streaming down her face.

Just as Sophia had expected, her mother kept her busy with chores while the *Mist Seeker* was at sea. She usually would have dreaded not having time to herself, but Sophia was actually a little grateful. She was afraid if she didn't stay busy she would fall apart from the pain of missing Nick. Her birthday came and went and she found that being seventeen made her feel much older than she had only a few short months before.

Sophia and Elsa were invited to the nearby home of Charles and Elenora Mason to share in the relatively new tradition of

Thanksgiving. They had a wonderful feast and Sophia found that she could actually smile and be happy. Without her father around, she and her mother were getting along better than usual, but it was nice to have someone other than Elsa to talk to and to break up the monotony of the increasingly colder days.

Unfortunately, after they dined with the Mason family her mother couldn't stop talking about their son, Michael, and how he would be such a good match for Sophia.

"Michael is a strong man that knows how to work hard, Sophia. Besides, look at the land he already owns and how much he will own as soon as his parents die," Elsa explained one December morning.

Michael had to be nearing forty years old and the idea of being paired with him sent shivers up Sophia's spine. He was an unusually large man and something about him made her feel uncomfortable, as if evil poured out of him in some unseen way.

"Mother, he barely spoke five words the entire time we were visiting and that was to grunt something about wanting more food passed down the table. I can't be with a man who doesn't know how to carry on a conversation," Sophia complained.

"But Sophia, dear, a girl in your situation is never going to find anyone better," Elsa snapped, ending their chat as she stomped out of the room.

For Christmas, Elsa and Sophia stayed at home. Her mother wasn't a particularly festive person nor was she one to celebrate God, but Sophia loved the excitement and joy that flooded out of everyone else during the holiday season. Her parents had never joined in the tradition of decorating a Christmas tree—that would just be absurd—but Sophia strung popped corn onto string and draped it around the house with little red bows fastened in the corners. She started sewing and mending for the ladies in town and it felt nice to have some money of her own that had been earned *honestly*. Her parents weren't exactly destitute, but they didn't spend much of their money on her. Sophia usually inherited Elsa's clothes when she became bored with them and she did her best to liven them up by adding bows and ribbons and other homemade accessories.

That is why Sophia was so surprised to find a package with her name on it, wrapped in brown paper, sitting on the kitchen table on Christmas morning. Inside, Sophia found a beautiful new burgundy dress with delicate white lace at the throat and wrists. She was speechless for some time and couldn't stop running her hands over the silky material.

"Oh, Mother. It's beautiful. Thank you." Sophia gushed when Elsa walked into the room.

Elsa's usually hard face softened. "I didn't have much money growin' up. And I never got nothin' new until I met your pa. I guess we haven't been good at gettin' nice things for you. I saw this in a store window and thought you might like it."

Sophia gave Elsa a hug. She couldn't remember the last time they had done that. It felt awkward and a little forced, but it needed to be done.

Elsa, unable to handle the physical contact pulled away first. "Come now. No need to get carried away. Our grandkids will be better off if their mother looks nice."

Sophia looked at Elsa in surprise. "Grandkids? I've never heard you say that word before." Sophia paused, continuing to finger the silky material of the dress. "Mother, why did you and Pa only have one child? Why don't I have any siblings?"

Elsa cleared her throat and busied herself in the kitchen, ignoring the questions. "You'll have a much better chance of marrying someone with money if you look nice. Your pa and I want to be taken care of in our old age, and that ain't gonna happen if you marry some poor farmhand."

So there it was—the motive. Just like Jeremiah, Elsa could do nothing unless she thought it would somehow benefit her. Sophia knew she should be more upset than she was, but she just couldn't be. It was Christmas and for the first time in a very long time she had a *new* dress. She couldn't wait for Nick to see her in it when he returned.

December made its way into January and then February and the cold windy weather continued, along with a lot of rain and snow. Living on the coast, the snow never stayed on the ground for very long, but that year it lingered. Everything was so wet and muddy that Sophia dreaded doing the chores every day. She considered it a good day if she only slipped and fell in the mud once while retrieving water from the well or feeding the horses in the barn.

One day in mid-February she was having a particularly difficult time carrying the water back to the house. It had rained most of the night and the trail she had worn from countless trips back and forth had completely washed away. She had already fallen twice and was so filthy that she knew she would have to change as soon as she got back to the house. Frustrated, she wiped at tears that threatened to spill out and left mud smears across her face wherever her hand touched.

Much to her horror, she wasn't the only one on the trail that morning.

"Well hello, miss. Would you like some help with that load you're trying to carry?" the newcomer said with a hint of laughter in his voice.

Sophia's head jerked up and her heart leaped as she saw that the boy she had been waiting for all winter had returned.

"Nick," she cried.

It was all she could do to keep from tossing the buckets to the ground and throwing her arms around him. She didn't want to appear desperate, after all. She lowered the yoke to the ground and he bent to pick it up. On his shoulders, the water seemed nothing more than a few drops. He easily carried it without slipping in the mud even once. Sophia was shocked at the difference a few months had made. Nick's arms were muscled and his shirt fit snugly across firm shoulders. She was convinced he'd grown taller, too.

"It looks like you've been swimming in the mud out here, Miss Sophia."

She quickly tried to brush the streaks of mud and dirt from her face, but her efforts only made matters worse. Nick threw his head back and laughed.

Trying to change the subject, Sophia said, "Did you just get back?"

"Yes, ma'am. We left the *Mist Seeker* docked in the shipyard north of here with Gus and Paul to watch her. Your father and I hired a wagon to bring us down here this morning and we just got in. You weren't in the kitchen with your mother and I reckon I knew exactly where you would be."

"The last telegram Father sent said that he didn't know when you would be back for sure, but that it might be spring before you were here. It's really good to see you." She was so happy she wanted to twirl around like a little girl.

"We ended up not being able to take the cargo we had hoped to run down into the Gulf of Mexico, but I'm fine with that." He smiled down at her.

She smiled back and they continued in happy silence until they reached the back door to her parent's home. As they entered the kitchen, they could hear Sophia's parents talking in hushed tones. The pair had papers spread across the kitchen table and upon seeing Sophia and Nick, they quickly swept them up and her father tucked them into a pouch at his side.

"Sophia, my dear, how I've missed you." He gave her an awkward hug.

Sophia wondered why he felt the need to continue putting on a show for Nick. In all of her memory she could not remember him ever having hugged her before, but for some reason he felt the need to prove to Nick that they were a normal, happy family.

"Father, it's nice to see you. I hope your journey was a good one."

"It was just as a journey should be. In the time we were gone we were able to run three loads of lumber down the coast and we have a contract for another load of cargo that we will take two weeks from now."

Sophia's heart fell. She'd known that Nick would have to leave again, but two weeks was such a short time for them to stay.

"How long will you be gone this time, Father?"

"I'm not sure, but this could be the beginning of a regular run for us. Maybe I'll have to start bringing your mother along with me so she doesn't get lonely." He winked at his wife.

"What kind of cargo will you be ferrying, Father?"

Jeremiah looked at Elsa who quickly pretended she wasn't listening to the conversation. "We will be taking goods down to Florida. They're building rail lines so fast in that state they can hardly keep in supplies."

The next week and a half flew by and Sophia found herself stuck in a horrible mood. She wanted to be happy during the little time Nick was around, but the thought of him leaving again made her sick. She didn't know how women, like her mother, could bear to be married to seamen who were regularly leaving. The pain of constant goodbyes must be devastating. Besides that, since they'd been back, something seemed to be bothering Nick and he didn't talk as much as he used to.

A few mornings before the *Mist Seeker* was due to sail again, Sophia found herself alone in the barn with Nick who was visiting his horse, Mabel.

"Did you think about me at all when you were gone?" she boldly asked.

Nick sighed. "Only every day. You were right, I didn't get seasick and I did enjoy being on the water, but I couldn't stand not seeing you every morning and evening like I did all last summer."

Sophia smiled.

"Sophia, do you think you would ever consider . . . down the road . . . maybe . . . perhaps . . . marrying me?"

Sophia's heart stopped. When it finally started beating again she managed to whisper, "Yes. I can't imagine anything that would make me happier."

"I am saving every penny that I'm getting from your father, but I'm afraid it will still be a long time before I have enough to get us a place of our own. Are you willing to wait for me, even if it is something we do far in the future?"

"I can wait as long as it takes." *But I don't want to wait another day.*

Nick reached down and took her hand, entwining his fingers with hers. He slowly lowered his head as if to kiss her again, and she felt herself leaning toward him on trembling legs, her heart beating faster with every inch of space that disappeared between them.

"What is going on in here?" Jeremiah boomed as he entered the barn behind the young couple.

Nick quickly dropped Sophia's hand and continued running a comb through Mabel's shiny black mane. Jeremiah's face quickly registered surprise, realization, and then anger.

"Father, I—" Sophia tried to talk, but she was cut off when Jeremiah grabbed her and shoved her angrily towards the barn door.

"I should have known this would happen. Get in the house, Sophia." He turned to Nick with raging eyes. "Don't *ever* let me catch you near my daughter again. Do you hear me, boy?"

"Yes, sir. I'm sorry, sir. It will never happen again."

"You're not good enough for her, boy, so keep your filthy hands off her."

Sophia didn't hear anything else as she ran for the house where she threw herself across her bed and sobbed.

Elsa came into the room and sat on the bed next to her, resting a hand on her back. "What happened?"

Sophia was too upset to respond, but she found she didn't need to. Jeremiah burst through the door at that moment, yelling about his tramp of a daughter who flirted with the hired help.

"Father. He's a good man. He treats me right and he's a hard worker. What more could you want from a son-in-law?" Sophia cried.

"Son-in-law? Are you out of your mind? The most important thing you should consider when choosing a husband is how much money he has and whether or not he will be able to support you. That boy out there in the barn is never going to be able to support himself—or anyone else for that matter."

She clutched at her stomach, willing away the need to vomit. It made her sick to think of the future her father wanted for her. He wanted *her* to marry into money so that *he* could try to get his hands on it.

For the next few days, Sophia did nothing but mope around the house. She barely ate and her usually creamy skin took on a ghostly pallor. Jeremiah and Elsa ignored her and she barely spoke a word. She desperately wanted to talk to Nick alone, but her father assured that their paths never crossed. Either she was outside doing a chore or he was, but never at the same time. Jeremiah made sure Nick was kept busy riding his horse, going for walks, or running errands in town until long after Sophia had gone to bed each night and then he would be allowed into the house for a cold dinner. Sophia never got a chance to talk to him about what happened in the barn. He never got to see her in the new burgundy dress with the delicate lace trim.

The day for Nick and Jeremiah to return to the ship came faster than Sophia could have possibly imagined. The last couple of days had been tense around the house. No one spoke, except Jeremiah and Elsa, who always did so in secretive whispers. The morning of their departure Sophia woke and dressed early, hoping that Nick would somehow find a way to talk to her. Perhaps he would meet her at the well again. She hurried out the door with her buckets that morning, looking around for the one person who could make her heart beat happily, but she never heard from him or saw him. When she got back to her house, her father bade her farewell, mentioning that Nick had gone ahead the night before. And that was it, she was alone again.

Chapter 10

Spring and Summer of 1888

Spring had once again found Virginia, but no matter how many wildflowers blossomed and released their scents into the air, Sophia could not bring herself to be happy. Her father would never give his blessing for her to marry Nick. All she could think about was running away, but she could never support herself on the miniscule amount of money she had saved from sewing for people in town. The more she thought about it, the more she realized that their only option was to con the con man. Somehow she would have to convince Nick to run away with her when he once again returned to port.

Elsa was more nervous and jittery during the men's second absence. She paced the house often and would sometimes stand at the window, staring at the bumpy road running past their home, as if she were waiting for someone to come. She was so distracted that she didn't even care when Sophia slacked on her chores.

One evening while Sophia was cutting potatoes for dinner there was a rough knock at the door. The sun was low and shadows danced across the room, making ordinary objects appear different somehow. Sophia's eyes widened in surprise as she spied Elsa cowering in a shadowy corner with one hand clutching her apron hem and the other covering her mouth, her face betraying the concern she felt. Sophia eyed her mother suspiciously before opening the door.

"Good evening, ma'am," the gentlemen at the door said.

"Good evening to you, too, sir."

"I have a telegram for Mrs. Jeremiah Goodwin."

Sophia raised her eyebrows and glanced in her mother's direction as she heard the tiniest of whimpers escape the shadowy corner.

"Thank you for bringing it all the way out here, sir. May I interest you in a drink or a bite to eat before you take your leave?"

"Thank you for your kindness, ma'am, but I need to be on my way. Good day." The gentleman tipped his hat toward Sophia and walked away.

"Give it to me," Elsa whispered, stepping from her corner.

Sophia obliged and handed over the small envelope.

Elsa held it for a moment before finally tearing into it with trembling hands.

Sophia watched her mother's odd behavior curiously and saw as the expression on her face changed from fear to relief.

"All is well with the ship. Your father and the crew are faring well and, more importantly, making money."

And that was the end of the conversation.

Elsa spent much more time with the Mason family on their neighboring land during that summer. Elenora Mason had a bout of bad health and Elsa would visit—taking food and gifts—and pretend to be highly concerned about her well-being. She usually forced Sophia to accompany her on those outings. Sophia was always told to wear her burgundy dress and to dab a little rose water on her neck and wrists before they left. Much to Sophia's disgust, Elsa made a point of asking about Michael and commented to Mrs. Mason more than once about "what a nice man he was."

"Hmph," Michael would grunt, looking Sophia up and down as if she were a piece of meat on his overflowing dinner plate.

She tried not to, but encounters like that were usually accompanied by a shudder and the taste of bile in her mouth. The idea of being with a man more than twice her age still made her sick.

The summer wore on and the days grew hotter and longer. Sophia started spending more time down by the water, letting the ocean waters cool her bare feet. Then, the air once again turned crisp and the leaves began to change. News from the sea was rare and far between. And then finally, after months of delays as outlined in infrequent telegrams, Nick and her father returned. By then it was mid-October and they again planned on staying for only two weeks. They arrived late in the evening when the sun had almost completed its descent from the sky.

"You're back," Sophia exclaimed joyfully.

Nick gave a polite nod without looking directly at her. She cried inside. Something was wrong. Something had changed. She could feel it.

Sophia and Elsa quickly made a small meal for the new arrivals and everyone turned in for the night. Just before she laid her head down, Sophia noticed a small piece of paper folded on her pillow. "See you at the well. Sweet dreams," she silently read to herself. It was a long, sleepless night.

The next morning, Sophia entered the kitchen to find Elsa already there with her father.

"It's about time you got up. The boy woke a long time ago and went riding. Your mother and I have private matters to discuss. Go fetch the water," Jeremiah snapped at her.

She arrived at the well a short time later and found herself continuously looking over her shoulder and into the groves of trees, trying to spot those familiar blue eyes. Just as she finished filling the last bucket, he emerged from the trees leading Mabel.

"You came," she exclaimed.

"Did you doubt me?"

"A little. You didn't even look at me when you got back last night."

"I'm sorry. I was afraid once I did I wouldn't be able to stop staring. I didn't want to upset your father."

"Nick, I can't stand being apart. Please don't get back on that ship. I don't care how poor we'll be. Let's run away together." Her voice cracked as she unabashedly pled with him.

Nick hurried to her side and took both her hands in his. "Sophia, I don't want to go either, but I'm almost more afraid of what will happen if I don't go."

"What do you mean?"

He hesitated before continuing. "Sophia, I don't want to speak poorly of your father, but there is something you need to know. When we were rebuilding the *Mist Seeker* last summer, your father had us assemble a lot of hidden storage compartments. I asked him about it once and he said that he liked to have places to stow extra supplies. Most of these cubbies are so hidden that you would never know they were there unless you had helped build them yourself. The first time we left Virginia we made a couple of what I believed to be honest runs, but after that your father started dealing with some men that I didn't trust. I figured it was his boat and he could do what he wanted. When we returned to the ship after our previous two-week stay here, Gus and Paul were having a lot of whispered, secretive conversations with your father. A few days into our trip I randomly opened one of the hidden compartments, expecting it to be empty. Sophia, it was filled with opium."

Sophia gasped. "Are you serious?"

He nodded.

"I think that's why your father brought me here with him last time. I'm pretty sure that while we were visiting you, Gus and Paul were loading all the illegal cargo onto the *Mist Seeker* and this was everyone's way of keeping me out of the loop. When we got to our destination in Florida, Jeremiah had me spend a couple of days on land with him . . . away from the ship. I'm sure that's when the opium was emptied because I checked when we were on board again and it was gone. I had a lot of time to ask around and think about it, and I've read a lot over the years. I think I figured out what your father is doing. The railroad industry is on fire in Florida right now. Many of the Chinese immigrants who helped build the transcontinental railroad twenty years ago have started helping there. They all want opium. Sophia, I think your father is acting as a middle man, picking it up from someone and delivering it to Florida. I've been trying to act normal, but I think your father suspects that I know more than I'm letting on. He said he wants to discuss a business proposition with me before we sail again. I don't want to be involved with this, but I'm afraid I know too much already." It all came out in a rush of words and emotions.

"Oh, Nick, I'm so sorry. My father has always been a deceitful man. I don't think he has an honest bone in his body. The very first day you arrived here all those months ago I wanted to tell you not to get involved with him, but . . . you were so nice to me. I wanted you to stay."

"It's not your fault, Sophia. All the warning signs were there—I was just too young and naïve to see them at first. Besides, once I met you I wanted to stay, too."

"So what do we do now?"

"I don't know. I've wondered about letting him know that I know what he's been up to, and that I want a cut of the deal since I'm taking risks, too, but then I think of you and I know that you would never agree with that idea."

"You're right, I would never be happy about you lowering your standards to his level. Besides, he doesn't like to feel threatened. If you tried to blackmail him it might make matters worse. You can't let my father be a bad influence on you, Nick. You have to get out. Now."

He sighed. "I don't know what else I'm going to be able to do. I'm not qualified for any high-paying jobs. If I have to work my way up from the bottom, it's going to be forever until I can take you away from here."

"Nick, I don't want you to take care of me. Let's take care of each other. Let's go to one of the bigger cities—like New York. We can both get jobs in the factories. We don't need fancy things and a lot of money as long as we're together. *Please.*"

"How could we ever get your parents to agree to that?"

"We could never convince them. We'll just have to run away together—before you get back on that boat." Sophia could feel the excitement rising inside her.

"Are you sure this is what you want?"

"Nick, I have been waiting to leave my entire life."

He was silent for a while as he mulled things over in his head. "Okay. Let's do it. Let's go to New York."

He picked her up and swung her around, kissing her on the forehead, both cheeks, and finally her lips. When he finally set her down she continued to float.

"You better get back. Your parents are going to think you fell into the well. Love, I can't carry the water for you today or they would know I was with you. I'm so sorry."

He was more than she deserved. No one had ever cared for her like Nick did and it touched her heart in a way she couldn't possibly explain.

Sophia hurried back to her house as fast as she could with her load of water, hoping she hadn't angered her parents too much for taking so long. Luckily, they were again hunched over the kitchen table in a whispered conversation and didn't appear to notice or care how long she'd been gone. She spread breakfast on the table for all of them and pretended she didn't care when Nick walked in a little while later. He avoided making eye contact with her and Jeremiah and Elsa were none the wiser to what had transpired earlier that morning.

When the morning meal had been consumed, Sophia stood and began to clear the table. Jeremiah reached out and pushed on her shoulder, forcing her to sit back in her chair. "Hold on, Sophia. Your mother and I need to talk to you about something." Had they figured out her secret plans with Nick already?

"Sophia, you will be turning eighteen in a couple of days and it's time you started a household of your own. Your mother will be accompanying me on the *Mist Seeker* the next time I leave and we aren't about to leave you here alone. We have made an arrangement with Michael Mason. You will be marrying him before we leave."

Sophia felt as if she had been punched in the stomach as all the air in her lungs left her body at once.

"Father . . . no. You can't do this to me. I'm not a possession you can just sell. Mr. Mason is so much older than me and I don't care for him at all. *Please* don't make me do this." She looked to Nick for help.

He sat in stunned silence and shook his head slightly as if he didn't know what to do. Elsa frowned, but wouldn't make eye contact with Sophia.

"Stop acting like a child, Sophia. The deal has already been made. You *will* marry Mr. Mason and you *will* do it next week. It's time for you to be someone else's problem."

Sophia ran from the room and out the back door of the house. She kept running even as her hair came unpinned and fell down around her shoulders, tangling in the wind. She didn't stop until she reached the shore and there was nowhere else she could run. She threw herself to the ground and sobbed. It felt like all she did was cry. There couldn't possibly be any tears left inside her.

She didn't know how long she lay on the pebble covered beach, but it must have been a long time because the water began to lap at her as the tide rose. She sensed a new presence and sat up to see Nick kneeling beside her.

"Oh, Nick. What am I supposed to do? I am so scared of Michael Mason." She was almost hysterical.

"Shhh . . . love. Your father has set your wedding day for two days after your birthday. We'll just have to leave before then."

"I don't know if we can pull it off, Nick. When we talked about leaving before, I thought Father would secretly be happy that I was gone, but if I break a contract he made he will be angry and will hunt for us."

"We'll just have to disguise ourselves, give ourselves new names, and lose ourselves in the city as soon as we can. If he catches up with us, we always have a secret weapon."

"What secret weapon?"

"We could threaten to expose his illegal activities if he doesn't leave us alone. It'll work. I'm sure of it. Besides, you'll be eighteen, Sophia. It's not like I'm stealing a child. You just have to pretend as if you are unhappily going along with your wedding to this Mason fellow until we leave. You will even be able to pack your bags without anyone being suspicious. I'll go to town this week and secure railroad passage for us under different names. We can do this, Sophia."

The two made plans to rendezvous on the morning of Sophia's eighteenth birthday. Nick had purchased two tickets to New York leaving town on October 31, 1888. If they met at the Goodwin well when Sophia went to fetch water that morning, they would have just enough time to get to town and board the train. By the time Jeremiah and Elsa realized she wasn't coming back to the house and went looking for the couple, the train would be gone. Their tickets were under the names of Neil and Samantha Jackson, newlyweds traveling up the coast. Once they got to New York they would look for work and rent a small apartment under the same names. In theory, it would be almost impossible to track them down.

The last few days before her birthday were some of the longest days of Sophia's life. She expected their plan to be uncovered at any moment and jumped every time either of her parents approached or spoke to her. The day before her birthday she went with her parents to discuss the upcoming nuptials with the Mason family. The affair was to be a small one—just the families of the bride and bridegroom and a nearby preacher. The vows would take place at the Mason farm. While they were there, Sophia received a tour of what was to be her new home and farm.

Michael's home was not far from his parent's large two-story farmhouse. His home was smaller, but still beautiful compared to the house she currently lived in with Jeremiah and Elsa. It would have been a dream come true if it weren't for the man she was supposed to live there with. While they visited he barely spoke to her, but he incessantly leered at her and she constantly pulled at the shawl draped around her shoulders, trying to cover every feminine feature she had.

The night before her birthday she met Nick in the barn for a brief moment. He reassured her that everything would be fine and he would meet her at the well with Mabel hitched to his two-seater buggy. They would follow a trail through the woods that met up with the road just past the Mason farm. All was well.

"I love you, Sophia. I can't wait until we get to New York so we can be married."

"I love you, too, Nick. Tonight is the last night I will ever have to be unhappy."

He looked through the barn door to make sure no one was coming and then quickly kissed her. Her whole body turned to mush and when he tried to pull away she leaned into him more, not wanting the kiss to end. He gently squeezed her shoulders and pulled her away.

"I will see you in the morning, love, I promise," he said as he slipped through the door and returned to the house. She watched his retreating figure and wondered again how a girl like her had become so lucky.

Chapter *11*

Modern Day
Evergreen Cemetery, Marion, Massachusetts

Sophia paused in the telling of her story. All of us were sitting upright on the blanket, hanging on every word she said, desperate to hear how her story ended. I for one couldn't imagine what it would have been like to live the life she had all those years before.

"Don't stop there, Sophia, you're just getting to the good part," Peter encouraged.

"You still haven't gotten to your death," I added.

"I know. I know. I've just never told anyone about it before. Sometimes ghosts compare how they died. Everyone has to one up each other, you know? But I've always avoided the question when people ask me how I passed on. It brings back bad memories that I've spent years trying to forget."

I looked at my watch. It was already midnight and we'd been sitting in the dark cemetery for hours. Halfway through Sophia's story Camille had texted her mom, telling her that she would be spending the night at my house. I was supposedly at Camille's home, she was supposedly at mine, and no one was home to wonder about Peter's whereabouts. We could stay there all night if we wanted and no one would ever know.

After sitting in silence for a few more minutes, Sophia finally began the conclusion of her heartrending story. "The morning of my eighteenth birthday I woke up early. Of course, I don't think I ever actually fell asleep the night before. I was too excited and nervous to sleep. What Nick and I were undertaking was potentially dangerous. Jeremiah seemed nice enough—until you crossed him. If he caught us there was no telling what he would do to me or Nick. Actually, I was more worried for Nick than myself. My sentence would be to marry Michael Mason, but his anger toward Nick could have brought any number of things. Anyway, I dressed in the burgundy and lace dress that I'd gotten for Christmas the year before. Then I pulled the oldest dress I owned over the top so that I wouldn't bring any suspicion when I left the house. With my shawl and apron covering you couldn't tell what I was wearing. I figured I could throw my worn dress into the well and travel in my best clothing. Jeremiah and Elsa were in the kitchen having a heated discussion when I grabbed the water buckets and left. It was hard not to look around, taking one last sentimental look at everything, but I didn't want to alert them that something wasn't right. I didn't have to worry—they barely even looked at me that day. I'm pretty sure I ran all the way to the well. I can still feel the water buckets swinging and jostling me as I ran. When I got there, I couldn't see Nick so I paced back and forth and quietly called his name into the trees. I wondered if he'd had trouble getting Mabel hitched up without my father noticing."

Sophia squirmed restlessly on the blanket. "Time wore on and I was starting to get nervous. My heart raced and I didn't know what to do. I ran around the edge of the trees calling his name. I even went farther down to the edge of the water to see if I had somehow misunderstood where I was supposed to meet him. There wasn't any sign of him and no sign that he had ever been there."

"What happened to Nick? Did something happen to Nick?" Camille panicked.

Sophia ignored her and continued talking. "Finally, after what seemed like hours, although I'm sure it wasn't, I decided I should go back up to the house. If my father had detained him, we might've still had a chance to leave and get to the train on time if I met him at the road near our home. It would be riskier, of course, but I didn't know what else to do. Since my plans had changed and I was going back to the house, I still had to fill the water buckets. I hurried as fast as I could. I'd never been more anxious in my life."

Sophia wrapped her arms around her legs and rocked back and forth. "When I got back to the house, Jeremiah met me at the back door yelling about how slow I was. 'I hope Michael Mason can knock some sense into you,' I remember him saying. I entered the kitchen and frantically looked around hoping that Nick was there, but there was no sign of him. 'What's wrong with you this morning?' Elsa asked me. Jeremiah followed me in and told me I needed to come help him hitch up his wagon. I asked him where he was going and he said he was headed to town to find someone else for his crew. He pulled out a piece of paper and waved it at me. 'It's a note from that boy,' he said. 'I found it on the kitchen table when I got up this morning. The boy says he doesn't want to live life on the sea anymore and he's left. The no-good, stupid boy didn't know how good he had it.' Jeremiah cursed about the inconsiderate way Nick had resigned and how he was forced to train someone new and how he might have to delay leaving on his next sea journey. He was so angry . . . he didn't even notice I was crying through it all." Sophia stopped to catch her breath.

"He really left you?" I asked in unbelief.

"He really left," Sophia answered.

"How could he do that? You were in love. It was the perfect love story." Camille had tears streaming down her face.

Peter continued to pick at the grass along the edge of the blanket, not daring to look any of us in the eye. He was definitely the odd man out.

"I wish I could answer the question of why he left. It's haunted me for more than a hundred and twenty years."

I was afraid to ask the next question, but I had to. "Sophia, did you have to marry Michael Mason?"

She nodded almost imperceptibly. "I was like a zombie for the next two days. I couldn't feel. I couldn't think. It was as if I was on auto pilot. The morning of the wedding I thought about running away myself, but I had nothing to run for. I'm ashamed to say it, but I even thought about taking my own life."

"Oh, Sophia . . ." I didn't think the story could get much worse.

"The ceremony was in the evening. It was early November and the sun was quickly dropping from the sky. I kept watching the road, hoping Nick would change his mind and come back for me, but he never did. I reluctantly exchanged vows with Michael. When he kissed me at the end, I was so repulsed I had to turn away to keep from vomiting on him. Just the sweaty smell of him made me sick. He leered at me every chance he got that evening. We shared a meal with our parents and then Jeremiah and Elsa left and Michael's parents returned to their nearby home. I was alone with Michael and I was so terrified I couldn't stop shaking."

Sophia struggled with her story. She still had her knees up with her arms tucked around them and rocked back and forth as she spoke, not looking up at all.

"When everyone was gone he escorted me to his bedroom and started to remove his clothing. Then he . . . he . . . he tried to remove *my* dress. I told him I was really tired and asked if we could just turn in for the night. He told me that I was his wife and I had to do what he said. I was there for his pleasure. I was scared so I tried to move away from him, but he was so much bigger and stronger than me. He grabbed me and began to tear at my clothing. It was so humiliating.

The man was old enough to be my father. All I wanted was to get out of there and I tried again to pull away from him, but he kept hold of me with one hand while the other one tore at my clothes. He kept touching me all over and it was awful. I wanted to die."

Sophia was crying so hard she could barely speak. Her words came out in stutters between her sobs. I put my arm around her and she tensed at first, but then relaxed and continued with her gruesome narrative.

"By this time I was so sick to my stomach that I . . . I . . . puked . . . all over the floor. He was so angry. He slapped me and cursed at me. I fell to the ground, but he picked me up and punched me in the face again and again. I was bleeding, but he didn't even care. I kept trying to pull away and he kept trying to touch me. I hurt so bad from him beating me that I could barely stand anymore. He finally shoved me so hard that I completely lost my balance and fell back against the fireplace. The poker that he used to stir the fire was propped up against it and I fell on it. It went right through my chest. I died instantly."

When her story ended no one spoke. I could hear Camille crying softly to herself and I wiped at the silent tears that streamed down my own cheeks. Even Peter tried to hide his emotions as he coughed, cleared his throat, and squirmed around on the blanket.

"Sophia, I'm so sorry you had to go through that. No person should ever have to be subjected to something like that. You had so much tragedy in your life. It wasn't fair." My voice cracked.

"It may not seem fair, but that's how it was. I've had a lot of years to come to terms with my previous life and I've learned to live how I want to, without anyone else telling me what to do. And now I'm ready to move on." She wiped the final tears from her eyes and smoothed her hair, composing herself once more.

"Please tell me Michael went to prison for the rest of his life," Camille said.

Sophia's lips formed a straight, emotionless line. "He claimed I tried to kill *him* with the fire poker. He told my parents I died in self-defense. They didn't push the matter so the local authorities didn't either."

"Could that have something to do with your unfinished business? Maybe you need to find justice for yourself," I said.

"Maybe, but I know that Michael never came back as a ghost. When he died, he actually died."

Peter attempted to ease the mood by changing the subject. I think we were all glad to have the heavy pall lifted from our little group. "So, if you guys came here to meet with other ghosts, what do we need to do to contact them?" he asked.

Sophia looked up. "Nothing, really. They've been watching us for hours now."

Chapter 12

W hat?" Camille screeched. "We're being watched?"

"Don't worry. If they were mischievous ghosts they would've done something by now. I think they've been watching us because I'm with you. They're probably wondering why a ghost is hanging out with a bunch of living teenagers—in a cemetery. I'm sure they think *I'm* the one who's up to no good," Sophia explained.

"Umm, how many are out there?" I asked hesitantly.

"I'm not sure. Some have come and gone since it got dark, but there's consistently been a group of five watching from behind that mausoleum over there." Sophia pointed to a memorial about fifty yards away.

The three of us who were living looked for the unseen spirits, turning our heads every way we could, searching the shadows for signs of movement. The tingling feeling in my spine returned and I began to shiver.

Peter, who was obviously a little anxious himself, scooted closer to me and whispered, "Hey, are you okay? Do you want to borrow my jacket?"

"I'm fine. If I took your jacket, what would you use?" I did my best to smile at him.

"I could stand up and do a bunch of jumping jacks to stay warm," he joked.

"Why don't you do that? I'm sure we wouldn't look suspicious at all." Somehow it was easier talking to him in the dark than it was in the light, when all my weaknesses and flaws were exposed.

"You guys wait here. I'm going to go talk to them. Maybe one of them has been around long enough to know if my brother is—or was ever—a ghost."

Sophia didn't wait for a response. She stood and vanished in the blink of an eye. I felt a slight change in the air and temperature around me when she did so, as if something unseen had passed by. The three of us sat on the blanket in silence. It wasn't nearly as scary when Sophia was there. After all, she *was* what we were afraid of. Without her there as a guide, we were all a little lost.

I kept checking my watch—five minutes passed, then ten, then fifteen. Finally, I sensed the air around us change again and Sophia reappeared with an unknown man and woman in tow. Camille gasped and grabbed my arm.

"Guys, this is Simon Rowan and Phyllis Hoffman. They've been hanging around here for a while," Sophia said.

I studied Simon and Phyllis. They looked as normal as any human could, but I knew their secret. We were nervous around the newcomers, but the funny thing was that I could tell they were just as nervous talking to the three of us who were still mortal. I wondered if they'd ever exposed themselves to living people before.

Sophia was still talking. "Simon died in 1926 and Phyllis died in 1935. Simon says he knew Arthur before they both died, but neither of them have ever seen him here as a ghost."

I frowned. I'd thought that Arthur might be left as a ghost because he would have the same unfinished business as Sophia, but I guess I'd been wrong.

Simon cleared his throat and spoke for the first time. He had a deep voice that echoed through the gloomy cemetery. "I was ninety years old when I died," he said proudly. "Arthur was a good man and I enjoyed talking with him at times around town when we were both alive. He always wondered why he'd been left behind when everyone else in his family disappeared. I was in my mid-thirties and remember well when the crew of the *Mary Celeste* was lost to the sea. Rumors of what had transpired were rampant. Everyone had a different opinion of what really occurred. People were scared to sail with a member of the Briggs family on board. They said the family had a curse." At that point he realized Sophia looked uncomfortable and he stopped talking abruptly, obviously remembering that she *was* a member of the family of which he spoke.

Phyllis perked up when Simon stopped talking. "I never knew Arthur when we were alive. I wasn't native to Marion or even Massachusetts," she said. "I was ailing for quite some time before I died and I came to live with my daughter's family here in Marion. I had two bouts with pneumonia that almost wiped me out, but I eventually got a little better. Then, wouldn't you know, I tripped over one of my grandchild's toys and broke my hip. I never could recover from that. The hospitals here are fine, but had I been back in Philadelphia at least my friends and neighbors could have come to visit. Rather than ship my body back to Philadelphia, my daughter decided to have me buried here. It was kind of selfish if you ask me. I would much rather be buried next to my Harold in Pennsylvania. I lived in Pennsylvania my whole life. Why wouldn't I want to live there when I was dead? Of course, the spirits in this cemetery are friendly enough and I fit in just fine, but I don't like leaving my body to go all the way back to Philadelphia to visit Harold's body. It makes me nervous. What if something happened to my body while I was gone?"

I think Phyllis would have continued with more useless information if Sophia hadn't jumped in. "When I was talking to you before, you mentioned that we weren't the first ghosts to ask about Arthur," she prompted.

"Yes. More than one, actually. The first time was about fifty years ago. I think it was around 1960 wasn't it, Simon?" Phyllis asked.

"I think that would be a good time estimate. Two ghosts came asking about Arthur, just like you, except they were curious if anyone else in his family was around, too. They particularly asked about you, Sophia," Simon said.

"They asked about me?"

"Yes, they asked if we knew if Arthur's sister had become a ghost and if she had been around at all. I remember because I thought it was strange. You died, or at least everyone thought you died, when you were two. Babies don't usually become ghosts," Phyllis added.

"What did these ghosts look like? Maybe you knew them when you were alive, Sophia," I said, finally finding my voice.

"I think they were definitely a couple. They acted as if they were married. I would guess that they were in their early seventies when they died. They never gave names and I didn't recognize them at all. Ghosts come and go quite often, you know," Simon said.

Phyllis jumped in again. "They looked to be about the same age as me at death. I was seventy-two. The man was robust and very grandfatherly. The woman was shorter, a little plump, and had long gray hair that she kept pulled back in a bun. I'm pretty sure I've caught sight of them in town every few years ever since then, but they've never approached me, and it's always been just the two of them."

"Phyllis never misses a thing around here," Simon joked.

"Sophia, does that description match anyone you know?" Peter asked.

"Not anyone that I can think of or remember. Most people I knew were younger. I don't think I ever even met Jeremiah or Elsa's parents, so I doubt it was grandparents. Maybe it was long lost relatives I don't remember from when I was young—I mean *real* relatives. Phyllis, you mentioned that they weren't the only ones to come asking about Arthur. Who else came?"

"Well, it was probably a year or two after the first couple came by. A man came and started asking questions—only he didn't really know what he was looking for. He was actually asking about the other couple and if we'd seen them. When we said that we had, he wanted to know what they'd been doing here. He was a suspicious fellow, if you ask me," Phyllis added.

"I don't suppose he gave his name?" Sophia asked.

"Sorry, no."

"Thank you so much for your help. Maybe I can find this couple somewhere. If you see them again will you call me?"

Sophia scribbled her cell phone number onto a slip of paper she pulled from her purse and handed it to Phyllis. Then, she reached out to shake the hands of the two accommodating cemetery ghosts. Phyllis decided to forego the handshake and opted for a hug instead.

"I'm really glad to finally find out what happened on that infamous ship. I hope you're able to find what you're looking for so that you can finish your business and be extricated, honey. I sure would like to finish my own business," Simon said sadly.

"Oh, Simon. You're always in such a hurry to leave. Who wants to leave to go to some unknown place when there's so much going on down here?" Phyllis quipped.

Simon rolled his eyes.

"Maybe I'll come by to visit another time," Sophia said and started walking back toward the mausoleum where she'd met Simon and Phyllis. They followed her and soon vanished into the thin night air.

Sophia came back to the blanket where the three of us were still huddled. Camille relaxed for the first time since we'd started talking to the other ghosts.

"Now what do we do?" I asked.

"I guess we'll just keep checking out places that were important to my family and keep an eye out for this mystery couple. I really can't think of who it would be."

"Does that mean we can go now? I'm pretty sure if I sit here any longer I'm going to freeze to death," Camille complained as she stood and rocked back and forth on her heels.

"Yeah. We can go now," Sophia answered.

I looked down at my watch. It was past two thirty in the morning. I couldn't believe we'd stayed out there as long as we had. Peter stood and folded the blanket, shaking the grass, dirt, and crumbs from it first. I wondered if he was over his shock yet.

He turned to me and handed me the blanket. "So, Jamie, do I get to come with you the next time you search out Sophia's past, or was this a one-time thing?"

"I'm sorry, Peter, but you're stuck with us now. We can't have you wandering around town potentially telling people about Sophia. Think what it would do to your reputation. You'd be the school idiot." I winked at him, trying to be flirtatious, but then realized that he probably couldn't see it in the dark. "Actually, I assumed you'd want to see this through to the end now."

He laughed. "Even if you told me I couldn't come, I'd probably follow you. This is the coolest thing that's ever happened to me."

We piled into Sophia's little white car. When Peter had come to the cemetery, he intended to walk to a nearby bus stop—after he left the obligatory flowers on his grandparent's graves—and take a late bus home, but then he met up with us and he never made it to the bus. Sophia drove him home and we promised to call him before we did anything else the next day. There was no way I *wasn't* going to call. As we pulled away from Peter's house it occurred to me that Camille and I had nowhere else to go that night. We were both supposedly sleeping at each other's homes. We couldn't exactly show up on our doorsteps in the middle of the night without one of our parents asking questions. I suggested we find a quiet street and sleep in the car. We all had jackets and it wasn't as if it were the middle of winter. Sophia, however, had other plans.

"It's time you met Jack and Rita, my fake parents. You'll love them. I promise," Sophia insisted.

After meeting Simon and Phyllis at the cemetery, and knowing Sophia, I wasn't really scared to meet more ghosts, but Camille moaned and muttered something about haunted houses under her breath.

Jack and Rita lived in a modest, well-kept home on a quiet street not far from our high school in nearby Mattapoisett. Flower pots filled with pansies sat on each of the steps leading to the front door. There was a shiny brass knocker and a peephole on the front door. For some reason that made me laugh. I imagined that Jack and Rita didn't really get a lot of use out of the peephole. Who needed one when you could walk through walls? Camille and I hung back a little as we waited for Sophia to open the door. She just stared at it as if she didn't know what to do.

"Uhh . . . I don't have a key. I guess I've never needed one before. Hold on a second." She disappeared and Camille and I silently looked at each other. We weren't really sure what to do next, but we didn't have to wait long because only a moment later the front door opened and Sophia's smiling face was there to greet us.

"Welcome to Casa Afterlife," she declared as she flung the door wide and we stepped inside.

I didn't really know what to expect, but judging by the look on Camille's face and the fact that she was clinging to me, I'm sure she expected to see coffins filled with vampires, bats hanging from the ceiling, cobwebs on all the furniture, and jars filled with body parts on the shelves. The house couldn't have been more normal and homey. There were beautiful landscape paintings on the walls, fresh flowers in vases on all the little tables, a curio cabinet full of knickknacks, and comfy bright-colored furniture arranged in an inviting manner. It could have belonged to any normal human family.

"Hello? Sophia, is that you?"

A lady that looked to be in her late thirties or maybe early forties stood at the top of the stairs wrapped in a fluffy purple robe. Her brown hair was pulled up into curlers and she looked as if she had just woken from a deep sleep.

"Rita, I'm so sorry I disturbed you. This is Jamie Peters—the one I've been telling you about. And this is her friend, Camille."

Rita hurried down the stairs and greeted us. "It is *so* good to meet you. It isn't often that Jack and I get to meet someone's soul saver." She turned back to the staircase and yelled. "*Jack*. Get down here. Sophia's brought Jamie over."

I quickly jumped in. "There's no need to wake him up. I can always meet him in the morning." I felt a little self-conscious. I still wasn't completely convinced that I really was Sophia's soul saver. I hadn't been of much help yet. The way Rita acted you would think I was a movie star.

"Don't be silly," she replied. "Ghosts don't really have to sleep. We just do it to pass the time. Jack and I try to live as normally as we can so that we don't make the neighbors nervous. If we had our lights on all night long they would start to talk. Besides, what would we do all night? I can only take so many games of checkers before I want to tear my hair out." She threw her head back and laughed.

I liked Rita immediately. She was full of life—even though she was technically dead—and genuine. Jack came down the stairs in a blue robe, almost identical to the one Rita was wearing, and put his arm around her shoulders. He was tall and had brown hair so dark it was almost black. He shook our hands with a firm handshake and a confident smile. I guessed that he had been some sort of businessman when he was still alive.

"Nice to meet you, Jamie and Camille. Sophia has been telling us about you. I know she was quite nervous about revealing who she really was. I'm glad to see you took it in stride," Jack said in a deep masculine voice.

"So what brings you to our doorstep at . . ." Rita looked at an ornate grandfather clock in the corner, "three-thirty in the morning?"

"We were hoping to find a place for Jamie and Camille to crash for the rest of the night. It's a long story, but neither of them can go home tonight," Sophia explained.

Rita wasn't fazed at all.

"By all means. I'll go grab some blankets and you can sleep right here on these couches if that's okay."

"That would be great," I said. I turned to Camille, but she had already sat on one of the couches and was in the process of removing her shoes. She was exhausted. Usually Cam and I stayed up late whispering when we had a sleepover, but that night was different. As soon as Rita gave me a blanket and a pillow I laid down on the other couch, and even though I was sleeping in a house full of ghosts, I fell asleep immediately.

I had no idea how much time had passed when I woke up, but I felt refreshed so I figured it must have been a while. I stretched each muscle slowly before I even opened my eyes. I was warm under the blanket—it smelled like lavender—and I didn't really want to get up. I finally sat up and looked over at Camille. She still slept deeply with her head turned into the back of the couch, her legs curled up in the fetal position with the blanket wrapped tightly around her body. The curtains were closed and all the lights were off, so I pulled out my phone to check the time. It was ten thirty in the morning.

It was about that time that I realized what must have woken me. The smell of sizzling bacon and fried eggs wafted in from the kitchen. I rose from the couch to follow the smell down the hall.

I entered the kitchen to find Sophia sitting on a barstool, watching Rita cook. Sophia had changed into a clean pair of shorts and a t-shirt. Her bare feet showed off her manicured red toenails. Rita, too, was dressed for the day in stylish jeans and a button-up blouse that showed off her slim figure. The curlers were no longer in her hair and it cascaded down her back in subtle curls. Her makeup made her look like a fashion icon. I could see why she and Sophia had hit it off with each other.

"Good morning. Welcome to my kitchen."

"You didn't have to cook for us, Rita. I know that it's not necessary for ghosts to eat."

"Honey, don't worry. It was no trouble at all. I love it when I have guests I can cook for. When I was alive, I owned a small diner called *Rita's Place* out in San Francisco. This was in the 50s, of course, and people actually knew how to cook back then," she said as she waved a spatula at me. "I miss getting to do what I did best. Sometimes I cook just to see if my sense of taste has returned, but sadly it never does. I just have to live through my sense of smell." She closed her eyes, tilted her head back, and breathed in slowly through her nose.

"So is your sense of taste the only thing that changes when you become a ghost?" I asked the two ghosts.

"Pretty much. Unless you count the whole not-being-able-to-age thing, that is. Our ghostly bodies function almost the same as a real body. If we eat, the food just moves right through us, but if we don't eat, we're still okay," Sophia explained. "It was the strangest feeling I had to get used to when I died."

I climbed onto a barstool next to Sophia, and Rita placed a plate full of perfectly cooked scrambled eggs, bacon, waffles, and fresh fruit in front of me. I took a bite and felt like I had died and gone to heaven. Ironic, I know.

"If you are ever out and about and get hungry, feel free to come over and Rita will happily feed you. We buy groceries to keep up appearances, so we might as well put them to good use," Jack said as he entered the room.

He walked straight to Rita and wrapped his arms around her. He kissed her so deeply that I became uncomfortable and looked away.

Sophia just smiled and looked on. There was a hint of sadness in her smile as she watched the two lovers.

I waited for them to separate before I asked, "Is it rare for two people who love each other to die and both come back as ghosts? Did the two of you die at the same time or something?"

Jack laughed. "Nope. I was killed on the beaches of Normandy during World War II. Rita here died when she crashed her car into a tree while trying to apply lipstick on her way to work in 1956."

"I've gotten better at driving since then." Rita playfully punched Jack in the arm.

He continued, "We actually found each other after we died—in 1992 to be exact. Neither of us ever married when we were alive, so we decided to move across the country to places neither of us had ever been so we wouldn't *accidentally* extricate and be separated from each other."

"Isn't that the sweetest love story you've ever heard?" Sophia asked with a giant grin on her face.

"It's definitely up there." I grinned back.

"I guess I better get going so I'm not late. I'm meeting a client at eleven." Jack gave Rita another peck on the cheek and walked out of the room, picking up a briefcase on his way out.

"You look bewildered, Jamie," Rita commented as she tossed another waffle onto my plate.

"Does Jack have a *job*?"

"Of course. How else would we pay for the house?"

"Wow. This just keeps getting crazier. Do you ever work, Sophia?"

"Sometimes. I look much too young to get any good paying career-type jobs. I can never pass for older than 21 or 22. The only people who want to hire someone who looks as young as me are fast food joints or big box retailers. Neither of those options appeals to me so sometimes I have to find alternative ways of earning money."

Sophia squirmed in her seat. The new topic of conversation made her uncomfortable.

I looked to Rita, but her head was down and she avoided eye contact with me.

"Alternative ways?" I prodded.

"You know, things that might not be the most honest."

I raised my eyebrows and gave Sophia a questioning look.

"Jamie, please don't judge me. I wouldn't do it if I had any other choice. When I don't have money I have to live an invisible life and that pretty much sucks. I get so bored. When I have money I can come and go as I please and interact with living people." She was so defensive.

"I'm not going to judge you, Sophia. In the last week or so my definition of reality has been turned upside down. I might as well reevaluate the definition of right and wrong while I'm at it."

"Jack might have an honest job right now, but we've had moments we're not very proud of, too," Rita said quietly. "It's pretty easy for a ghost to shoplift and pickpocket, you know. We've never felt good about it, but sometimes it has to be done if we want to live in a world where we can be seen. We were pretty creative for a while. We discovered that if we tried really hard we could see through lottery tickets at the convenience stores. One of us would go to the register in our human form while the other one would remain invisible and prompt us on which tickets to buy. When that worked out so well we got even more creative. Sometimes we would go to those bingo halls that are usually only frequented by senior citizens and rig the outcome in our favor. We convinced ourselves that most of the people there had social security checks and retirement accounts and didn't really *need* the prize money." She stopped talking and looked right at me, gauging my reaction.

"That *is* pretty creative," I said slowly.

"I've been known to dress up in rags and beg on the street corners. You'd be surprised at what people are willing to give you if you have the right words written on your cardboard sign," Sophia said. "I'm ashamed to say it, but back in the 20s I was at a low point. I had long given up on haunting Jeremiah and Elsa and I'd been wandering the world trying to find a purpose. I discovered that men were willing to buy anything for a pretty face if they were drunk enough."

"*Sophia*. Did you . . . *prostitute* yourself?" We all turned our heads to the doorway where Camille stood with a horrified expression on her face. I wondered how long she'd been standing there listening.

Sophia's face fell as if she were hurt. "No. Of course not. I mean, I would flirt and pretend to be interested, maybe let them kiss me once or twice so that they would buy me things, but I would never stoop to that level, Camille. I promise. I've honestly never cared about anyone since Nick left me. Besides, this was the roaring 20s. Women were starting to be a little looser and guys were taking advantage of it. Have you ever heard of a speakeasy?"

"Isn't that where they would sell illegal alcohol during prohibition?" Camille asked as she sat down next to me.

"Yes."

I laughed out loud.

"Why is that so funny?" Sophia asked.

"I'm just picturing you in a flapper dress on the arm of Al Capone."

"Al Capone was overweight and he totally wasn't my type."

I wasn't sure if she was being serious or not, so I didn't respond.

"I never drank at those establishments. Actually, I've never drank anywhere. I watched my parents—I mean Jeremiah and Elsa— drink enough when I was alive. I've never liked the way people act when they're drunk. It makes them too vulnerable. I'm sure it wouldn't affect me now that I'm a ghost, but it's just never seemed like the right thing to do. Anyway, when the men were drunk they were pretty willing to give me a wad of cash and tell me to go buy myself something pretty."

"For someone who isn't actually living, you've led a pretty full life," I said.

Sophia smiled. "I know. I've had some pretty neat experiences that I wouldn't trade for anything, but now I feel like it's time for it all to be done. That's why I'm trying so hard to finish my business and be extricated. I've done everything I can here and I'm ready to know what comes next."

Rita reached over and squeezed Sophia's hand. "I'm sure you'll know soon, honey."

After Camille and I had eaten enough to feed a small army, we thanked Rita for her hospitality and announced that we'd better go home.

We started to walk out the door, but as an afterthought, Sophia turned around and asked Rita if she'd ever seen any ghosts around Marion that fit the description of the couple in their seventies that Phyllis had told us about.

She thought about it for a second and then perked up. "Yeah. I think I know who you're talking about. Jack and I met a ghost couple when we were out taking a walk one evening a couple of years ago. They would probably fit that description. They introduced themselves as John and Elizabeth Godfrey."

Sophia dropped the car keys she'd been holding and grabbed for the doorframe to keep herself from falling. She was as pale as a—for lack of a better word—ghost.

I grabbed her arm to help steady her. "Sophia, what's wrong?"

She took a moment to compose herself and then in a very soft voice whispered, "John and Elizabeth Godfrey are the names Jeremiah and Elsa used when they were conning people."

Chapter 13

"Oh my gosh. Are you serious?" Camille blurted out.

The four of us stood in Rita's doorway staring at each other, not moving.

"For obvious reasons the Goodwins couldn't use their real names, so they went by John and Elizabeth Godfrey. Sometimes they would force me to be part of the con. A decently dressed couple with a young child in tow was always believable. They made me call myself Suzanne Godfrey," Sophia explained. "The last time I haunted them they were in their fifties. I never actually saw them die so I didn't know when it happened. Apparently they found each other in death."

"Sophia, it terrifies me that they've been to town multiple times looking for you and your family," I said.

"It scares me, too. If they're anything like they were when they were alive, they aren't the type of ghost you want to be around."

"What do we do now?" Camille asked.

"I guess we just keep doing what we've been doing and keep our eyes open. I sure wish it was possible to make *myself* invisible from ghosts. You two shouldn't have to worry, they won't know who you are or that you're trying to help me. We'll have to limit how much I'm seen with you in public."

We said our goodbyes to Rita, who promised to keep watch for us, and climbed into Sophia's car. She was unusually quiet on the drive to our side of town. I thought about Sophia's situation and couldn't help but wonder if Jeremiah and Elsa were supposed to be part of her extrication process. I kept my thoughts to myself as we dropped Camille in her driveway and headed for my house. I said goodbye to Sophia and promised to call her later—after I'd showered and changed my clothes. I found my dad sitting at the kitchen table with his laptop in front of him. He was concentrating and did little more than greet me as I walked through the room and headed for the stairs and a warm bath. While I waited for the tub to fill with water, I texted Peter and let him know about the latest development. I was sitting on the counter in my bathroom and I jumped when my phone started playing the song that was my latest ringtone.

"Hello?"

"Jamie?"

"Peter?"

"How was your night? Where'd you guys go after you dropped me off?"

"It was fine. Sophia's been staying with a couple of friends on the other side of town and we spent the night on their couches. They were really friendly. I think you'd like them." It felt weird to be talking to the boy I'd been in love with for years while I sat on my bathroom counter waiting to get into the tub. I grabbed a towel from the rack and wrapped it around me, as if he could actually see through the phone.

"Do you really think that the mystery couple might be Sophia's kidnapping pirate parents?"

I laughed at his description. "Yeah, we're pretty sure it is. It would make sense."

"What are you going to do?"

"I think we're just going to continue what we're already doing and try to avoid them if they come back to town."

"Okay. Keep me posted. And Jamie, I really had fun last night. It was nice to hang out with you."

"You, too."

There was an awkward silence for a few seconds before Peter said goodbye and we hung up. I was utterly happy. Part of me hoped that Sophia would never finish her business so that I wouldn't have to say goodbye to her *and* I would continue to have an excuse to spend time with Peter.

I stayed in the bathtub until my whole body was as wrinkled as a prune and my dad knocked on the bathroom door, interrupting my thoughts.

"Are you okay in there?" he asked.

"I'm fine. I was just about to get out," I called back through the door.

"I have to pick up some papers at my office. Are you interested in coming with me?"

I thought about it for a second. I'd been wondering what happened to the *Mary Celeste* after the Dei Gratia towed it to Italy for salvage rights all those years ago. The information I searched on the internet was vague on the subject. Newton University, where my dad worked, had an excellent research library. I needed an excuse to look through their material.

"Sure. Just give me a little time to get ready."

I quickly dried off and dressed in clean clothes. The one feature I did like about myself was my legs. It was easier to show them off in the summer when you could wear shorts every day. I pulled on a pair of red walking shorts with a white t-shirt. The shirt wasn't fancy, but it was gathered in the sleeves and had a feminine neckline. I thought I looked pretty good in the outfit. I used the blow dryer on my hair and pulled it up on the sides with two silver butterfly barrettes. I applied a little eye makeup and examined myself in the mirror one last time. *If only Peter could see me this way instead of bundled up in a dark cemetery . . .*

The drive to Dad's office in New Bedford was relaxing. Instead of taking the I-195 like he usually did, he took the slightly longer route past the cemetery and through the town of Mattapoisett. Technically, our high school was across the border in Mattapoisett, but we still claimed it. I liked that route better because you could see more life than you could while driving on a busy interstate. I especially liked the part where the road crossed over the Acushnet River and I could look out over Buzzards Bay with water as far as I could see. I'd always felt like the sea held mystery. After meeting Sophia, I had become part of that mystique.

We pulled into Dad's reserved parking space in front of the administration building and got out of the car. The campus was well-maintained and had many tree-lined sidewalks around the buildings. I'd enjoyed visiting campus with Dad ever since I was little. I figured there were only three more years until I would be a student there. I informed Dad that I wanted to look something up in the library and would meet him at his office soon. He agreed and we parted ways.

I walked across a large common area to the two-story library and entered through the front door. Only a few students milled about outside, and the library itself was almost completely void of life. I guess I shouldn't have been surprised. After all, it was a Sunday afternoon *and* it was Memorial Day weekend. I sat down at a reference computer and typed in the name *Mary Celeste.* A few options came up, but most of the books were the same ones I'd found at our little library in Marion. I continued to scroll down the screen until I saw a reference number for a maritime research journal that I hadn't seen anywhere else before. I scribbled down the number on a piece of paper I found next to the computer and walked up and down the aisles until I found the journal. The magazine was wrapped in a plastic protective cover, its pages tight and crisp as if it had never been opened. I scanned the library for a place to sit and chose a table near a large window in the back. I hurriedly skimmed the table of contents, flipped to the pages about the *Mary Celeste,* and soon found myself completely engrossed in the article.

When the *Mary Celeste* was brought back to America after it was found adrift, the owner sold it and the ship changed hands many times over the next thirteen years or so. The final Captain was a man by the name of G. C. Parker. He was in over his head and decided to purposely sink the *Mary Celeste* so that he could collect insurance money from her. He ran the ship into a reef off the western coast of Haiti in 1885, but the ship *still* failed to sink completely and he was found out. Captain Parker went to trial for fraud and the ship was eventually burned down to the waterline, its remains slowly sinking down into the ocean. *But*, in 2001 it was rediscovered off the coast of Port-au-Prince by some sort of research team.

I couldn't have been more excited about reading the article. *This information has to be helpful.* If only we could find a way to get to Haiti . . .

"Hello."

I was startled from my thoughts by a person standing over me. He was one of the most handsome boys—men?—I had ever seen. He had piercing blue eyes that made my heart flutter a little. It was the first time I'd felt some an attraction to an older college student. The thought made me a little nervous.

"Umm . . . hi."

"What are you reading?"

"An article." My heart still fluttered.

He laughed. "I can see that. What's it about?" He leaned over and read the title. "Ahh. The infamous *Mary Celeste*. Why are you so interested in something like that when it's so beautiful outside?"

I glanced at the windows. I didn't want to reveal too much to the prying individual so I tried to refocus the conversation on him. "Why are *you* in the library on a holiday weekend?"

He laughed again. "Touché. Actually, I came here for the same reason as you. Research."

I didn't say anything. I hoped that if I just stopped talking he would take the hint and move on. I wasn't so lucky, and he sat down in the empty chair next to me.

"I saw you outside. I thought you looked like the kind of girl I'd like to meet."

The tacky pickup line made me uncomfortable and I looked around for an excuse to slip away. Dad would not be happy if he thought I was trying to flirt with a college student, and of course I'd chosen a table all the way in the back where no one else in the library could see us.

"My dad should be here any second to meet me," I lied and stood up quickly, closing the journal and picking it up off the table.

"I'm sorry. I've made you uncomfortable. Let me start over." He stood up, too.

There was something in his eyes—a look that was almost pleading. I felt oddly drawn to him. I don't know why, but I sat back down again.

"The truth is, I did see you outside, but I was going to come in here anyway. You left the reference computer pulled up on your search and I saw that you were researching the same subject as me. I followed you, but I'm not a stalker. I promise."

"You're researching the *Mary Celeste?*"

"Yes, ma'am."

I smiled at his formal tone, although I was pretty sure he was mocking me. "Why are *you* researching an old ship?"

"Well, someone else I know has been studying it and I decided to see what all the fuss was about. I think I remember hearing something about it a long time ago, but I don't remember the details."

"You must not be from around here, then."

"No. I'm just here for school. What can you tell me about the ship?"

"Well, there's a lot to the story, but I'll just give you the short version. Back in 1872 the *Mary Celeste* was found adrift in the Atlantic. There were no signs of any of the crew, the captain, or his family even though the ship was in sailing condition. No one ever heard from them again. Basically, it's one of the greatest unsolved mysteries of the sea."

"Remind me of the names of the Captain and his family?"

"Captain Benjamin Spooner Briggs, his wife Sarah Cobb Briggs, and their daughter Sophia Briggs. You know, you could easily find out that much information by doing a simple internet search."

He appeared thoughtful. "I know, but I like to do things the old-school way. There's a lot more satisfaction in that. I'm sorry, I didn't catch your name."

"I'm Jamie."

"It's nice to meet you, Jamie. My name is Nicholas Trenton, by the way."

I jumped up so fast I knocked the wooden chair I was sitting in over and it clattered to the ground, shattering the peaceful silence of the library. I hastily scanned the room in search of an escape route and wondered if I should scream. Sophia said ghosts *could* hurt humans and I did not trust that one, deserter that he was. He had to be working with the Goodwins.

"Stay away from me," I yelled, panicking. *How did he find me and how does he know I'm helping Sophia?*

I grabbed my purse and ran. I didn't get very far before Nicholas cut me off. I should have known that outrunning a ghost who was much bigger than me was probably impossible. He grabbed me and covered my mouth with his hand, preventing me from making any noise. He pulled me behind the last of the tall shelves of books and pressed my back up against the wall, holding me there with the arm that covered my mouth.

"*Shh,*" he hissed. "I don't want to hurt you. Honest."

I whimpered and he loosened his grip just a little.

"Why did you run?"

I couldn't exactly answer him since he was covering my mouth. I blinked a few times instead and I think he understood what it meant.

"I'm going to let go of you now, but you have to promise not to scream . . . or run. I just want to talk to you. *Please.*"

I blinked again and he slowly let go of me. I folded my arms and hugged myself in an attempt to form a barrier between us.

"Why did you run?" he repeated.

"Because."

"Because, why?"

"Because I know who you are." I had no doubt. He looked exactly like Sophia had described him.

"Who am I?"

"You're a ghost."

He looked genuinely stunned. "You know about ghosts?"

"I've met one or two."

"Really? Maybe that's why I felt compelled to follow you today. I think you might be my soul saver."

I couldn't believe what I'd heard. *His soul saver?* There was no way I was helping the jerk. He ruined Sophia's life. Literally. For all I cared he could just continue to rot in his miserable shadow of a life.

"Why are you so angry?" he asked.

"Because I know who you are, Nicholas . . . Nick . . . whatever you call yourself."

"You know *me?*"

I nodded.

"How could you possibly know who I am? I didn't have any family left when I died."

"Well I guess that's your fault, isn't it?"

"What are you talking about?"

"Sophia. You left her. *You're* the reason she was killed." Tears spilled from my eyes and ran down my cheeks, but I didn't care. I felt so much hate for the ghost in front of me that I forgot to be afraid of him.

"Sophia? You know about Sophia?" He was unexpectedly baffled.

I didn't say anything, but I could tell by the look on his face the exact moment that realization struck.

"Sophia became a ghost," he whispered.

I nodded slowly.

"Were you her soul saver? How long has it been since she was here?" he asked quietly.

It was my turn to be confused. He acted as if he didn't know that Sophia was still around. *Isn't that why he's been following me—to get to her? Am I really supposed to be his soul saver, too?*

"Why did you leave her on her eighteenth birthday? You were supposed to marry her and you deserted her. She wouldn't have died if you had just kept your promise to her."

"Jamie, I don't know how or when she died. How could I have killed her?"

"You left her and she was forced to marry the old bachelor, Michael Mason. He attacked her on their wedding night. She tried to get away, but she fell on a fire poker and it went through her chest. She died instantly," I snapped at him.

Nick took a step back until he bumped against the bookshelf. He slowly slid down until he was sitting on the ground, his head in his hands.

"Sophia . . . Sophia . . . I had no idea." He was crying and I wasn't sure what to do. Half of me felt sorry for him and half of me loathed him. I wondered if I should try to run again.

"I didn't leave her. Honest, Jamie. Her father, Captain Goodwin, somehow found out about our plan to run away together and he had two of his men from the *Mist Seeker* kidnap me that night. I tried, *believe* me, but I couldn't fight them both off. They tied me up, threw me in a wagon, and hid me in town until they could stow me away on the *Mist Seeker*. I was there for a couple of days before Jeremiah came to tell me that Sophia had just been married. I remember him laughing and mocking me. He called me a snooping fool and told me he didn't want a poor nobody like me working for him anymore. Then . . . he pulled out a pistol and shot me in the head. He didn't even hesitate. It was as if he'd done it a million times before. They threw my body into the Chesapeake Bay. It sounds like I died the same night as Sophia."

It was my turn to slide down to the ground. I struggled to process everything I'd just heard. I'm sure we made an odd-looking pair sitting on the floor in the back of the library, tears streaming down both our faces.

"After I died and became a ghost, I thought about going back to Sophia's new home so I could see her one last time. I decided against it. I thought seeing her with her new husband would hurt too much. We may be ghosts, but we still have feelings. I spent the next decade and a half haunting ships at sea, biding my time until I could finish my business. I hit a low point and decided to go back and spend some time haunting the Goodwins, but I never dared venture over to Sophia's farmhouse. I figured by that time she must have children of her own. I never heard the Goodwins discuss her and she never came to visit. Now I know why."

"Nick, she's spent a hundred and twenty years thinking you left her and didn't want to be with her."

"Oh, man," he moaned and shook his head. "I can't even imagine her pain. I assume she's gone now. How long has it been since she was here?"

I hesitated for just a second and then decided he had a right to know. "I was with her just a few hours ago. She's still here, Nick."

He jumped up and let out a whoop. He pulled me to my feet and threw his arms around me, picking me up off the ground as he twirled. I couldn't help but laugh a little. His eyes were sparkling just like Sophia's always did.

"Where is she? Can you take me to her? I never dared dream that I would actually see her again."

"Nick, remember, she thinks you left her. I don't know if it's a good idea for you to just waltz back into her life without warning."

"Will you help me, Jamie? Convince her that I'm telling the truth. When her parents died I was there and I saw that they became ghosts. I've been following them off and on for years. They're up to something and I feel like I'm always just one step behind them. After talking to you, I'm pretty sure it's her they're looking for and I don't want them to find her."

"I'll try."

"Thank you." He hugged me again. "Let's go."

"Nick, I really did come here with my dad. He doesn't know anything about ghosts so I think maybe you should just disappear for a while. Give me a chance to talk to Sophia and then we'll meet you somewhere tomorrow."

"Okay. That makes sense. Gosh, it's going to be a long night." He ran his fingers through his hair and paced back and forth in front of the shelf. "Where should we meet?"

I thought about the cemetery back in Marion, but realized that the next day would be Memorial Day and it would be full of people paying tribute to their loved ones. I didn't think it was a good idea to bring Nick to my house so I gave him the address of our high school and told him to meet us by the football field at two in the afternoon. I really hoped Sophia believed him—because I did.

I started to walk away, but Nick grabbed my arm once again.

"Wait . . . Jamie. Is Sophia Goodwin really Sophia Briggs?"

I nodded.

He nodded back. "I get it now. I couldn't figure out why the Goodwins were spending so much time trying to find ghosts that had connections with the *Mary Celeste*. Was Sophia kidnapped by them as a girl? Did they take all of the Briggs family?"

"I think you better wait and have Sophia tell you the story herself. She's not the person you thought she was all those years ago."

"Okay." He paused. "Thanks, Jamie. I really appreciate this."

I smiled at him before stepping out the door. I met my dad at his office and we began the drive home.

"You're mighty quiet this afternoon," he said after we'd driven in silence for five or so miles.

"I'm just thinking. That's all."

"That must have been some book you read back there at the library to have you think this much." He playfully jabbed me in the arm.

"It was about long lost lovers finding each other again."

"I thought you were more into mystery and suspense than you were into romance."

I laughed. "There're a whole lot of secrets and suspense involved in this story, too. I haven't gotten to the ending yet and I guess I'm trying to solve the mystery in my head."

With the return of Nick, I thought I knew what Sophia's unfinished business was. It scared me. I wasn't ready to say goodbye to her.

When we got home I excused myself and ran up the stairs to my room. I really hoped I wouldn't find Sophia there. I whispered her name and then said it a few times a little louder, just to see if she was lurking in the shadows somewhere. I didn't get a response so I called Camille and told her everything that had happened at the library in New Bedford. She was just as shocked as I was. When I got to the part about Nick actually being a "good guy" she squealed into the phone. She was definitely the romantic in our little duo.

It grew late and we agreed to meet to tell Sophia in the morning. I flung myself across my bed, stared at the ceiling, and called Peter. He answered on the first ring.

"Hey."

"Hey, yourself."

"Any ghost business going on?"

I loved that it was such a casual subject with him, as if he did that kind of thing every day. "Actually, yeah. Peter, Sophia's old flame is alive. I mean, he's dead, but he's a ghost."

"Do you mean Nicholas Trenton or Michael Mason?"

I cringed at the thought of Michael still being around. "Nick. Nick's still here. I met him in New Bedford today."

Except for Peter's breathing, the other end of the line was quiet. Finally he spoke. "What's he doing here? Is he trying to hurt Sophia again?"

"That's what I thought, but it turns out he's been following the Goodwins, who are also ghosts. Peter, they're bad news. Jeremiah had Nick kidnapped and then killed him so he couldn't marry Sophia."

"Wow . . . this story just keeps getting crazier."

"I know. I can barely believe it. I keep hoping I'm going to wake up and find that I've been having a wicked crazy dream and it's still the last week of school."

There was silence on the other end of the line again. "I don't think I want this to be a dream. I'm kind of having a good time."

I paused. "Actually, I'm having a good time, too."

Peter agreed to meet with the rest of us in the morning as well. I texted Sophia and then I quickly fell asleep, once again dreaming of kidnappers, lovers, and old ships.

Chapter 14

Physically and emotionally drained the next morning, I forced myself to get up, get dressed, comb my hair, and put on some makeup. After all, I *would* be seeing Peter. I trudged down the stairs to where Dad stood in the kitchen, loading the dishwasher.

"Good morning, sunshine," he greeted me.

"Mornin', Dad," I mumbled.

"What are your plans for the day?"

"Cam and Sophia are coming over in a little while. We'll probably hang out somewhere."

"Sounds fun. I need to get some paperwork done this morning and then mow the lawn this afternoon. The rain we got last week is making the grass grow like weeds."

I sat down with a bowl of cereal and noticed for the first time the bouquet of brightly-colored tulips sitting in the middle of the table, reminding me it was Memorial Day. My eyes skimmed past the vase and into the living room where the urns of my father's parents sat on the mantle of our fireplace. They both died when I was very young and their cremated bodies had always sat in a prominent position in the living room, but I hadn't ever really given them much thought. My mom's parents were dead, too, but I think they were buried in Ft. Lauderdale or something like that. I wasn't exactly sure. Since Dad's parents were cremated and we didn't have a headstone to visit on Memorial Day he always brought home a bouquet of fresh flowers for the house instead to help us remember. I thought it was a sweet gesture. As I sat there eating my cereal, I wondered if Grandpa and Grandma Peters had ever been ghosts, hanging around their bodies in our living room. I hoped not. The thought gave me the creeps.

Peter arrived first. We'd all agreed to meet at 10:30 and he rang the bell at 10:25. Dad's eyes widened when he saw who was standing on the front porch and he looked at me quizzically.

"Mr. Ashby. It's nice to see you. I don't think you've come over since you and Jamie were in grade school. How have you been?"

I blushed. My dad was completely embarrassing me. There had been one birthday party of mine when I was young—ten, maybe?—that Mom actually planned and attended. She invited everyone in my class so that included Peter. It was true that the party was probably the last time he'd been over even though his parents and my dad were acquaintances in the academic world. Peter's parents were archaeologists and traveled the world researching this and that, often presenting their findings at the nearby universities. They went on a lot of speaking tours across the country and I think Peter was alone a lot.

"It's nice to see you, Mr. Peters."

"How are your parents doing?"

"Great, I guess. They're on a cruise ship somewhere in the south Pacific right now."

"Ahh . . . research or pleasure?"

"Supposedly pleasure, but if I know them they'll find something to study when they get off the boat."

We were still standing in the doorway when Sophia pulled up to the curb. I was glad there would be someone else to join in the awkward conversation. Camille jumped out of Sophia's car, too. I was relieved that the two of them had become friends. It made my job as the supposed soul saver a little easier. They greeted my dad and the four of us ventured into my backyard where we took up residence on the patio furniture. Camille lay down on a chaise lounge chair and Sophia sat at the table. I sat on the porch swing and blushed yet again when Peter sat down next to me.

"So what's the big news you have for me?" Sophia asked.

Camille was about to bubble over with that news, but I wanted to tell Sophia gently.

"Well, there're a couple of things. First, I did a little more research at the Newton library in New Bedford yesterday. I found out where the final resting place of the *Mary Celeste* is."

"Seriously?"

"Seriously."

"That's so neat. Where is it? Can we all go there together? Maybe I'm meant to say goodbye to the ship and the memories of it before I'm extricated. This could be my unfinished business."

"It's in Haiti."

"*Haiti*?" Peter exclaimed.

I guess I'd forgotten to tell Peter and Camille that part of the story. The part where Nick suddenly reappeared kind of overshadowed the rest of what I'd learned.

"I don't think there's any way my parents would let me take off for Haiti," Camille said. "Besides, don't you have to have some sort of special visa or something like that to even get into that country?"

"I'm not sure. Are you thinking of Cuba? I think maybe you can get into Haiti with just a normal passport, but that doesn't really matter. Dad would never let me go either."

"The sad thing is that my parents would probably think it was a great idea for me to go, even with the cholera, kidnappings, and crime they have there." Peter sighed.

"I think this is something Sophia is going to have to do on her own," I said.

"I can't believe it. This could really be the answer. I would miss all of you if I disappeared, though," Sophia reassured us.

"There's more, Sophia, but I'm not really sure how to tell you. Umm . . . have you ever wondered if Nick didn't come back for you because maybe he couldn't?"

"What are you talking about?"

"You said he gave Jeremiah a note when he left. What if that wasn't true? What if he wasn't really the one that wrote it? Did you actually see the note?"

Sophia raised her eyebrows and shook her head.

"That's what I thought." I smiled.

"Jamie, if you have something to tell me, please do so. Now."

"Sophia, Nick is still here."

"What? That's not funny."

"I saw him yesterday, Sophia. He's a ghost."

"I don't believe you."

"It's true. He found me in New Bedford. He thinks I'm *his* soul saver, too."

"You're not going to help him, are you?" she said accusingly.

"Actually, I am. Sophia, you need to listen. He told me what happened all those years ago and I believe him. His story is just as tragic as yours."

"Tragic? Let me guess. He met someone in town that was prettier than me so he decided to run away with her instead, but then she didn't want him after all and he was left all alone. Oh . . . poor Nick." She mockingly put her hands on her cheeks and shook her head. Apparently she hadn't forgiven him.

"Sophia, he was killed at the same time as you."

"You're not making any sense," she yelled.

"Your father, I mean Jeremiah, found out about your plans and had him kidnapped. Then, on the night of your wedding, he *shot* him." I yelled, too.

My dad opened the patio door and stuck his head out. "Is everything okay out here?"

"We're fine, Dad. Sorry if we disturbed you." I didn't sound very sincere and I wouldn't look him in the eye.

His eyes lingered on Sophia, who was wiping away tears, but he didn't say anything and went back inside. I continued. "Sophia, it might sound like a made-up story, but I believe him. He was really upset when I told him about what happened to you and he feels awful. He didn't know you were a ghost. He wants to see you today."

Camille and Peter had remained silent during our exchange, but Peter finally chimed in. "Sophia, I think you should see him. What if Nick is the reason why you haven't been able to move on? Maybe the two of you were really meant to be together and it just took this long to find each other again."

"I'm scared."

"If he's as cute as you described, what's there to be scared of?" Camille asked.

We all looked at her like she had lost her mind, but then Sophia laughed, and the rest of us joined in. It helped.

"Sophia, he still loves you. He's been following the Goodwins for years because he wanted to stop them from hurting other people."

"Wait . . . is he the other person that the cemetery ghosts said was asking about Sophia?" Camille asked.

"I hadn't thought about that until now, but I'm sure you're right, Cam."

"Where's Nick now?" Sophia whispered.

"He's planning on meeting us at the high school at two."

"Oh, man," Camille moaned.

"What's the problem?" I asked.

"My parents made me promise to be home by one. We're having our annual Memorial Day barbecue with my mom's sisters and their families."

"That sucks. I'm glad I'm not you." Peter grinned at Camille who glared at him in return.

"This is going to be the reunion of the century—literally—and I'm going to miss it." Camille was distraught, but the rest of us found her reaction kind of funny.

"You better promise to bring Nick over as soon as you reunite. I'm dying to meet him. Uhh . . . no offense about the whole dying thing."

"No offense taken." Sophia stood up. "Okay, if I'm really going to go through with this, I want to go change my clothes and freshen up a little before it's time to go. Do you need a ride home, Camille?"

I couldn't think of anything Sophia could possibly do to make herself look better. She had her thick blond hair pulled into a ponytail that showed off her long neck, and she wore cute khaki capris with a yellow tank top. As usual, her makeup was impeccable.

"Yeah, I guess I'll go with you," Camille grumbled. They excused themselves and I found myself alone with Peter on the patio swing. We gently kicked our legs and swung back and forth. The light breeze blew my hair around and brought with it the faint smell of the last of the lilac blooms. The birds were chirping—or was it angels singing—and I smiled. We weren't alone for long before Dad reappeared and asked what we'd done to chase away our other friends.

"I was just about to make sandwiches for everyone," he said.

"Thanks, Dad, but Cam had to get home. Their family has a yearly Memorial Day barbecue at her house."

"Oh, that's right. I forgot they do that. Can I make the two of you something to eat?"

"Sure. Thanks."

Dad brought ham sandwiches and a green salad out to the patio table and the three of us began to eat. He and Peter conversed easily, but I found myself continuously blushing. I thought I'd gotten past that. I think it had something to do with my dad seeing me with a boy for the first time. I struggled to hide how I felt about Peter, and I think Dad realized that I wasn't his innocent little girl anymore. I was relieved when Sophia returned and we had an excuse to leave.

I'd previously thought Sophia didn't need improving, but when she came back she was absolutely stunning in an orange sundress with little white flowers embroidered on the hem. Her hair was curled and gently cascaded down her back, tied with an orange ribbon the color of her dress. I was excited for her, but she was a nervous wreck, continuously clasping and unclasping her hands.

We piled into her car with Peter riding shotgun. I was getting anxious myself and my palms began to sweat. I worried that maybe Nick had been making up stories and was just trying to find a way to ferret Sophia out. *What if we show up at the football field to find the Goodwins waiting for us?* I would feel horrible if I'd led Sophia into more pain and possibly danger.

The football field looked a lot different than it did when school was in session and games were being played. It was usually full of students and laughter and noise. That afternoon it was eerily quiet. Sophia parked her car near one of the entrances and we all climbed out. I unlatched the gate separating the parking lot from the bleachers and field. I wasn't really sure how to proceed so I led our little group out to the fifty yard line and we looked around, waiting for something to happen.

I saw him first. He appeared about ten feet behind us, looking just as nervous as Sophia. He wore dark blue jeans and a button up shirt. His dark hair was combed in a stylish haphazard way. He looked like a male model on the cover of some magazine standing there with such a serious look on his face. He gave me a questioning look and I smiled and nodded, trying to assure him that it was okay.

"Sophia?"

She closed her eyes before turning around.

"Nick?"

Twelve and a half decades melted away in just moments. Nick closed the distance between them in the blink of an eye and then they were embracing—laughing, crying, hugging.

I watched the happy couple for a moment before Peter grabbed my hand and gently pulled me away.

"Let's leave them alone for a while," he said.

I thought he would let go of my hand once he got my attention, but he held it all the way to the bleachers and my heart fluttered the entire way. I hoped that my palms wouldn't start sweating again. We walked up the stairs and sat at the top of the stadium, watching Nick and Sophia below us.

"Do you think that reuniting them was enough? If this was their way of extrication, how long before they disappear? Do they just vanish?" Peter asked.

"I have no idea." I hesitated. "This might sound stupid, but I feel like this is just the beginning. I felt drawn to both of them, and they felt drawn to me, but I don't feel like it's ended yet. I still have this burning desire to help them, but now that they're together I'm scared that one of them is going to finish their business and leave while the other one is still here. I don't want them to be hurt even more by having to leave each other again."

We were interrupted by the beeping of my cell phone alerting me that I had a new text. It was Camille, of course, wondering if we'd found Nick yet.

"Do you two ever do anything without each other?" Peter asked.

I thought about it for a second. "Not really."

He chuckled. "What's going to happen when you end up going to different colleges or one of you gets married before the other one?"

It was my turn to laugh. "Actually, we both plan on going to Newton University since my dad works there . . . and maybe we'll marry twins. Don't worry, though, both of those things are a loooong way off. Cam and I can think about it later."

"How exactly did you two meet?"

"In first grade—long before you even moved here. We were assigned to sit next to each other on the first day of Mrs. Novak's class."

"Girls become closer to each other than boys ever do."

"Cam is almost like a sister to me, I think. I wouldn't really know since I don't actually have any siblings."

"I don't have any siblings either, but you don't find me constantly attached to any of my friends."

"Does it bother you that we're so close?"

He looked away. "No. I've just noticed that it's hard for anyone to ever talk to you without Camille being there. She talks a lot more than you do and sometimes it's just nice to hear what you have to say."

"Thanks—I think. Camille's not here now, what do you want to talk about?"

"Hmm . . . good question." We sat in silence for a moment while Peter contemplated his subject matter.

I thought of all the classes we'd shared, all the field trips we'd gone on together, and all the childhood memories that were ingrained in my mind. For some reason, I kept thinking of all the comedic moments. Apparently Peter did, too.

"Remember that time in sixth grade when Mrs. Anderson had toilet paper trailing from beneath her skirt all through class?" he asked.

I laughed. "How could I forget? No one had the guts to tell her. I don't think anyone learned anything all day because we were so preoccupied with the TP dangling from her backside."

"Do you think it eventually fell out on its own or did she find it when she went home that night and put her pajamas on? She was probably humiliated."

"Probably. I would've been mortified for sure. If it had happened to me, I would have tried to convince my dad that we needed to move—to another state."

"I'm sure we all had our fair share of embarrassing moments growing up."

"Oh come on, I had more than my fair share."

"What did you ever do that was embarrassing?"

"Uh-uh. You first."

"Okay. Let me think." He tapped his fingers on the bleacher. "I know. One time I was at the park with a bunch of friends. We hadn't been there in a while and I decided to go down the slide. I climbed to the top and announced to everyone down below that I would be going down the slide head first. I got down on my stomach and pushed myself forward—only my shorts got caught on the handrail and they came off. I went all the way down the slide without pants . . . and everyone watching."

I laughed so hard I could barely sit upright. It was a good thing I didn't have to pee.

"When was this?" I managed to ask between giggles.

Peter looked a little sheepish. "I wish I could say it was when I was young, but I'll be honest—it was last summer."

I laughed even harder. "I think that's the greatest story I've ever heard."

"What about you? It's your turn to tell me something embarrassing."

I turned red. I'd hoped we could skip over my embarrassing moments. "Okay. One time in fifth grade I went to a fall carnival up in Boston with Camille's family. We pigged out on all the fried foods they have at those kinds of places and then rode a bunch of rides. I was starting to feel kind of crappy, but we went on the Gravitron anyway. I totally puked when we got off."

"Come on. You've got to have something more embarrassing than that. Everyone pukes at carnivals."

"Yeah, well, I puked all over Camille's dad."

"Eww. Okay, that's pretty bad. I can just see the look on Mr. Spencer's face. He's such a serious guy."

Peter and I spent the next half hour talking about school and memories of growing up in Marion. Every once in a while we glanced down at the field where the young lovers sat and talked. I saw them kiss a couple of times, but I didn't say anything about it to Peter. That was a subject I did *not* want to bring up with him.

"Where'd they go?" Peter asked a while later, looking down at the field where Nick and Sophia had been sitting.

I looked down to see that they were no longer on the overgrown fifty yard line. Had something happened to them? What if they'd finished their business and they were gone forever? *I didn't get to say good-bye.* I stood up in a panic just as they both reappeared right in front of Peter and me, holding each other's hand tightly.

I breathed a sigh of relief. "So?"

"We're good," Sophia said, looking up into Nick's eyes.

"Jamie, I can't believe this has happened. I'm so glad I met you yesterday." Nick turned to Peter and stuck out his hand, introducing himself. "Hi. I'm Nick Trenton."

"Peter Ashby. I'm a friend of Jamie's."

"So what do we do now? How do we know if you guys have finished your business?" I asked.

"I've never actually seen it happen before, but Nick says he was with someone once when they extricated. They described a pulling sensation and then they only had a few moments before they disappeared. He said their aura disappeared with them," Sophia answered.

"Do either of you feel a pulling sensation?" I was scared to ask.

"Nope," Nick responded.

"Good. I mean, I wouldn't want you to have to leave each other already. What do we do now?"

Sophia and Nick exchanged glances again. "We're going to take a couple of days and go down to Haiti together. I want to see the wreckage of the *Mary Celeste*."

"That's probably a good idea. I can keep looking into things here while you're gone. Maybe I'll uncover something that will help us—if you come back."

We all knew that the "if" was the most loaded word of that sentence.

"When will you leave? What kind of travel arrangements do you need to make first?" Peter asked.

Sophia laughed in her tinkling way. "We're ghosts, remember. All we have to do is pick a flight and hop on. Customs can't hold us back. I really don't think we'll be gone for more than a couple of days, but we thought we should leave as soon as possible, before the Goodwins find either of us."

"I understand."

"Don't worry. We'll drop you off at home first," Nick teased. I was thankful that our relationship felt so natural already.

On the drive back to our neighborhood Peter sat in the back with me while Nick took his new place in the front. He kept his hand on Sophia's knee as if she would disappear again if he wasn't touching her. My hand lay on the seat next to me and Peter reached over and covered it with his own, giving it a little squeeze. I turned in surprise and he smiled and winked. Neither of us moved our hands and we sat in silence, no words needing to be exchanged, all the way to Peter's house.

When we arrived at my home, Sophia and Nick both got out. I hugged each of them tightly, not sure if that was our final goodbye.

"Keep me posted, will you?" I said.

"Of course. Don't have too much fun without us, either," Nick said.

He opened the passenger side car door for Sophia and helped her climb in before walking around and getting in the driver's seat. He was backing out of the driveway when Sophia rolled down her window and called to me.

"Hey, Jamie, text Camille and tell her to meet me in her tree house in about ten minutes. She'll kill me again if I don't let her meet Nick before we leave."

Chapter 15

I lay on top of my bed, staring at the ceiling. It was the middle of the night and I should have been sleeping, but I couldn't stop thinking about Sophia and the chance that I might never see her again. Since she'd been around, my life suddenly had a purpose. I tried to picture what it would be like when everything went back to normal—whatever normal was—but I couldn't do it. I predicted that I would find myself pedaling to the library multiple times a week again, but I didn't think I would find the same joy in books as I used to. Would Peter and I still hang out or would he go back to being the casual acquaintance that he'd been before he got caught up in the insane ghost business with me? Would I find myself constantly looking over my shoulder for someone hiding in the shadows?

After lying in bed for what felt like an eternity, I got up and flipped the switch of the lamp on my bedside table. I pulled out my laptop and looked up flights, wondering if Sophia and Nick had already left. There was a Delta flight going to Port-au-Prince via Washington D. C. and an American Airlines flight going to Port-au-Prince via Miami. Both were leaving around dawn. I tried to imagine Sophia and Nick huddled in the baggage compartment, completely invisible, but who was I kidding—they would totally be riding invisibly in first class.

I must have eventually drifted off to sleep because the next thing I remembered was Dad knocking softly on my bedroom door. In my blurred state of mind, it took me a while to figure out what the tapping noise was and where it was coming from. My lamp was still turned on, but my computer had slid off my lap and rested next to me on the bed.

"Yeah?" I called groggily.

"It's Dad. Sorry to wake you."

"It's fine. Come in."

I looked at my alarm clock. It wasn't even six yet. I rubbed my eyes as Dad entered the room fully clothed in a black suit with a red and grey paisley tie.

"I didn't want to leave without saying goodbye. Sorry I have to leave so early."

I'd completely forgotten that he was leaving for Chicago. "It's alright. I wasn't sleeping very well anyway."

"I made sure there's plenty of money in your household account and I left a list of things I'd like you to get done in the next couple of days. I hope to be back Friday, but it might be as late as Saturday."

"Okay."

"I'll keep my cell phone on in case you need to reach me. *Please* make sure you take yours if you go anywhere."

"I will." Early morning conversations weren't really my thing. Dad was used to my short answers.

"I love you. Be good." He disappeared into the hallway and shut the door behind himself.

I lay back against my pillows and sighed. I wasn't sure if I should even try to go back to sleep at that point. It seemed useless. Instead, I opened my computer again and made notes of things we could do while Sophia and Nick were gone. There were still a couple of museums that we could visit. They might have something in their collections that would be helpful. I decided that our goal for Tuesday would be to visit the Sippican Historical Society and maybe take a bus up to Salem to visit the Peabody Essex Museum. If I remembered correctly, the museum had some of Captain Briggs' belongings that had been found on the *Mary Celeste*. I forced myself to stay in bed until seven and then got up. I blared the radio while I showered and dressed. I could handle quiet when Dad was around—or when he was at work—but there was something about him being out of the state that always made me want to have background noise so that I didn't feel completely alone. That was the first business trip he'd gone on since I found out about the existence of ghosts and I didn't feel all that safe.

I decided to look at the list Dad left so that I could get most of it done before I met up with Cam and Peter. Dad always left "chore lists" when he went out of town. They made me laugh because most of what was on them were pointless things I did normally without ever having to be asked. I knew he trusted me, but I figured it was his way of trying to be a parent, rather than a roommate. The list was small:

> Water the plants
> Check the mailbox
> Wash any needed laundry
> Take out the trash if you fill it up
> Love you, Dad

Yep. It was definitely one of Dad's typical lists. I could have it all done in fifteen minutes. We had a couple of houseplants on a stand in the living room. I quickly watered them, pulled off a few dead leaves, and then re-filled the water of the Memorial Day flowers still on the kitchen table. I threw a load of my clothes into the washing machine, dumped some soap in, and turned it on. I slipped my feet into a pair of pink flip-flops and walked to the curb. No mail. I'm sure Dad had checked it the day before anyway. There was never anything for me so I could probably wait a few days before I needed to check it again. I went back to the kitchen and opened the garbage can lid. All that was in there was an empty yogurt container which my father must have eaten before he left. There—I was all done with chores. I looked at the clock. It was only 8:07. *What am I supposed to do all day?*

All I could think about was Sophia and Nick. I convinced myself that they were in the air somewhere. I wandered back into the living room and opened the cabinet holding our television. Neither Dad nor I watched much TV, but right then it seemed like a good way to kill some time. I flipped through a few channels before I settled on a morning news show.

Two anchors—one male and one female—were seated at the large news desk. He had black hair that was plastered to his head in such a way that I couldn't decide if it was real or a toupee. She had a poufy hairdo and wore so much makeup that it probably took her an hour to remove it every night. I didn't find the male anchor particularly interesting, but every time he would say something the female anchor would toss her hair back and laugh. That movement was usually followed by a dumb comment. When they got to a serious story (a car accident that killed a mother and her son) she put on a sad pouty face, as if she hadn't been laughing just a moment before. The whole thing felt staged and I wondered if she—or they— had majored in drama instead of journalism.

My phone beeped at me around ten. It was Peter.

"Got any plans for today?" he texted.

"I thought we could check out a couple of museums," I texted back.

"When you say 'we,' does that include me?"

"Of course. LOL."

148

I hit send and immediately wished I could take it back. I usually prided myself in not using annoying teenage slang like LOL or ROFL. Oh well—it was too late.

We agreed to meet at the Sippican Historical Society at 11:00. I threw a few things in a backpack and headed to the garage for my bike. My hand was on the doorknob before I decided to double-check the locks on the front and back doors. They were secure, not that it mattered if any ghosts decided to visit. I rode to Camille's house and walked up the stone path to her house. She opened the door and came out before I even had a chance to ring the bell.

"Grrr. Allison is driving me crazy this morning. Her latest boyfriend, what's-his-name, gave her a promise ring last night and she can't stop talking about it. What does a promise ring really mean, anyway? There's no way she's ever really going to marry him or even get officially engaged. I predict they break up before the 4th of July. My guess is that he just gave her the dumb ring to let other guys know to keep their hands off her until he gets bored with her. Nick is sooo cute. He and Sophia are the cutest couple *ever*."

The Camille I knew was back. She could talk up a storm without even knowing it. I often wondered how she was able to say so much without coming up for a breath of air. I think I even caught her turning blue once before she stopped talking. I wanted to tell her I'd held hands with Peter, but I didn't know how to bring the subject up. Guys were her area of expertise—not mine. She always held guy's hands and I'd lost track of how many she'd kissed. She'd had her first kiss in seventh grade. For me, though, it had been a new experience and one that I didn't know how to talk about.

The Sippican Historical Society was only a few blocks from the library and a short bike ride from Camille's street. Peter was already there, sitting under a large shade tree, when Camille and I showed up. I appreciated his promptness, but I wondered how much of it had to do with boredom from being alone so often.

The museum wasn't large, but it had a treasure trove of information about Marion and the history surrounding our city. The three of us were greeted by an elderly docent the moment we stepped inside.

"Hello and welcome," she gushed.

I looked around. I hadn't been inside the museum since the fourth grade when we went there for a class trip as part of a unit on local history. Camille and Peter had been with me then, too, and I wondered if either of them had been back since. The woman introduced herself as Rebekah and offered to give us a tour. She was obviously excited to have patrons and we agreed. For the most part, the information she gave us didn't really pertain to why we were there, but I learned some things about our town's history that either I hadn't known previously or I'd forgotten. Everyone perked up when we got to a small replica of the *Mary Celeste*.

Rebekah was fascinated by the legend as well and her storytelling became a lot more animated. She explained what had been found on the ship and gave a little description of each of the theories that had been thrown around about the fate of the Captain and his family and crew. Some of the theories were new to me, which probably meant they weren't widely accepted, but it didn't really matter. I already knew the *truth* of what happened that day. When the docent had told all of her stories she excused herself to help someone standing in the gift shop area and invited us to continue looking around.

I looked at the model ship and tried to picture Sophia there as a little child. She would have been two years old and just learning to talk. I wondered if her little laugh back then brought as much joy to people as her laugh did now. I bent over and looked into the windows of the ship's miniature cabin, trying to picture her mother playing music and singing while Sophia sat on the wooden floor playing with a doll. Unfortunately, I also pictured Jeremiah and Elsa boarding the ship with a band of unruly pirates to take the crew hostage. I pictured Sophia's reaction as she was yanked from her mother's arms and I jumped when I heard imaginary gunshots signaling the end of her parent's lives.

"You okay?" Peter asked.

"Yeah. Sorry. I was trying to imagine what it must have been like to be in Sophia's place back then."

"Do you realize that I'm old enough to have been a cabin boy on a ship back then? I guess guys my age are pretty lazy these days."

"Can you imagine trying to cook on a ship like that?" Camille asked. "It would have been hard enough in a house in those days without an oven or a microwave, but on a boat it had to have been so much worse. All that rocking back and forth probably made it hard to eat, too. I bet the food was super boring."

"I did learn something new that I don't remember hearing before. I wonder if Sophia even knows it. Did you read the paper talking about the Brigg's family curse?"

Camille and Peter shook their heads.

"A few days ago Sophia told me about all the Brigg's family members that had died at sea, but I don't remember her mentioning her Uncle Oliver Briggs. Apparently he died only a month after Sophia's family disappeared. His ship got caught in a storm and sank. He survived by floating on some of the wreckage for a few days, but died shortly before the only remaining crewman was rescued. Sophia's grandmother was still holding onto hope that Benjamin, Sarah, and Sophia would be found alive when she found out about Oliver's death. That poor lady."

"That *is* sad," Peter and Camille replied in unison.

An awkward silence hung over us for a few moments. Nobody spoke because none of us knew what else to say.

Finally, Camille cleared her throat. "Is anyone else hungry?"

"I'm starving," Peter replied gratefully.

"I could definitely eat. Want to go to Grandma's Cafe?"

We left the museum and rode to the library where we chained our bicycles to their bike racks before crossing the street to the restaurant.

"I miss Sophia. I like being friends with someone who has a car and a license," Camille complained.

"You better not get too attached to it. I don't think she plans on sticking around forever."

"Where will her car go when she dies? I mean when she's extricated."

"I honestly have no idea. Maybe Jack and Rita will do something with it. When a ghost is living in mainstream society it's probably difficult to cover up their unexplained permanent disappearances."

The usual crowd of kids from school filled the café. Just as we walked through the door a couple of Peter's good friends, Scott and Jason, walked out.

"Peter. Where've you been, man? Aren't your parents out of town? You usually hang with us when they're gone, but you haven't been home. I thought maybe you went with them this time," Scott said.

"Nope. I've just been . . . umm . . . busy." Peter looked down at me.

I blushed.

"Oh. I see." Scott got a silly grin on his face and nodded.

"Well, call us sometime, bro. Don't be a stranger." He high-fived Peter and he and Jason walked out the door.

We claimed a booth by leaving my bag and Peter's gray hoodie on the table before going to the counter to place our order. While we stood in line my cell phone rang.

"It's Sophia," I whispered loudly as I placed it to my ear.

"Hello?"

"Jamie?" Her voice was quiet and distant.

"Yes."

"How are you?"

"I'm fine, but what about you? Did you make it to Haiti yet?"

"Yeah . . . we're trying to find someone to take us out to the site now." The connection was fuzzy and I could tell I was about to lose her.

"Okay. Call me when you can." The call dropped before she could respond. I wondered if it would be the last time I'd hear her voice.

Chapter 16

One thing I learned by watching Peter that day was that teenage boys are never satisfied. Camille had a half sandwich with a bowl of chicken noodle soup. I had a turkey sandwich with fries. Peter had a double cheeseburger with chili cheese fries and a large Coke. When he finished all of that he ate what was left of my fries. He was in good physical shape so I couldn't figure out where he hid it all.

"Where are we going now? Didn't you say there were two museums to visit?" Camille asked as she pushed her dishes away and leaned her elbows on the table.

I looked at my watch and sighed. "It's already 2 o'clock. The other museum is in Salem so we'd have to take a bus. Even if we left now, we couldn't get there before they close at five. Besides, I kind of feel like we're just spinning our wheels and not getting anywhere. I doubt going there would be of any help. I'm so confused about how *I'm* supposed to help Sophia and Nick. Maybe they were wrong and I'm not really their soul saver."

Peter leaned back and put his arm across the back of the booth. His arm wasn't actually around me, but it made me blush anyway.

Camille giggled and I kicked her under the table hoping Peter wouldn't notice.

"Jamie, Sophia's been hanging around as a ghost for over a hundred years. I don't think you should expect to solve her problem in just a few days. Give it some time. Something will come up," he said.

"If we're not going to Salem, what else could we do? Please don't make me go home to hear Allison babble on about her boyfriend. I'm not ready for more of that yet," Camille pleaded.

"I guess we could go back to my place and hang out. We could rent a movie and get pizza and give this whole soul saver thing a rest for a while," I offered.

"I'm game," Peter said without any hesitation.

"Count me in, but can I invite Travis, too?" Camille asked.

I hesitated. I'd promised Dad I wouldn't have any parties, although I don't think he seriously thought I ever would. *Does this count as a party?* Camille and I did that kind of thing all the time when Dad was at work, but there weren't usually guys involved. Besides, I didn't want it to look like a double-date because I didn't want Peter to feel pressured to *act* like my date.

"Uhh . . . that would probably be okay."

"Good. I'll text him right now."

We ditched our bikes on my lawn and climbed the stairs to the front door. My heart skipped a beat as I reached for the doorknob. The door wasn't open, but it wasn't closed either. It was as if someone had pushed it shut behind them and it didn't quite latch.

Camille scrunched up her nose as she looked at me. "What's wrong? You look scared."

"Guys, I know the front door was shut and locked. I double-checked it before I left my house. Someone's been here."

"You're *positive* you locked it?" Peter asked with concern.

"Yes!" I snapped at him without thinking. I was scared.

"Is there any chance your dad missed his flight and came back already?" Camille asked as she slowly backed down the stairs.

"He would've called me. Guys, someone has definitely been here. What if they're still inside?" I was freaking out.

Peter put his hand on my shoulder. "Let's check it out. It's probably fine. Maybe the wind caught it."

He led the way while Camille and I hovered close behind. He threw the front door open and peered inside before stepping over the threshold. We looked around the living room first and didn't see anything amiss. My heart thumped loudly in my chest and I was sure if anyone was hiding inside they would be able to hear it. We stepped through the kitchen doorway and collectively gasped. Someone sat the kitchen table drinking a glass of ice water.

"*Mom*?"

"Jamie."

"You scared the crap out of us."

"Why?"

"You left the door open. We thought someone was in here."

"Someone *is* in here. Me." She laughed.

"Hi, Lillian," Camille said as she stepped out from behind Peter. She loved my mom and always called her by her first name—which my mom insisted on. I think their personalities were more similar than mine and my mom's. I was more like my dad.

"Hey, Cam. I'm loving your new hairstyle." Mom gave Camille a little squeeze on her way to give me a hug.

"She cut her hair in November, Mom."

"Well, it's new to me. Who's this?" she asked, looking at Peter.

"I'm Peter Ashby. I live nearby."

"I remember you. You came to Jamie's birthday party when she was little. Wow, you're all grown up now. You even have muscles." She playfully patted him on the arm.

I was mortified. I didn't know who was more embarrassing when it came to boys—my dad or my mom.

"That was a fun party," he offered. I'm sure he barely remembered it.

"Mom, why didn't you tell me you were coming?"

"I dunno. I thought you might like the surprise. Is Dad at work?"

"He's in Chicago."

"You mean he just left you here—by yourself?"

I didn't respond because I knew she didn't actually care. If she did, she wouldn't have left me all those years ago. Dad referred to Mom as his Wildflower. She was full of life and made the world prettier and happier wherever she went, but you couldn't control her. Her seeds fell where they may and sprung up in random places just when you least expected it. I thought of her as a gypsy. She went from one job and one town to another, trying new things and exploring the world. She phoned or wrote a letter now and then, and sometimes she even dropped in unexpectedly. I loved seeing her, but after every visit my dad would retreat to his office for weeks and I was left even more alone.

"So, Jamesie, what are you guys up to? I came to town to see some friends and thought I'd pop in for a visit."

First, I hated the pet name she had for me. Second, I loved the fact that visiting *me* was the secondary part of her reason for being there. I tried to stay calm. I knew that was how she operated and I couldn't let it get to me. *Just try to enjoy her while she's here. This situation is probably still better than having her here permanently, fighting with Dad.*

"We were thinking about renting a movie this evening—maybe getting a pizza, too," I said.

"Fun. Can I come?" Mom was a perpetual teenager.

"Of course you're invited," Camille insisted before I had a chance to tell her no.

Well, I guess I didn't have to worry about getting in trouble for having a "party." There would be "adult" supervision. I just hoped Mom didn't try to flirt with Peter or Travis—I would definitely have to find a new town to live in if that happened.

The four of us sat down in the living room and listened to Mom tell stories about her current life. The woman knew how to live—I could give her credit for that. She had just started to tell about the month she spent on a cattle ranch in south Texas when we were interrupted by the buzzing of the doorbell.

"Oooh, it's probably Travis." Camille jumped up and opened the door.

"Hi, Camille. Is Jamie around?"

I couldn't believe who stood at the door. It was Rita, looking very anxious. *How does she know where I live and why is she here? What should I tell Mom?* I'm sure I looked like a deer caught in the headlights.

"Uhh . . . hi. Come in, Rita," I opened the door wider for her. "Mom, this is Rita. She's the mother of one of my friends." I hoped Rita would play along with my charade.

Mom didn't stand up, but greeted her warmly from the comfort of the couch. "Hi. It's good to meet you. I'm sure Jamie has told me all about your daughter . . . or is it son?"

Rita looked at me. "Oh . . . that would be daughter. Sophia."

"What a beautiful name? Is she here with you?"

"No. That's actually why I came to see Jamie."

We had the attention of the entire room. Three other sets of eyes were on us and Rita seemed hesitant to proceed.

"I was wondering if you'd heard from Sophia, Jamie. She's not answering her cell. I needed to tell her something. You know how she is about keeping her cell charged, though." She raised her eyebrows.

"Oh yeah—I know Sophia. I heard from her a couple of hours ago, actually. She was hanging out with Nick in Hai . . . Hartford, you know."

"Oh good. I hoped she was still with him. I thought she might have left him by now. If you talk to her again, can you give her a message for me, please?" she asked.

"Sure, I can do that."

"Will you tell her that her Goodwin relatives are in town and I think they would like to see her?"

I could feel my eyes clouding over as I understood what Rita was trying to tell me. We exchanged knowing looks and Rita nodded. I was sure Cam and Peter caught on, too. Camille sat on the couch biting her nails, something she only did when she was really nervous. I hoped Mom wouldn't notice the concern rapidly spreading through the room.

"Well, I better get going. My husband's probably wondering where I disappeared to. It was nice to meet you, Mrs. Peters," Rita said.

"It's just Lillian. Call me Lillian. Oh, and it was nice to meet you, too, Rita," Mom gushed.

I showed Rita to the door and she squeezed my hand and whispered, *"Be careful,"* right before I shut the door. I stepped back into the room and plopped down on the chair I had previously occupied. Camille, Peter, and I exchanged looks, but none of us dared say anything. You could have heard a pin drop in the room.

"She was nice. And *very* pretty. How come I've never heard you talk about Sophia before?" Mom finally spoke up, breaking the silence.

"She's kind of new to town. I guess she hasn't come up in conversation, yet."

Mom seemed to be okay with that answer and a thoughtful look spread across her face. "Did Rita say that their Goodwin relatives were visiting?"

"Yeah, I think that's the name she said."

"Huh. I wonder if you're related to your friend. That would be really funny, wouldn't it?"

"What?" I asked.

"You know, because you have Goodwin relatives, too."

"What are you talking about, Mom?"

"My mother was a Goodwin. I'm sure you knew that, honey."

"Why would I have ever known that? You never talk about your family. Why haven't you told me about them before now?" I yelled.

Mom's mouth dropped open at my outburst. "Jamie, why are you getting so upset? I didn't know you cared about your ancestors, I guess. Sorry."

"Do you remember any of their names?"

"Sure. Grandpa and Grandma Goodwin." She laughed before looking around at her audience to see who would be amused by her joke. Camille was the only one who took the bait.

"Honestly, Jamie, I can't remember anyone's name right now. I just remember Grandpa Goodwin talking about his crazy relatives sometimes. I think there were a pretty wild bunch of people in his family line. If you really want to know their names you can look through their stuff. I think when Dad moved you over here from the other house he just put everything that had been in the attic there into the attic here. Grandma Goodwin saved everything and she passed it on to my mother. When my mom passed away, I inherited all the junk."

I looked toward the stairs. "What kind of stuff is up there?"

"I can't really remember. Most of it was in old boxes that probably haven't been looked through in decades. I'm sure it's mostly paperwork and maybe a few old pictures and trinkets. Maybe you should go through it—there might be valuables up there. Remember to share with me if you find anything worth a lot of money." She laughed.

Every part of my body begged for a race up to my room to climb the curving staircase leading to the attic. I was afraid if I acted too anxious Mom would question my motives even more—or worse, she might offer to help. I did *not* want her around if I found something important.

"So how long are you staying, Mom?"

"Do you want to get rid of me already?" she asked, pretending to be hurt.

"Of course not. I just wondered how much time I get to spend with you," I lied.

"Well, I think my friend wanted to leave kind of early in the morning. That's his car outside. I dropped him off at another friend's and he let me borrow his car to come over here."

I looked outside and saw a blue SUV with New Jersey plates parked across the street. I'd noticed it when we first came home, but assumed it belonged to someone visiting a neighbor. I was glad Dad wasn't there to witness Mom talking about other male friends.

The doorbell rang again and that time it really was Travis. Mom offered to drive us all to rent a movie. After the week and a half we'd been having, we opted for a comedy rather than a horror movie, although normally that would have been more fun. I vetoed anything romantic, hoping to avoid watching any awkward love scenes while sitting at my house with the boy I was infatuated with and my semi-estranged mother. Mom offered to spring for the pizza, but I picked up the tab knowing she lived on borrowed money half the time.

We were soon back at my place enjoying our pie dripping in cheese and the latest comedic release. Mom stayed in the room and watched the movie with us, but thankfully she behaved herself. I had fun, but my mind was on one thing only and it wasn't the movie. I couldn't wait to get into that attic, and I desperately hoped Mom didn't change her plans and decide to stay longer. At the end of the night she offered to drive everybody home so that Camille and Peter wouldn't have to ride their bikes in the dark and Travis wouldn't have to walk. I was sure Peter and Cam would be over in the morning and they could just get their bikes then.

Mom and I stayed up late talking that night—girl to girl and woman to woman. It was nice. It had never happened before. I ended up admitting to her that I liked Peter, and she sincerely told me she hoped it worked out for me because she liked Peter, too. I fell asleep happy that night.

Chapter *17*

Even though I stayed up late, I felt great when I woke up and nearly jumped out of bed. I had a good feeling about the day. I used the bathroom first because there's just no avoiding that in the morning, but before I showered I went downstairs to see if Mom was awake yet. Whenever she visits she makes a bed for herself on our pull-out sofa sleeper. We always offer the guest room, but she never takes us up on the offer.

Mom wasn't in the kitchen or dining room so I quietly tiptoed into the living room, not wanting to disturb her. Instead of finding a snoozing mass on the hide-a-bed, I found a neatly folded pile of blankets with a pillow on top. On the coffee table was a note.

Jamesie   I ended up needing to leave earlier than I expected and I didn't want to wake you up to say goodbye. I had a fun time seeing you. Good luck with Peter this summer.

Love you   Lillian.

She ended the note by drawing a heart and a bunch of X's and O's. That was one of the biggest differences between Mom and Dad. He would always wake me up to say goodbye no matter what time it was, but Mom would rather sneak out in the night to avoid "uncomfortable" goodbyes. Oh well. I didn't really care. She'd pop in again eventually, and with her out of the house I could get up to the attic and see if my Goodwin relatives had any link to the Goodwins that raised Sophia. I remembered Sophia telling me that soul savers often had a family link to the ghost they were trying to help. I might have been grasping at straws, but it was worth investigating further.

My stomach growled and I decided to make myself some breakfast before I headed back upstairs. I scrambled an egg and toasted a couple pieces of bread while it cooked. I flipped on the annoying morning news show in the living room again and ate my food on the couch while I watched it, careful not to drop any crumbs. What Dad didn't know couldn't hurt him. After my morning meal I headed upstairs for the shower I'd been putting off. I didn't spend much time in there, but chose to hurry instead—I was a girl on a mission. I threw on a pair of jeans and a lightweight long-sleeve shirt. It wasn't my typical summer attire, but there might be creepy crawlies in the attic and the more skin I covered, the less chance I had of one of them deciding to make a meal out of me.

After I'd given sufficient attention to my appearance I checked my phone for messages. Apparently I'd missed a call from Dad while I showered. I called him back and he answered almost immediately.

"How was your day yesterday? Are you staying out of trouble?" I could almost hear amusement in his voice.

"Of course, Dad. I only broke three or four laws."

"Did you hang out with your friends?"

"Yeah. Mom came by, too."

There was a pause. "She did?"

"Yeah. I was out with Camille and Peter and when I got back she was here waiting."

"Is she there now? Maybe I should talk to her."

"Actually she left already. She spent the night, but she was gone by the time I woke up this morning."

"That sounds about right." Disappointment tainted his voice. "Do you have any plans for today?"

I wasn't sure whether I should tell him the truth or not. I knew how he felt about me going into the attic by myself. He always worried that I'd go out on the widow's walk and fall off or something. I wasn't ten years old anymore, though. I decided to go with a half-truth.

"Actually, Mom was talking about some of her ancestors while she was here. They sounded interesting and I thought it might be fun to do some research on them today."

"Really? That sounds like a worthwhile project. You'll have to let me know what you find out."

"I will."

"Okay, well I better go. I need to get over to the conference center for a breakfast meeting. I'll call you tomorrow, honey."

"Sounds good. Love ya, Dad."

"I love you, too."

I pressed the button to end the call just as it beeped, telling me I had a new message.

"When do I get to come over???" Camille texted.

"As soon as you can," I responded.

"On my way."

I started to text Peter, too, but I stopped. *What if he's starting to get tired of hanging out with me?* I didn't want him to feel pressured. The whole boy/girl thing was kind of out of my realm of social skills.

While I hesitated, he called me.

"Hey." His voice sounded gravelly that early in the morning.

"Good morning."

"Camille just texted me and told me I have to walk to your house with her. Is that okay?"

"Sure—if you want to come. I was just about to invite you, anyway."

"Good. We'll be there soon I guess."

I was glad that I wouldn't have to spend the day alone in the attic. I looked at my room, suddenly realizing that I needed to do a little cleaning up—and fast. The only entrance to the attic was through my bedroom and I would seriously die if Peter saw one of my bras on the floor. I made my bed carefully, smoothing all the wrinkles, and tossed the clothes from the floor into the hamper. I cleared everything that had carelessly been strung over the attic staircase's railing and looked around quickly. It would have to do.

I was just heading downstairs to look for a flashlight when I heard the doorbell ring. I opened the door for Peter and Camille, and together we searched my garage for Dad's heavy duty flashlights. Dad liked to stockpile emergency supplies and I was grateful for it. The attic had a light, but if my memory served me correctly, it was pretty dim. We stopped in the kitchen to grab a bag of potato chips and some sodas out of the fridge. I didn't know how long we'd be up there and I didn't want to starve my friends.

"Your house is really cool, Jamie," Peter said as we walked up the stairs. "I like how old it feels—in a comfortable way."

"That's what Dad and I try for."

I led them through my room—which Camille had been in a million times before—and headed straight for the spiral staircase. Peter looked around a little, but he respectfully didn't stare at any of my personal things.

"In all the years you've lived here, I've never done more than sit on these stairs," Camille said. "We aren't going to find ghosts up there, too, are we?"

"The thought hadn't crossed my mind before, but now you've made me nervous. Thanks, Cam."

"I do what I can."

I inserted the key I'd taken from Dad's desk drawer into the lock and opened the smaller-than-normal door. We were greeted by a musty smell and a puff of dust. I flipped the switch of the flashlight I carried and shined it around before I stepped up into the attic. Nothing but stacks of boxes and stuff Dad and I couldn't quite part with . . . yet. I stepped forward and pulled the cord of the light bulb, illuminating the space in a yellow light. I was surprised. Between it and the light coming from the balcony window, there was enough light that we probably wouldn't need the flashlights until we reached the back corners.

"Hey. Is this how you get out on the balcony?" Peter asked, peering through the window at the world below.

"Yeah."

"I bet you spend a lot of time out there. You have an amazing view of Marion from up here."

"Actually, I rarely go out there. Dad's always afraid I'll fall off." I felt like a little kid admitting that to him.

Peter laughed, but didn't say anything.

"Where do we start?" Camille asked as she brushed at the dust covering a tote near the entrance to the attic. I knew that it held Christmas decorations and wouldn't contain anything pertaining to our search.

"We should probably start in the back. The storage containers in the front are the ones that actually get used occasionally."

The three of us weaved our way through a maze of boxes and clutter to the back corner. Each of us claimed a carton and opened it up.

"What exactly do you think we're looking for?" Cam asked.

"I'm not sure, but if you come across anything that looks important, set it aside and we can look at it in more detail later."

"Have you heard from Sophia?" Peter asked quietly.

"Nope. I texted her again last night and told her about Rita's warning, but I didn't get a response. I'm hoping she's either out of cell range or just having so much fun with Nick that she's lost track of time."

"I'm sure you're right." He didn't sound convincing.

The box I opened first held old household items, most of which were for kitchen use. There were wooden spoons, a tarnished tea kettle, and measuring cups. I removed the tea kettle and examined it closely. It was unusually ornate for a tea kettle and I sensed it would look nice after it was polished. The antique collector in me decided to keep it out when I closed up the box. I planned to take it downstairs and display it on the stove in the kitchen.

Camille's first box contained assorted linens—tablecloths, pillowcases, and dishtowels. Some of the items were hand embroidered and we checked them thoroughly to see if any initials had been sewn into the handwork. Nothing.

When Peter opened his box we were greeted by the smell of old leather. It contained multiple pairs of old work boots in various degrees of disrepair. It only took a second to realize that most of the stuff up there could probably be thrown out or donated to the Salvation Army or some other secondhand store. Dad and I would *never* use any of it. When we moved, Dad had a hard time getting rid of Mom's things so he saved them all. She obviously didn't care about the stuff, so I didn't think we needed to hang onto it.

I'd just started digging into another box of kitchen items when Camille let out a blood-curdling scream.

"What's wrong? Did you find something?" Peter and I were by her side in a split second.

"Look." She pointed to the box she'd been rummaging through.

"I don't see anything," Peter said.

"Look closer . . . at the bottom." She shivered as if something had just crawled up her spine and hopped from one foot to the other.

He peered over the box and shined his flashlight at the contents. At the bottom of the box was a little clump of fur amongst a pile of chewed up paper and black droppings. From the look of it, the mouse had been dead for a *very* long time.

"Why did I have to be the one to open *that* box?" Camille moaned.

"There's probably more where that came from. Jamie and I will most likely find our fair share," Peter said.

I kicked him in the shin. "Way to make her feel better, Mr. Ashby."

"Oops."

"I'm sure there aren't mice everywhere, Cam. Do you want me to get you some gloves?" I offered.

"Yes, please."

"Okay, I'll be back." I walked back down the attic staircase and then down the main stairs into the kitchen. I had just pulled some rubber gloves out from under the sink when my phone beeped. It was Sophia.

"*Still here. We're fine. Can't talk now.*" It was a short message, but exactly what I needed to hear to know that the project going on above me wasn't in vain.

I took the stairs two at a time on my way back to the attic to tell Peter and Camille the news. They seemed to have a renewed purpose as they continued digging through the endless stack of boxes. At one point, Peter uncovered a box full of clothes that looked like they were from the first decade of the twentieth century. He and Camille put on a fashion show and tried on the moth-eaten clothing. Some of it was pretty cool—I just wished it had been preserved better. Peter looked pretty good in the long-tailed suit coat and top hat he picked. Camille twirled around in a long blue dress that was close to the right size. The dress was trimmed in age-yellowed lace around the sleeves and neckline and she complained that it was horribly itchy. I laughed at their antics, but didn't want to stop searching long enough to try anything on myself.

We continued like that for almost two hours. Eventually we uncovered a few papers containing Goodwin names and set them aside for closer inspection later. We were just talking about taking a lunch break when Camille let out another one of her famous screams.

"That's it! I'm done. I'm not staying up her another second."

"Now what happened?" I asked with less concern than the first time.

She pointed to the top of the box she was about to open and stepped back. That time it was the shriveled up body of a dead spider. I'll admit it looked as if it had been large when it was alive, but that was obviously a long time ago. Peter came over and flicked the spider off the box which made Camille scream for a third time.

"I can't believe I'm wearing flip-flops up here. I'm sorry, Jamie, but I don't really want to do this anymore. Can you just call me if you find something important?" Camille asked.

"Yeah. That's fine. I understand."

The work would be slower with only two of us, but it might be better than listening to Camille scream and complain every few minutes. Peter and I waved as Camille pedaled off on the bike she'd left at my house the night before.

"Want some lunch?" I asked.

"Sure. What're we having?"

"I don't know. We can raid my kitchen and see what sounds good."

After searching the fridge, freezer, and cupboards we opted for a myriad of foods not limited to leftover pizza from the night before, orange juice, chicken nuggets, and Oreos. I figured I could eat healthy again when Dad got home. When we'd completely consumed all the junk we set before ourselves, we wound our way back up to the attic. I felt much more comfortable being alone with Peter. Conversation came naturally and there weren't any awkward moments, which is what I feared most.

"So . . . how often do you get to see your mom?" he asked when we were once again surrounded by cardboard and dust.

"Depends. Some years I might see her every month and other years I might only see her once or twice."

"That sucks. How long had it been this time?"

"Hmm . . . she came over and brought a Christmas gift in December so I guess it's been five or six months."

"Wow. That's a long time. I'm sorry."

I looked up quickly. "Don't feel sorry for me. I'm used to it. Besides, my parents don't get along very well so it's best if she stays away. They do okay if she only comes around once in a great while."

"I still feel sorry for you. I know your dad works a lot and you probably get lonely."

I shrugged.

"Does your dad ever date? Do you think he'd ever consider getting remarried?"

I laughed. "My parents are still married and Dad is very proper. Dating would require him to be officially divorced and I don't know that he would ever do that. I'm sure he still loves my mom. Deep down I think she must still love him, too, because she's never asked for a divorce. Why are we only talking about me, though? I'm not the only one who's constantly being abandoned."

"What're you saying?"

"I'm saying that your parents ditch you all the time, too."

"Maybe so, but my parent's problem is that they're still madly, deeply in love. Sometimes I think they'd rather be alone *all* the time without having me around."

"Well aren't we just a sorry lot of orphans," I joked.

"I guess we'll just have to stick with each other then."

"I'm okay with that."

He smiled at me over the big box he was tearing into. "Oh, wow, Jamie, look at this."

I stood up and had to pause for a minute to steady myself. I shook my legs one at a time, trying to wake them up from the sleep I'd put them in by kneeling for so long. He scooted the box closer to me and I folded back the flaps.

"Yes. This is what I've been hoping for."

The entire box was full of letters. Most of them were in coarse envelopes and were brittle with age. I could see right away that they were addressed to various Goodwins.

"I bet we'll learn *so* much from these."

I glanced at the remaining boxes and wondered if we should finish going through them or start reading the letters. There were only five or six boxes left and I decided we should just get all the work done in the attic at once, but I was anxious to get to the box of letters.

It was in the final box that I found it. I pulled out a book with old black and white photos and newspaper clippings pasted inside. The pages were full and the book could barely stay shut. There had to be generations of photographs and memorabilia inside. I stood to show Peter and one of the photos slipped out of the book, falling to the attic floor. I bent to pick it up and gasped as I saw the picture. My hands were shaking when I finally dared touch it. The black and white photograph was small, maybe two inches by three inches and curved slightly around the edges. Looking back at me from the paper were the serious faces of a man, a woman, and a girl of about thirteen or fourteen years. The girl was a younger version of the one I knew, but there was no doubt in my mind that I was looking at Sophia. I turned the picture over and in a flowing script was written *Jeremiah, Elsa, and Sophia Goodwin— December 1883*.

"Peter." My voice caught in my throat as I squeaked the one word I could actually get out. He looked up from the box he was closing and saw me standing above him holding out a picture. He looked at my face, noted the concern, and took the picture from my trembling hands. He flipped on his flashlight and trained the bright beam at the old print, staring at it for what felt like an eternity.

"This is it, Jamie. This is our connection."

I nodded.

"Now I guess we just need to figure out what to do with this knowledge."

I nodded again.

"You don't look like you're very happy with this information. I thought you'd be excited that we had a lead."

I sat down on the nearest box. "I would be excited, but Peter, this find means that it was *my* family and *my* ancestors that did this unspeakable thing to Sophia." My voice shook a little as I said her name.

Peter stood in a flash and stepped over to where I sat on one of the dusty boxes. He took both of my hands in his and crouched down in front of me. "Jamie, do *not* do this to yourself. You had nothing to do with what happened to Sophia. Of everyone she's ever known, you are the one who is helping her the most. Don't blame yourself for something that was done ages ago. Besides, you don't even know yet how closely Jeremiah and Elsa are related to you. For all you know they could be twelfth cousins or something. I'm sure if we all dug around, we would find that we all have ghosts in our family tree—I mean—well, you know what I mean." He squeezed my hands for emphasis.

"I know what you're saying is true, but I still feel bad. Now more than ever I want to help Sophia."

"Good. Let's carry all the letters and papers downstairs and we can go through it down there. Okay?"

"Yeah. Sounds good." I stood and reached for one of the boxes we'd set aside, but Peter reached out and gently laid his hand on my shoulder before I could pick it up.

"Actually, can I ask for one thing first?"

"Hmm . . . depends on what it is."

"I've been dying to go out on the widow's walk. Can we go out there for just a minute?"

I laughed. "Sure. Just don't fall off or my dad will kill me."

We unlatched the tall window and stepped out onto the small balcony.

"I bet I can see my house from here."

We both looked in the direction of Peter's street and sure enough, we could just make out the roof of his home a few blocks away. It was a beautiful June afternoon and the sun shone brightly on everything below us. Trees and yards were fully green after their winter's nap and the world was alive with color. We could hear children laughing somewhere below and I remembered spending summers—when Dad was home—on my swing set in the backyard. Camille had a trampoline and we would spend hours and hours jumping on it, seeing who could bounce the highest. I always won and Camille was always upset. Peter leaned over the small railing and looked away from me.

"How come we haven't hung out with each other much in the past?"

"I don't know. I guess we just never took the time."

He turned back toward me and slowly slid his arms around my waist. I looked at him with surprise as my heart thumped in my chest. He pulled me closer to him until our faces were just inches apart. I didn't know what to do with my hands so I rested them on his chest.

I knew what was going to happen and my whole body felt as if it would melt at any second. Finally, when I thought I might die of anticipation, Peter leaned forward and kissed me. It was a small, gentle kiss. There was nothing demanding about it and it only lasted for a second. We smiled at each other, laughed a little, and then holding my hand, he helped me step back into the attic through the window. There were no words exchanged—there didn't need to be.

We carried all the stuff we'd kept out for further inspection down to the dining room table. It took us two trips. We thought it would be best to start with the letters since they'd probably contain the most information. We laid them out in order of the dates they were written as best we could. I grabbed a notebook and pen so that we could jot down anything that seemed important or interesting. Peter started reading the letters with the latest dates first since they were most likely to be from people closely related to me. I took notes.

The first letters were written to my grandmother. It must have been before she'd married my grandfather because they were still addressed to Betsy Goodwin rather than her married name of Betsy Calder. Most of them were from childhood friends, and didn't contain anything important. A few were from cousins who lived in various states across the eastern seaboard. Betsy Goodwin's family lived near Boston at the time most of the first letters were written.

As we progressed through the stack we started finding letters addressed to Betsy's parents. Again, most of these letters were from family that lived elsewhere. I'd decided to make a genealogical chart of sorts in the back of the notebook I was using so that we could keep track of the barrage of names coming at us. So much of the handwriting was flowery and faded that it took both of us to interpret some of the words. I felt like a genuine detective.

About midway through the box we came across the first mention of Jeremiah and Elsa. It was addressed to Betsy's father Henry (my great-grandfather) and was written by his older sister, Genevieve Goodwin Slate. The date at the top was July 17, 1926.

> Dearest Brother,
> It was so lovely to receive the last letter you wrote to me. It brings me great pleasure to know that you are well. Please give your sweet wife and baby hugs from Aunt Gen. My little family is faring well too

and we hope to be in our new home by fall. James works hard on it every day. You will need to come stay with us for a while once the work is complete.

You might be interested to know that I was recently given an old sea trunk that belonged to fathers cousins Jeremiah and Elsa Goodwin. Do you remember them. I recall meeting them once as a very young girl perhaps five or six. You might not have been old enough to remember that day.

Anyway it seems that they both passed many years ago so the trunk was brought here and left by an elderly man whose name I did not catch. He said I was the nearest kin to them that he could find and thought I should have their trunk. It is locked and perhaps one day James will find enough time to open it for me. I found it to be a strange incident and thought you might get a laugh from it. I hope all is well and that your family is having a wonderful summer.

Love always. Genevieve Goodwin Slate

"I would love to know what was in that trunk," Peter said as he folded the letter and put it back in its aging envelope.

"Me, too. I wonder if any other letters will say."

He shuffled through the letters and shook his head. "The rest of the ones we haven't read yet are dated before the letter that mentioned the trunk. I don't think we're going to find anything else about it."

"Darn."

"Let's keep reading though. We might find something else important."

Apparently Genevieve had a passion for writing letters, because we had to make our way through a great number of ramblings about her children and husband before we got to letters from the previous generation. The stack of letters was beginning to dwindle before we finally found another one that mentioned Jeremiah and Elsa.

It was written by Henry and Genevieve's father Phillip and it was addressed to someone by the name of Sally Hart. For some reason it had never actually been sent to the recipient. I wondered who she was, but I never did get an answer. The best guess I had from the wording in the letter was that she too was a distant cousin of Jeremiah and Elsa.

Dear Sally,

Congratulations on the arrival of your new child. We wish you and your little one the best of health in the days to come. I am happy to share the news that Laura has accepted the offer of my hand in marriage and her father has agreed as well. We shall be married sometime in the fall if all goes as planned. She is a lovely girl and I couldn't be luckier. Father has been keeping me busy on the farm and I fear I might never get a break to enjoy the fine spring weather we have been having here.

We were recently visited by our cousins, Jeremiah and Elsa Goodwin. They are surely a strange couple. I recall father taking me to visit them when I was about fourteen and they had a beautiful daughter. I believe Sophia was her name. She was friendly enough and I think her parents would have liked to see us married, but I definitely did not want to be paired with them, nor would my father have ever allowed it. I overheard him talking with Mother about "trusting

Jeremiah about as far as I could throw him." I suppose Father does not hold much regard for him.

They came here without their daughter this time and did not mention her so I suppose she has been married off to some other poor fool. I do not know what business they had with my father, but he was very upset when they left. I shall try to avoid contact with this family in the future and I suggest you do so as well if you ever chance to meet up with them since you now live so close to them. I pray for your continued health and happiness.

Best regards, Phillip Goodwin

I felt like I'd been taken back in time. In just one letter there was the happiness of a new baby being born and the joy of an engagement. The man who wrote this letter would have been my great-great grandfather and the Laura he mentioned would be my great-great grandmother. Being an only child and coming from parents who did not have much family, I found myself fascinated with the history of it all and I felt a closeness to the people I'd never met. I hoped that Peter wasn't getting bored.

"When was that letter written?" I asked.

Peter unfolded it again and looked at the date. "It looks like it was May of 1895."

"Hmm . . . so this was written after Sophia had been dead for a while. I think she told me she quit haunting them after five or six years or something like that. I don't think Nick started haunting them until sometime in the early 1900's. Apparently this visit fell sometime between the two of them keeping tabs on Jeremiah and Elsa."

We finished the last of the letters without finding any more references to the "strange cousins" and decided to look through the photo album where I'd found the picture of Sophia with Jeremiah and Elsa. I found it fascinating to see what my dead relatives looked like. Some of the women were absolutely beautiful in their elegant dresses with high collars and long sleeves. I hoped that some of their genes had been passed on to me. Some of the pictures were a little eerie since no one ever smiled in pictures back in those days. I could only imagine what my ancestors would think if they saw the goofy poses and silly faces we made in modern photographs.

"Have you ever heard of post-mortem photography?" Peter asked as he flipped through the album.

"Umm . . . I'm not sure."

"Have you ever seen *The Others?* It's a Nicole Kidman movie. Looking at all these old pictures makes me think of it."

"I don't think so."

"Oh. The movie talks about it a little bit. It's kind of a freaky movie. We should watch it together some time."

"Okay, but if it's a scary movie can we wait until this whole thing with Nick and Sophia is done?"

He smiled. "Of course."

"So what *is* post-whatever-you-called-it photography?"

"Post-mortem. Years ago, when photographs first started to become available, people would sometimes take pictures of their deceased loved ones."

"Eww."

"It wasn't creepy to them. Their culture was different back then. Regular people didn't own cameras or have cell phones with video capabilities like they do now. It cost a lot of money to have your picture taken so people would sometimes wait until a family member died before they splurged on it. They wanted to preserve the memory of their loved ones."

"So . . . were they decaying when their pictures were taken?"

"No. They took the pictures within the first couple days of the person dying so that they still looked somewhat normal. They posed them, too, you know."

"Posed them? What do you mean?"

"Well, since photographs were such a rare occurrence, they usually wanted the whole family in the picture so they'd prop up the dead body, make sure their eyes were held open, and pose as if it were a normal family portrait. A lot of times they'd take pictures of dead kids with their favorite toys and sometimes if a mother died in childbirth, they'd prop her up, sit her baby on her lap, and then cover her face with a shroud of some sort. Those are the pictures that disturb me most."

"That is so creepy. How do you know all this anyway?"

"You're forgetting who my parents are. I'm sure I have a different feeling toward dead people than most kids my age. I grew up looking at skeletons."

Suddenly I had a whole different perspective while looking through the photo album. I found myself analyzing every person in every picture to see if there were any signs of death. I questioned a couple of them, but Peter didn't agree with me. Apparently he'd seen a lot of those pictures. I was fine looking at ghosts, but I didn't want to stare at their real bodies.

Toward the back of the album we started finding newspaper clippings and other small mementos. I found a few birth records and death notices of some of the ones whose letters we'd read earlier. Peter restlessly tapped his feet and squirmed atop his perch before finally standing up. He stared aimlessly out one of the windows into the backyard and I decided it was time to call it a day.

But then I turned one more page.

There was a clipping with the headline, "Couple Feared Lost At Sea." I leaned in for a closer look. It was from the Newport News Daily Press and was dated September 28, 1912. I skimmed the first couple of lines.

"Peter, listen to this."

He returned from his post at the window and sat next to me at the table. I began to read:

"Former Newport News resident, Captain Jeremiah Goodwin, is believed to be lost at sea. The elderly Captain Goodwin's ship, The Mist Seeker, was found smashed into the rocks near Sunset Cove after the large storm on the 16th day of September 1912. At first it was feared that no survivors would be found, but a young man by the name of Hans Bowman was discovered floating on a bit of debris the next day. Bowman claims he was the only person on the ship to survive. It is believed that the elderly Mrs. Goodwin was also aboard the ship at the time of its sinking.

Captain Goodwin had recently sold his property on the south end of Newport News where he had been a part-time resident for the last thirty years. Captain Goodwin was known to be a shrewd businessman in the area. He and Mrs. Goodwin do not have any surviving descendants and no memorial services are currently being planned."

"Wow. They totally got what was coming to them," Peter said when I'd finished reading the article.

"I don't think any kind of death would make up for the pain they put countless people through when they were alive."

"I guess we know how they found each other in death—they died at the same time and place. When you read that it was 1912, I thought you were about to tell me they died on the Titanic."

"Why?"

"It sunk in 1912, too."

"You're just a walking history book, aren't you?" I joked.

I really didn't mind. I enjoyed history myself and found Peter's little trivia facts to be kind of interesting.

I was silent for a minute, thinking. "Why do you think they became ghosts? Sophia said it's rare for people who did something bad on earth to become ghosts when they die. Usually it's for them to right a wrong, but I don't picture Jeremiah and Elsa doing that. They were completely heartless and I don't think there's any way they could ever right all of the wrongs they did."

"I don't know. I just hope we don't ever have to find out. As long as we can keep Sophia and Nick away from the Goodwins until they extricate we shouldn't ever have to cross paths with them."

I looked at the clock. It was already after five and I was completely exhausted from everything we'd been doing that day.

"Let's just leave everything spread out here for tonight," I said as I waved my hand over the mess of papers on the dining room table. "We can show it to Camille tomorrow . . . and Sophia if she comes back. I don't know about you, but I'm starving again."

"I have an idea. You've been feeding me for the last few days and I think it's my turn to return the favor. Cooking is a hobby of mine. Are you willing to taste *my* food?" Peter suggested.

"Sure. I have nothing better to do so I might as well give it a try," I joked.

"I make a pretty mean Alfredo sauce if you like that kind of thing."

"It sounds delicious. What ingredients do I need to have?"

"Actually, I think I have everything that I need at my house. Want to go over there?"

I hesitated for a second. For some reason it didn't feel weird to be alone at my house with Peter, but the idea of being alone on his territory made me nervous.

"I guess that would be okay," I said slowly.

"Great. Let's go."

We made the walk to his house in less than fifteen minutes and let ourselves in through the garage. Peter's house was filled with old things just like mine, but the things occupying the shelves in his home were artifacts, not antiques. I spent the first twenty minutes we were there going from glass case to glass case admiring everything I saw. Peter was able to tell me the history of every single piece. His parents had taught him well.

He stopped at a hall table and hit play on the answering machine. There were a couple of messages for his parents that he quickly skipped over and then listened when he heard his mom's voice come on the machine.

"Peter? Hello? I guess you must be out with friends. Don't have too much fun without us. We were able to take a ferry out to a little tropical island today and it was blissful. You would have really liked it. Anyhoo, enjoy your evening. We'll call again tomorrow. Love you."

Peter rolled his eyes and laughed when the machine beeped that the message was over. "If they'd really wanted to talk to me they would have called my cell phone instead of the home number."

Peter chatted as he pulled out pans, utensils, and ingredients and began to work on dinner—obviously in his comfort zone. I offered to help and he instructed me to cook the fettuccine noodles. I could handle that—it only required pasta and water. I shouldn't have hesitated in going to his house because he was a complete gentleman the entire time we were there and never did so much as hold my hand. He was right—he made a delicious Alfredo and there were no leftovers when we finished.

We were trying to decide whether to return to my house and continue searching through documents or call it a night when my phone rang.

"How'd it go today? You never called me so I guess that means you didn't find anything?" It was Camille. I'd completely forgotten about her.

I quickly filled her in on all the information we'd uncovered. She was impressed. "I want to see the picture," she said when I told her about the photo we'd found.

"Would you be interested in coming back over to my house tonight or do you want to wait until tomorrow?"

"I know it's only seven-thirty and bright as day outside, but I'm already in my pajamas. We better make it tomorrow."

"Okay. Is ten good?"

"Yeah. I'll be there."

I hung up with Camille and walked with Peter back to my house. He didn't come inside again, but he said goodbye and left on his bike. I let myself inside the house and leaned back against the closed door.

I couldn't believe everything that had happened that day. I'd discovered that I was related to murderous villains and I had my first kiss—all in the same afternoon. Not bad.

Chapter 18

It was tempting to continue going through stuff on my own, but I decided against it. I might miss something important if mine were the only eyes looking. The chances of three of us missing the same thing were slim so I figured it could wait until the morning. I straightened up the dining room the best I could and went upstairs to get in my own pajamas. It was only 8:30 and the sun had barely gone down, so there was still a faint light coming through my bedroom window.

I thought back to earlier in the day and the kiss I'd shared with Peter on the widow's walk above me. I climbed the stairs to the attic once more and unlatched the window to the balcony. I stepped out into the cool night air and looked around. It was even more beautiful at that time of night. I could see the waters of Buzzards Bay way off on the horizon and I thought about all the ships that had sailed in and out of the waters there over the years. After my adventure was over I would never look at the sea the same way again. I closed my eyes and tried to remember the way it felt when Peter had touched my lips with his. The memory was still close.

I opened my eyes and as I turned to go back inside I spied a couple out for an evening stroll on the sidewalk just down the road from my house. It was sweet that they were still holding hands at their older age, but as they grew ever nearer to my house my world came crashing down. I was not very close, and it was fairly dark, but there was no doubt in my mind that it was Jeremiah and Elsa. I was so scared that my knees started knocking together. I probably should have immediately gone back down into the attic, but I was frozen in place, too scared to move.

They were almost directly in front of my house when they looked up and saw me staring at them. My heart pounded as our eyes locked. They stopped walking and waved. My arm felt as if it weighed a hundred pounds, but I was finally able to lift it in a gesture of hello and managed to fake a half-smile in return. They continued walking and I let out my breath loudly. I jumped back into the attic and locked the window. I ran down the attic staircase, locking the door behind me and then ran down the main staircase and peered out the living room window. I couldn't see the Goodwins anymore and hoped they'd gone on down the street.

I continued my crazy run through the house checking every window and door lock, turning on lights, and closing all the curtains before I realized it wasn't doing me any good—if they wanted in, they would come in. I was just about to dial Peter's number when the doorbell rang.

My heart raced and it took every ounce of courage I could dig up to step toward the front door. *Please let it be Camille, or Peter, or Sophia. Please let it be Camille, or Peter, or Sophia. Please let it be Camille, or Peter, or Sophia,* I chanted over and over in my head as I stood on tiptoes to look through the round peephole.

"Aaggh!" I tried to stifle the scream that escaped my mouth before the couple on the other side of the door could hear it. My mind raced, trying to decide what to do. I could run through the back door and hide in the yard until they left, but maybe they would just come in if I did that. All the information Peter and I had gathered about them lay on the dining room table. It wouldn't take a genius to find it and know what we'd been up to. If I ran out the back door I could try to escape to Jack and Rita's and maybe they could come back with me and check for ghosts since they could see their auras and I couldn't. But I really didn't want to get them involved. They deserved to be happy without getting mixed up in all the other crap. I was still trying to decide what to do when the doorbell rang again, followed by a knock on the door right near my head. I jumped and moaned again.

Finally, I made a decision. I'd wanted adventure and I was going to get it. If I answered the door I'd be able to see them and know what they were up to. If I didn't let them in, I'd spend the night wondering if they were invisibly following me around my house. I quickly dialed Peter's number on my cell phone and then slipped it into my pocket with my finger hovering over the send button. I unlocked the bolts on the door, the noise sounding much louder to me than I'm sure it actually was, and opened the door slowly.

"Hello, honey," Elsa said in a sing-song way.

"Uh . . . hi."

"We're the Godfreys. This is John and I'm Elizabeth," she said as she pointed to Jeremiah standing next to her. "We saw you standing on your roof and we were wondering if you could help us with a problem."

"What kind of problem?" I stood with the door only partially opened, not wanting to let them all the way in. Elsa peered past me into the room as if looking for something.

"Well, dear, our granddaughter has gone missing and we've been combing the neighborhoods around here looking for her. She's run away before, but we're really worried about her this time. Some others we've talked to thought she looked like a girl that had been seen at a bus stop near here recently. You look to be about her age so maybe you've seen her?"

Jeremiah, who hadn't yet said anything, stretched out his hand. I looked down and saw that he held a picture. When he spoke his voice was gruff and deep. "This is what she looks like. Have you seen her?"

I reached down and took the picture with the trembling hand that wasn't in my pocket. It was definitely Sophia. It looked like it had been taken sometime within a year or two after the one I'd found in the attic. The picture was cropped to only show her face and looked as if the color had been added later. Some sort of photo editing program had definitely been used.

The question remained. Should I lie or tell the truth . . . sort of?

I handed the picture back to Jeremiah. "She looks a little familiar. What did you say her name was?"

"Sophia," Elsa said at the same time Jeremiah said, "Suzanne."

"What we mean is, her name is Sophia Suzanne Godfrey. She could be going by any name, though," Elsa explained.

"Oh, I do remember her. I saw her at a restaurant in town. I overhead her talking with another girl that I don't know. She said something about leaving and going up to Boston I think." I really hoped they couldn't see through my poor lies.

"When was this?" Jeremiah questioned.

"Oh, I dunno. Maybe a week or so ago? I'm sure she's long gone. I haven't seen her since."

"Well, thank you for your help, honey. Can you do us one more favor? Will you give us a call if you see her again? We're desperate to know that she is safe. You can call us any time of the day."

"Sure. I could do that," I lied again, taking the little card on which Elsa had just scribbled a phone number and started to shut the door.

"We didn't catch your name, dear?"

"Jamie," I said without thinking. "Uhh . . . have a good night." That time I quickly shut the door and locked it again. I watched through the peephole as Jeremiah and Elsa walked down the porch stairs and down the road, continuing on their way. When I couldn't see them through the hole in the door anymore, I ran to the window and peered out through a gap in the curtains, watching as they rounded the corner at the end of the street. I breathed a sigh of relief and pulled out my phone, quickly dialing Peter's cell.

"Hello?" He sounded surprised that I called again so soon.

"Peter. It's Jamie." I didn't mean to and I tried to stop it, but I couldn't. The tears started falling and I sobbed into the phone.

Peter was on high alert. "What's wrong? Jamie, what happened? Is it Sophia?"

I tried to explain the best I could through the tears and was finally able to calm down.

"I'm sure they've moved on to another neighborhood. That was smart to try to lead them in the wrong direction," he said, his voice coming out kind of choppy.

"What if they circled back and snuck into my house? They could be standing behind me listening to everything I'm telling you." I shivered and looked around.

"Jamie, just stay put. If they're lingering around and they see you bolt, you're going to look suspicious. I'm sure if they really thought you knew something they would have stayed longer or done something to you." For some reason he sounded out of breath.

"I don't think I'm going to be able to sleep tonight. I'm so freaked out. I really wish Sophia was back so she could be on the lookout for spirits floating around."

"Jamie, don't freak out, but your doorbell is going to ring again."

"What?"

"I ran over as soon as you called. I'm almost to your door so don't freak out when I ring the bell."

"Are you serious?"

"About coming over or about not freaking out?"

I looked out the window. Peter was starting up the front walk. I opened the door before he even had a chance to ring the bell and stepped into his arms. The tears came again.

"I feel like such a baby. You didn't have to come all the way back here," I said when I'd finally composed myself and let go of him.

He laughed. "I don't mind at all. Guys like to play the role of protector, didn't you know that?"

"Did you pass the Goodwins on the way over?"

"No, but there are multiple streets they could have turned down. I'm sure they're well out of our neighborhood. Or else they went invisible."

I shuddered. "So what do we do now?"

Peter looked around. "Let's hide the stuff in the dining room first. In case they do come back, secretively or not, we don't want to risk them seeing anything."

We quickly stuffed the boxes in the small kitchen pantry and then looked around like lost puppies.

"Do you think we should call Jack or Rita?"

"I haven't met Jack yet, but I think you were right about not getting them involved."

"You'd like him." I managed a smile.

"It sure is bright in here. Why are all your lights on?"

I blushed. "I was nervous."

"Let's turn some of them off. If any of your neighbors know that your Dad is out of town, they'll wonder why the place is all lit up. If your neighbors come over, you can bet I won't be spending the night."

"You're spending the night?"

"There's no way I'm leaving you here by yourself."

My night had just become very interesting. I looked down then and realized I was standing there in my fuzzy pink pajama pants and an old t-shirt with dancing teddy bears. My face burned even more. I couldn't exactly go upstairs and change without Peter noticing and possibly saying something so I decided to just stick it out. The damage had already been done.

It was 10:30, but I was wide awake. I didn't know if I would ever be able to sleep again. Together Peter and I grabbed a pile of blankets and pillows from an upstairs linen closet and made beds for ourselves in my living room. I took the couch and Peter, ever the cavalier one, took the floor. We popped a bowl of popcorn and sat down in front of the TV. There were a couple of late night comedy talk shows on and we watched them without much enthusiasm. The last time I remember looking at the clock it was about 1 a.m. I don't know which of us fell asleep first, but I didn't wake up again until my phone started ringing and vibrating around five-thirty. I'd never been so glad to hear Sophia's voice in my life.

"Sophia," I yelled into the phone. The sudden noise woke Peter and he jumped up and looked around. I covered the mouthpiece and mouthed happily, "It's Sophia."

"You're mighty chipper for this time in the morning. I figured I'd be leaving a message on your voicemail."

"There hasn't been a lot of sleeping going on lately."

"How come?"

"Well, for starters, Jeremiah and Elsa paid me a visit last night."

"Are you *kidding* me?"

"I wish I was." I could hear Nick in the background asking what was wrong. Sophia whispered to him and then came back on the line.

"What happened? Are they still there? What do they want? Why won't they stop following me?"

"One question at a time, please."

She paused before answering and inhaled sharply. "I heard a voice in the background. Are they there now?" she whispered into the phone.

"No. That's Peter."

"Peter's there this early?"

"I was scared to be alone last night . . . so he stayed with me."

191

"Oh. That was nice, I guess."

I couldn't see Sophia through the phone but I could sense a sly smile spreading across her face. I'm sure she patted herself on the back for pulling Peter into the crazy adventure and successfully getting us together.

"So, tell me everything that happened. And please, start at the beginning."

I related to Sophia everything that had gone on the night before, starting when I stepped out onto the widow's walk by myself after Peter had gone home. She was understandably upset that Jeremiah and Elsa were passing her picture around town. Many of our friends had seen Sophia with us around Marion and we were sure that if Jeremiah and Elsa kept pushing the subject, someone would eventually finger us. When Jeremiah and Elsa returned to my house, they would most likely not be as "friendly" as they had been the first time.

"Jamie? Nick and I are in Miami right now. We should be home in a few hours. Is there somewhere you can go until then so that you're safe—somewhere with a lot of people?"

"Uhh . . . yeah. We'll find someplace. Call as soon as you get here."

"I will. Be safe."

We hung up and I explained to Peter what the plan was. I wasn't sure exactly how to proceed with my morning rituals. *Should I shower while he's here? It might be weird—plus, I don't want to go upstairs alone.*

I decided instead to change into some clean clothes and do a quick freshen up in the bathroom. I washed my face and pulled my hair into a ponytail. I used deodorant and a little mascara, glad I didn't have an acne problem because otherwise I wouldn't be able to get away with so little makeup. Finally, I dabbed the smallest of drops of perfume on my wrists and neck and ran back down the stairs, looking over my shoulder the entire way. Peter was just coming out of the kitchen, his face shining as if he had just splashed water on it. Now that the sun was up, my house didn't feel quite as scary. I reversed what I'd done the night before and went around opening curtains and shades. If our visitors were going to return, I wanted to see them coming.

It was still early—barely after six—and I wasn't sure where we should go. Peter's stomach was already growling so we made packets of instant oatmeal for breakfast, taking it to the front porch to eat. The morning was a little cool and the air smelled salty from the breeze rolling in off the ocean. Usually I loved those kinds of mornings. When we finished our meager breakfast we packed the letters mentioning Jeremiah and Elsa, the photo of the Goodwin family, and my notebook into a bag and left my house.

We walked to a nearby park, stopping at Peter's house on the way so he could change into some clean clothes. A lot of people liked to go for morning runs on the park's paths and we thought it would be a good place to wait until stores started opening for business. We'd decide then where to go next.

I spent the time in the park reading one of the books I'd checked out from the library more than a week before. I wanted to lose myself in the story so that my mind would stop replaying the events of the night before. I offered another book to Peter, but he opted to lie in the grass and take a nap instead.

At eight o'clock my phone rang again. That time it was my dad, checking in with me for the day.

"How was your night?"

"It was okay," I lied.

"You sound tired. Are you still in bed?"

I decided I better tell him the truth since I ran the risk of him hearing background noise. "Actually, I'm at the park right now."

"The park? What in heaven's name are you doing at the park this early in the morning?"

"I thought it would be a good idea to get some exercise. A lot of people come here to run or walk."

My dad's side of the phone was quiet for a moment. "Is someone there with you?"

"Uhh . . . Peter met me here. He wanted to exercise, too." I kicked Peter as he snickered beside me on the grass. It was a lame excuse and we were definitely not getting any exercise.

"Well, okay, I guess," Dad said hesitantly. "How was your day yesterday? You mentioned looking into your family history. Did you end up doing that?"

"Yeah, I did. Mom told me where to find some letters written by some of my great-grandparents. They were kind of interesting. One of the letters mentioned a mysterious trunk that was locked and the person who owned it couldn't open it. It read just like a mystery and you know I like that, Dad."

He laughed. "That does sound like something right up your alley. Maybe it's the mystery trunk your Mom inherited from her parents that wouldn't fit into the attic."

"Huh?"

"You know, the trunk in my den."

"No, I don't know."

"You really don't remember? When we moved into the house we tried to haul that big old trunk your mother inherited up to the attic with the rest of her leftovers, but it was too hard to maneuver it up the spiral staircase in your room and up into the attic. We put it in the closet in my den—behind the bookcases."

"Do you know what's in the trunk?" I asked, trying to sound nonchalant. Peter perked up and turned toward me with questioning eyes at the mention of the word "trunk."

"Nope. Lillian just mentioned something about old family stuff. I don't know that I've ever looked inside it."

My heart raced. "Dad, would it be okay if I tried to open it? Mom told me I could go through her stuff." I crossed my fingers and closed my eyes tight, hoping he would say yes, but knowing that if the answer was no I was going to open the trunk anyway.

"That's fine with me and I'm sure your mom won't care, either. It will give you something to do today, but please don't make a mess of my den."

"I won't, Dad. I promise." I grabbed Peter's hand and squeezed it tight, nodding my head up and down as I did so. He could only hear my part of the conversation, but I think he'd gotten the gist of it.

"I better get going. It looks like I *will* make it home tomorrow rather than Saturday."

"That's great. I can't wait to see you."

I wasn't sure if I was ready for Dad to come home or not. I didn't like having to explain my odd behavior to him, but I liked the idea of not being alone at night. That night, Sophia and Nick would be back and then the next night Dad would be home.

"Did your dad just tell you that he knows where the trunk is?" Peter asked excitedly when I'd hung up.

"*Yes,*" I squealed. "I knew there was more to that part of the story. I had a strange feeling about it. The trunk in my dad's den has to be the one that belonged to the Goodwins."

"Want to go check right now?"

"No. I mean, yes, but we can't. I promised Sophia we would stay in public view until she got here. Grrr, this is going to be a long day," I groaned.

"We should probably tell Camille what's going on."

I looked at my watch. "You're right, but I guarantee she's not awake yet. Unless we want her to be a grouch all day, we better wait at least another hour until we call."

"Fine, but now I'm anxious again. We need to do something to keep my mind busy."

"We could actually exercise like I told my dad."

"I don't want to get all sweaty—and I'm in flip-flops."

"I offered you a book to read."

"Ha. Ha. Ha. Just what I hoped for," he said sarcastically.

"Don't you ever read?"

"Sure, whenever I have to in order to pass my classes at school."

"Really, Peter? That's just sad. You can learn so much from books. I thought you liked history."

"I read the National Geographic. And honestly, I do read an occasional book for fun. I just don't know how some people can read a book and, immediately upon finishing it and closing its cover, open up another one and begin to read again."

"By 'some people,' you mean me." It was a statement, not a question. I didn't really take offense to it, though. It was pretty much the truth—until I met Sophia.

"There could be worse habits, I guess."

I laughed. "Please don't tell me you're one of those guys who spends all his days playing video games."

"I won't lie. I do play video games, but I consider myself to be a well-rounded person. I already told you I read once in a while. I have a few favorite TV shows I watch. I get exercise when I'm hanging out with the guys . . . kicking a soccer ball around, hitting a baseball, throwing a Frisbee. Oh, and you know I'm great at going down slides."

"How could I forget?" I laughed.

"Do you still like to play sports?"

"Honestly? Not that much anymore. I used to be somewhat of a tomboy. Whatever the guys were playing at recess, I was playing, too. The last few years I haven't been as active, I guess. I pretty much get all my exercise from riding my bike everywhere."

"Maybe we should change that. You can exercise with me this summer."

"We might have to get our exercise running from scary ghosts, you know."

"I hope we don't ever have to see the 'scary' ghosts again," Peter said, using his fingers to make the shape of quotation marks.

"That would be nice, but Peter—the more I think about it the more I'm convinced that Jeremiah and Elsa are somehow part of Sophia and Nick's unfinished business."

"Really? You don't think it has anything to do with the *Mary Celeste*?"

"Honestly, no. I don't. Every lead we've tried to follow about that ship has ended in nothing. We've gone over all the known facts a million times and there've been no new revelations. I don't know for sure yet, but Sophia most likely even saw the remains of the *Mary Celeste* and she's still here. *But*, every time we found something concerning the Goodwins yesterday, I had the sensation that we were on the right path. What if her way of extrication is somehow connected to the ghosts who were her captors for most of her real life?"

"Have you told Sophia about your idea?"

"Not yet. I didn't start thinking about it until after she left for Haiti."

"What do you think the business might be? Oh wait—never mind. I bet you think there's something in the trunk." He smiled.

"Yep."

"Okay. It's been an hour. Can we call Camille now?"

"Go for it."

Chapter *19*

I called Camille and tried to explain everything to her, but by that point the events of the previous evening were such a blur that I felt like I was making up a story. She was shocked that the Goodwins had come to my house and told me she was relieved she'd gone home early. Nice. I hoped I never needed her in an emergency because I was sure she'd be the first one to turn around and run away.

Peter and I instructed her to meet us at a nearby fast food joint as soon as possible. We thought about meeting at Grandma's Bakery and Café, but concluded that we should avoid the places we'd been seen with Sophia for the time being.

"I swear you have a curse, Jamie," Camille said when we were all seated in a booth eating a late breakfast or early lunch, however you wanted to look at it. It had been hours since Peter and I had eaten our oatmeal and we were starving. Apparently anxiety made me burn calories faster. Who knew?

"Why do I have a curse?"

"I don't know *why*. All I know is that there are an awful lot of ghosts following you lately."

"Come on—you like most of the ghosts. If Sophia wasn't in the picture, you'd have a secret crush on Nick. Admit it," I teased.

"*Jamie*, take that back." Camille blushed and pretended to be mad. I grinned. It was usually *her* making *me* blush.

Peter and I told Camille about the mystery trunk that was supposedly in the back of a closet somewhere in my dad's den. She was excited to open it with us once we told her she wouldn't have to go into the attic again. I couldn't guarantee there weren't spiders in the back of Dad's den, though.

"I think we need to have a plan in case Jeremiah and Elsa come back," Peter said seriously. "If they didn't take the bait and head to Boston to look for Sophia, you can bet the first place they'll go is back to Jamie's." He turned to me. "They'll assume you lied and have something to hide. I doubt they'll be very happy."

"Probably not, but I don't think they'd want to expose themselves as ghosts, so would they really do anything to me?"

"I don't know. If they find out that you were lying for Sophia, they might guess that she also told you who and what she really is."

"Can we do anything to ghosts that will affect them?" Camille asked.

"I'm not sure. When I first met Sophia, she told me that she could hurt me, but I couldn't really hurt her. I don't know if she meant there was absolutely, positively nothing I could do to her, or if she just doesn't feel pain the same way as living humans do."

"I think the most important thing we need to do as soon as Sophia and Nick get here is to find out how to protect ourselves against their kind," Camille suggested. Peter and I agreed.

We spent the rest of the morning wandering around Marion. We browsed through some of the quaint specialty stores aimed at tourists that we didn't usually frequent—including some I'd never been in—and then made a stop at the grocery store for snacks and a few things for dinner. Once Sophia and Nick arrived, we'd probably hole up in my house for a while, not wanting to be seen in public.

It was just after one when Sophia finally called to let us know they'd just gotten on the I-195 coming from Boston. That meant they were about five miles from town and I was ecstatic. I would feel a whole lot safer having someone who could see through walls by my side. Peter, Camille, and I immediately headed to my house and reached my driveway at the same time Sophia's little white car pulled up to the curb. I was surprised at the lump that grew in my throat and the joy I felt from seeing her and Nick again. The whole soul saver thing really messed with my emotions. I didn't want to seem like a baby so I didn't rush to her side like I wanted to.

"Hey, everyone. We're back." Sophia beamed as she stepped out of the passenger door of her car and Nick emerged from the driver's side.

"How was your trip?" It was kind of a dumb question. They'd gone there in hopes of finding answers to some really old questions and they hadn't succeeded. It wasn't exactly a pleasure trip. Of course, it *had* been over a hundred years since they'd seen each other . . .

"Well, it was definitely a culture shock. I've traveled quite a bit in my years on earth, but that was my first time in Haiti. It's a poor country and it was sad to see the poverty there."

"Did you see the *Mary Celeste*?" Camille asked, getting to the point.

"Yes . . . and no. We hired a man to take us out to the site by boat, and we did a little scuba diving, but with the guide there we couldn't do any exploring invisibly. There's only so much you can do in your human form. We did see some pieces of wreckage that were supposedly from the boat."

"How did you feel?" I asked.

"Just fine. I didn't feel any connection to it whatsoever. I expected to feel more passion than I did, knowing how much a part of my past the ship was, but I felt nothing."

"The water was beautiful, though. We *were* in the Caribbean after all," Nick joked.

"That's true." Sophia smiled as she gazed into his eyes. I guessed they'd done a lot of catching up while they were there.

There was a lull in the conversation for a second while we all watched the recently reunited lovebirds. I suggested we go inside instead of standing in the middle of my front yard.

"Umm . . . do you think you could check the house out for us first, though?" I asked.

"That's probably a good idea. We'll be right back."

I sensed that Sophia was about to vanish and I quickly jumped in. "Wait. Go around back. You can slip in there and any neighbors who happen to be looking out their windows won't see you disappear."

"Oh wow. I can't believe I almost did that. I've lived as a human for a long time, but these last few days I haven't had to be so careful. Oops."

We let ourselves through the gate and through the side yard to the back patio. Peter, Camille, and I sat on the patio stairs while we waited for the two ghosts to complete their inspection. Nick opened the glass patio door about ten minutes later.

"You guys can come in. We checked all the rooms and closets and didn't see anything. I think we're okay," he said.

We trailed after Nick as we followed him to the dining room and sat down. I pulled the letters and photo of the Goodwins out of my bag and tucked them closely to my chest.

I took a deep breath. "Sophia, I've been thinking—a lot, and I don't think your unfinished business has anything to do with the Mary Celeste. I think it has something to do with the Goodwins."

Sophia and Nick didn't look surprised like I'd expected them to. They exchanged glances and then Nick cleared his throat. "We've already come to that same conclusion. We think our extrication is somehow related to each other *and* to the Goodwins . . . and, as bad as it may sound, we think we're here until we get some sort of revenge on them."

"*Revenge?*" I couldn't picture either of them exacting revenge on someone. "Huh . . . Okay. If we're all on the same page maybe we can move forward, but first you need to know something. I don't know how to tell the two of you this, but I'm afraid it was my family that had you both killed."

"What are you talking about?" Nick was perplexed.

I unfolded my arms and began to read the letters. When I finished, I explained that they were from my ancestors and had been in my attic the whole time.

"I'm so sorry for what they did to you," I blurted out.

"Jamie, don't you dare think for one moment that because you are distantly related to these evil people that we would be upset. This is a *good* thing. Maybe we can find answers because of it. In fact, I'm sure this is why you're our soul saver. You have a connection to our unfinished business," Sophia insisted.

"We found this, too," I said as I produced the picture of Sophia and the Goodwins that I'd kept tucked in my lap.

"Oh my goodness, look at this. I was so young." Sophia gingerly touched the picture and traced the outline of her face. "I remember when we had this done. Jeremiah wanted a family photo for some con he was currently working. I can't recall the details of the whole con, but I do remember seeing Jeremiah pickpocket the photographer and it embarrassed me. Elsa had given me one of her old dresses to wear for the picture, but at that time she was starting to plump up and it didn't fit me very well." She lifted the picture up and looked at it more closely. "That old thing is pinned on everywhere. I was so scared I was going to get jabbed with a needle that day." She laughed and then sighed. "I think it might be the only photo we had taken together. I can't believe you found this."

Nick reached over and picked up the photo. "That's exactly how I remember the Goodwins looking when I first met all of you. You look a little young, though, Sophia."

"There's more," I said. "Remember in the letter I just read that an unopened trunk was mentioned?"

"Yes," Sophia and Nick spoke together.

"I think it might be in my dad's closet." I motioned toward the closed door of the den.

Sophia's mouth dropped open. "Are you serious?"

"Dad said he put an old trunk that belonged to my mom's family in there when we moved into the house. He's never opened it so he doesn't know what's in there. I don't think my mom has ever opened it either."

"What are we waiting for? Let's get that thing out of the closet." Nick jumped up.

Peter, Camille, and I stayed in our chairs.

"First, we need to know how to protect ourselves," Peter said.

"What?" Nick's confused look returned.

"What if we meet up with the Goodwins again and this time they aren't so friendly?"

Nick sat back down slowly. "What do you want to know?"

"Sophia, you once told me that you could hurt me, but I couldn't hurt you. Is that true in all circumstances?" I asked.

"Usually, but I guess there are exceptions. When a ghost is in its human form, it can feel pain, but in a muted way. For instance, if you were to shoot me I would feel it, but it wouldn't be like the extreme pain *you* would feel because it would heal so quickly. If you were to gun me down with a machine gun, it would hurt a lot worse because it would be continuous jolts of pain until you stopped."

I cringed. "A machine gun? Where am I supposed to get one of those?"

"Jamie, I'm not saying that's what you have to do. I was just using it as an example. Something that would kill or seriously injure you is just a momentary pain for a ghost. It just stalls them for a little bit. But remember, that's only if they're in their human form. If we're in our ghost form, nothing hurts. It's like we're just made of air or something."

"Okay. I guess that makes sense. So as long as we attack the Goodwins in their human form we should be okay?" Peter asked.

Nick cleared his throat and crossed his arms over his chest. "Not necessarily. If they were under attack, they'd just vanish into their ghost form and then *you're* the one in trouble because you won't know where they are. Besides, how and why do you plan on attacking them, Peter?"

"I don't know. I hadn't thought that far ahead. I just think those of us who are still living are getting kind of tired of not knowing what to expect."

Sophia frowned. "I'm sorry I dragged all of you into this giant mess."

I jumped in. "Don't get us wrong. We're happy to help and it's been an adventurous couple of weeks, but we just need to know what to expect."

"Well, if we're going to get revenge on the Goodwins we have to get them where it hurts. Sophia, what would you say matters most to them?" Nick asked.

"Money—hands down," she answered without any hesitation.

"Okay. Knowing them as much as I did, I would have to agree with you on that one. Other than trying to track you down for the last fifty or sixty years, we don't really know what they've been up to. I would assume they're probably still conning people because that's what they do best. It's probably a lot easier when they can vanish into thin air, too, so I would assume they're doing pretty well for themselves."

"Is there something in the past that involved either of you and their money?" I asked.

"Not that I can think of. I was the low man on the *Mist Seeker's* crew. I didn't get paid enough to really make a difference to Jeremiah," Nick answered.

"And I didn't get Jack Squat from them, so I doubt they're mad about that," Sophia added.

"If either of you remember anything, please tell the rest of us."

They both nodded.

The five of us entered Dad's den. I doubt if that many people had ever been in the little room at one time before. In fact, I don't know if Camille had ever even been in past the entrance in all the years I'd lived in the house. Sometimes when she was over we would poke our heads in to talk to my dad, but we didn't usually make ourselves at home in there.

Once our group was in the den I headed straight for the double-doors of the closet behind his big wooden desk. I think the room was originally intended to be an additional bedroom, but there were no bathrooms on the lower floor and we didn't need any more rooms, so naturally it became Dad's den. I opened the closet, revealing Dad's overflowing bookcases, sagging from the weight they bore. They were filled with books, which would usually excite me, but Dad's books were about business, management, ethics, and other boring stuff. I never read any of *his* books.

"Dad said the trunk was in the back of the closet behind the bookshelves." I stepped forward and peered into the space. I turned my cell phone on and aimed its light toward the right side of the closet. I saw nothing but bare wall. I aimed it toward the left side and there, behind the bookcase, I could just make out a large object half buried in books. It had to be the trunk.

"It's here," I squealed.

"Pull it out," Nick replied.

"Yeah, right. We're going to have to take this whole bookcase out first," I sighed.

"Really?" Camille whined. "I just painted my nails this morning."

I rolled my eyes. "Unless you can squeeze yourself back there and open it up, we have to move the bookcase."

It didn't take very long for five people to relieve the shelves of their books. We made sure to leave the books stacked in order of where they went on the shelves. Dad arranged his books alphabetically and I wanted them returned just as he had left them. Once the shelves were clear, Peter and Nick were able to slowly inch the bookcase forward until they could get on either side of it to push and pull it out into the den. As soon as they were clear of the doorway I slid past them and into the back of the closet. Sure enough, a big black trunk was in the very back corner. It was bigger than I'd expected. A person could stuff a lot of things into something that size. I grabbed the books piled on top of it and handed them back out through the doorway like an assembly line until the lid of the chest was completely clear.

"That's definitely their trunk." Sophia said as she stepped in behind me.

"Really? You can tell that even in the dark?" My heart was racing.

"Yes. They brought it with us every time we moved. It used to be in their bedroom when we lived in the house where I met Nick, although I think Jeremiah might have taken it with him after he restored the *Mist Seeker*."

"He did," Nick said, squeezing in behind Sophia. "I remember because I had to haul the dang thing onto the ship."

"If you look in the lower left corner, you'll see the initials JG," Sophia added.

I fell to my knees in front of the trunk and again aimed the light from my cell phone toward it. There, on the bottom left corner, was a little brass plate engraved with the letters 'J' and 'G'. I felt like the drumroll that had been going on in my head ever since my dad mentioned the trunk that morning had finally come to its climatic end and the cymbals were crashing.

"This is it," I yelled and jumped up. "We've got to get it out of here. We can open it in the living room because there is no way five of us are going to fit in this closet."

I stepped back out so that Peter and Nick could again work magic with their muscles. I was sure they didn't mind showing them off for us.

"Does it feel heavy or do you think it's empty?" I asked, hovering closely behind them while they ungracefully made their way out of the den and into the living room.

"It's definitely heavy," Peter grunted.

"Maybe for mere mortals like yourself," Nick teased.

The two guys carefully set the trunk in the middle of the living room floor and us girls were on it in a second.

"It's locked," Camille said. "Maybe that means it's still never been opened."

I rattled the padlock of the trunk. It was old, but very thick and sturdy. There was no way we were getting into that thing without some tools. I ran to the garage with Peter and we rummaged through Dad's things. He wasn't the world's best handyman, but he owned the basics. We managed to find a crowbar and a hammer and ran back inside. I let Nick and Peter take over from there and they pounded and beat at the stupid thing for what seemed like forever. Finally, after half an hour of failed attempts, the lock broke off and we leapt toward the trunk.

"You open it, Sophia," I urged. "It belonged to your parents . . . sort of."

"As you discovered, they're more closely related to you than me," she winked.

Sophia knelt in front of the trunk and pulled the remaining piece of the padlock out of the latch. "Here we go," she said breathily as Camille took a step back. I think she expected something to jump out at her.

Covering the contents of the trunk was a gray woolen blanket. Sophia pulled it off and tossed it to the ground. Like marionettes being controlled by some unseen hand, we all leaned forward and peered in. One by one Sophia began to remove things. There were a couple of well-worn changes of clothing for a man and a woman first. Then, out came a pair of tarnished silver candlesticks—closely followed by a silver serving tray.

"I don't remember these. Elsa must have gotten them after I died," Sophia remarked and set them on the coffee table. It fascinated me how casually she talked of death.

Next she pulled out a family bible that looked as if it had never been opened. "We weren't the best churchgoers back then. I think that made some people mistrust us."

"Really? Not the fact that Jeremiah cheated everyone?" Nick pretended to be shocked.

I turned the book over and flipped through the pages of the bible, hoping something would fall out just like the picture of Sophia had fallen from the photo album up in the attic. No such luck.

There were a few names and dates printed in the back cover, including the name of Jeremiah Goodwin and his date of birth. Some sort of genealogy had been recorded there. I knew with that information I would probably be able to figure out exactly how I was related to Jeremiah and Elsa if I wanted to. I set it on the coffee table next to the candlesticks figuring I could always look at it later.

I turned back to Sophia and saw that she had pulled out a packet of some sort. It was wrapped in cloth and tied with string. She set it on the floor carefully, gently untied it, and slowly pulled back the fabric. It was more letters.

"Do you want to read these now or wait until we've emptied the trunk?" Sophia asked.

"*Now*," Camille yelled.

We all turned and stared at her.

"I'm sorry, but this is intense. You've got to read them before I explode."

Nick chuckled and took the packet from Sophia. He gingerly flipped through the aged paper. The letters were in even worse shape than the ones we'd pulled out of the attic the day before.

"These are really old," he said.

"I know—we can tell," Camille responded anxiously.

"No. I mean these are *really* old. I think they're in order of dates. Look at this one, it's dated 1718. Here's one from 1712. And look at this one—1692," he said as he slipped the bottom letter from the stack.

"Let me see," I said as I reached for the letter. "Wow. I don't think I've ever held anything this old."

"That's more than a hundred years before Jeremiah and Elsa were even born. Go ahead and read it, Jamie, but I doubt it's going to have anything to do with us," Sophia said.

I carefully unfolded the brittle paper and began to read. I struggled as some of the ink was faded and the script was a flowing, fancy kind that I wasn't used to interpreting.

Dearest Catherine,

I am Afrayd that things have taken a turn for the Worse. I now Feare for my Life as many before me did as well. As much as it Hurts me, I do not wish you to be Invollved any more than you already have been in my Affayrs so I will no longer have any Contact with you. I have Hidden it all and left Instrucshuns for you. Do with it what You will. Please know that I am sorry for any Harm you may come upon because of your Involvement with me.

Love, your Dearest Friend, H

"H? Who is H? And who is Catherine?" I asked.

"I have no idea. I doubt it really matters though, they lived way before my time."

"It matters a lot more than you think." I whirled around as the gruff voice spoke from behind me. There was a loud scream that echoed again and again. I think it was Camille, but I couldn't know for sure because I was screaming in my head and for all I knew the sound was actually coming from my throat.

I watched in paralyzing fear as Jeremiah and Elsa slowly appeared before us. Camille was huddled in the corner with her head buried in her knees in the blink of an eye. Peter grabbed my hand and pulled me with him, as far back as we could get in the room. Jeremiah and Elsa blocked our exit. Sophia was still kneeling in front of the trunk when Nick jumped in front of everyone with his arms out, as if to protect us all.

There was fire in Jeremiah's eyes and Elsa had a smug look of satisfaction on her face. Both were brandishing pistols and I felt myself going weak in the knees. Peter put his arm around me and held me tight.

"What do you want from us?" Sophia yelled. "You ruined my life. Why can't you just stay away?"

"I want what's rightfully mine, you ungrateful little wench," Elsa yelled back.

"Ungrateful? Are you serious? You murdered my parents."

"If it wasn't for us you would have died out in that ocean right along with them," Elsa spat back.

"If it weren't for *you* we would have happily finished our journey to Italy and I would have been raised by my real parents along with my brother. You raised me as your daughter, why don't you care about me now?" Sophia grew bolder and rose to her feet. Nick stuck out his arm and held her behind him. For a brief moment, Elsa looked hurt, as if she actually might care about something.

"And you, Nicholas Trenton," Jeremiah put in. "I trusted you, gave you a great job, and how did you repay me? By secretly planning to steal our daughter away from us. I guess you got what was coming to you, though, didn't you?" He nudged Elsa and laughed.

I felt like I stood in the presence of pure evil. Camille still sobbed in the corner, her hands covering her eyes. I don't know if she ever even looked up. I had no idea how we were going to get ourselves out of the situation. No one was around to wonder where Peter was, Dad wouldn't be home until the next day, and Camille's parents probably wouldn't try to contact her for at least a few more hours.

"Do you realize how long we've been trying to track you down?" Elsa continued.

Sophia didn't say anything.

"We heard rumors in the ghost world that the poor little girl lost on the *Mary Celeste* had actually survived and was living as a ghost. Oh, how *tragic*." Elsa cupped her hands over her heart in mock pain.

"You're one hard girl to find, missy," Jeremiah threw in.

Elsa ignored him as she continued speaking. "We obviously can't kill you again. We should have done that the first time we had a chance. So . . . we'll make a deal with you."

"A *deal*?" Sophia hissed.

"Yes. You give back what you stole from us and you'll never have to see us again. You can keep living in your happy little world with your little ghost boyfriend and you'll never have to cross paths with us again, which would make us very, very happy."

"What could I possibly have stolen from you?"

"Stop playing dumb and tell us where you put the map," Jeremiah bellowed.

Camille started sobbing in the corner again and Peter tightened his grip on me.

"I don't know what you're talking about." Sophia was almost hysterical as Jeremiah moved toward her. Nick stretched his neck and puffed out his chest. It didn't matter that there was a size difference—there was no way Jeremiah would get through him to Sophia.

"How 'bout I make you tell me?" Jeremiah swung his arm around and raised it, aiming his pistol right at Camille huddled in the corner.

"*Nooo.*" I was the one screaming for sure that time and I tried to jump toward her. Peter wouldn't let go of me and I pounded on his chest, trying to break free from his grasp.

"Or, maybe I should get rid of your little friend over here. If she really is your soul saver, you'll *never* be able to leave your crappy existence." That time Jeremiah swung his pistol arm around and aimed it right at me. I'd never felt such terror in my life and I shook uncontrollably. Peter continued to hang on tight, holding me in a bear hug.

"Let's just all calm down for a minute," Nick cut in. "Maybe if Sophia knew what you were looking for she could give it to you and then you could be on your way. Everyone's emotions are high right now. Let's just talk about this like reasonable people."

"Reasonable people don't steal other people's stuff," Elsa muttered.

"*Really?* You're going to say that to me after you spent your whole life conning people out of their hard-earned money?" Sophia was flabbergasted.

Nick took Sophia's hand and kissed her on the forehead. Then, he turned back to Jeremiah and Elsa. "What kind of map are you looking for?"

"The map that was with that letter you just read," Jeremiah said angrily.

Nick came over and took the letter from me. I gladly relinquished it to him. He unfolded it and showed it to the Goodwins. He then turned the envelope upside down and showed them that it was empty.

"Obviously the map's not in there. *She* took it years ago." Elsa jabbed her thumb toward Sophia.

"This is the first time I've ever seen that stupid letter. I have no idea who Catherine or 'H' even are," Sophia said.

"When you got married you stole my leather pouch and the map was in there, you stupid girl. Where did you put it?" Jeremiah was angrier than ever.

"The only things I took when I got married were the few rags your wife couldn't stuff herself into anymore," Sophia said coldly.

"*You witch.*" Elsa lunged at Sophia, but Sophia set her jaw and held her ground. Elsa looked to Jeremiah for help, but he just shook his head.

"I'm telling you the truth. I want nothing more than for you to leave me alone. If I had any clue whatsoever about where this mysterious map was I would tell you. I swear it," Sophia pleaded.

Nick cleared his throat. "If I might say something, sir, when I worked for you I know that Paul, your first mate, used to talk sometimes of mutiny when he was drunk. I once heard him say something about getting your treasure before you had a chance. I had no idea what he was talking about and ignored him since he was drunk. I honestly don't think Sophia had anything to do with this. Perhaps you should take a closer look at your other crew members."

The room was silent, except for the thudding of my heart and a few random sobs that still escaped from Camille. Jeremiah and Elsa exchanged glances and kind of nodded at each other. I was scared to breathe.

Jeremiah stepped closer to Sophia. His face was just inches from hers. "You probably wouldn't have been smart enough to steal anything back then anyway. We'll go for now, but if we *ever* find out that you double-crossed us, it will be the end of your little living friends here—and don't think I won't do it. I have nothing to lose anymore."

"Really? I can't imagine *you* killing anyone," Nick said sarcastically. Jeremiah glared at him and then took Elsa's hand. Together they vanished from my living room as quickly as they'd appeared.

Chapter 20

I didn't dare move after the Goodwins vanished. Luckily, Peter still had has arms wrapped around me. Nick and Sophia both ran to the window and looked out.

Nick was the first to speak. "I can see their auras. They're actually leaving."

I breathed a deep sigh of relief. Camille started crying again and Sophia knelt beside her and wrapped her arms around the girl's shaking shoulders.

"I'm so sorry, Cam. I should never have gotten so many people involved in this mess. You can go home without feeling bad. I'll stay away from you from now on," Sophia whispered to her.

Camille looked up. I was surprised to see fire in her eyes as she spoke slowly and deliberately. "I am *not* leaving now. We are going to get revenge on those jerks."

"That's the spirit." Nick grinned.

Much to my dismay, Peter released me from his grip and I felt oddly alone. "You okay?" he asked gently.

"I'm fine—or at least I will be." I tried to smile at him.

Nick still stood at the window and kept glancing out every few seconds. "They're gone. I can't see them anymore."

"I *honestly* have no idea what map they're talking about," Sophia said. "I can't believe they've been trying to track me down for all these years over something like that."

I stepped to the middle of the room where Jeremiah had let the letter to the mysterious Catherine slip from his fingers and slide to the floor. I was thankful that he hadn't crumpled it up in his rage. I began to read the letter aloud again.

Dearest Catherine,

I am Afrayd that things have taken a turn for the Worse. I now Feare for my Life as many before me did as well. As much as it Hurts me, I do not wish you to be Involved any more than you already have been in my Affayrs so I will no longer have any Contact with you. I have Hidden it all and left Instrucshuns for you. Do with it what You will. Please know that I am sorry for any Harm you may come upon because of your Involvement with me.

Love, your Dearest Friend, H

"What do you think she hid? She said she left instructions so I assume it was the map Jeremiah was talking about, but she doesn't really say what was hidden. Do you think it was some sort of treasure?" I asked.

"Maybe. It could have been anything. I'm sure the Goodwins *believed* they were on the verge of some big find when they found that letter," Peter said. "How do we know that 'H' is a she? Couldn't it be a he?"

"That's a good point. Does it make a difference, though? We still don't know anything," I pointed out.

Nick left the window where he'd been standing quietly, walked to the couch, and sat down. "Guys—I think I know where the map is."

Four heads whirled to look at him. He leaned forward with his elbows resting on his knees and nodded his head as he spoke.

"The night before Sophia and I were supposed to run away together I decided I should have more insurance for us. I thought if I could find proof of Jeremiah's illegal dealings I could use it as blackmail if he ever found us."

Sophia's mouth dropped open. "You did?"

He nodded. "I'd seen Jeremiah tuck the leather pouch that he always carried his important papers in behind that old writing desk just outside your kitchen. I thought there might be something useful in there. I grabbed it and headed to the barn. My plan was to quickly look through the stuff and then return everything exactly how it was when I found it. I heard Paul's voice outside calling for Jeremiah and I was scared he'd come into the barn so I pried up one of the loose planks of the floor and stuffed the pouch under it. That was about the time they came into the barn and knocked me out. I still don't know how they found out about our plan, Sophia. I hadn't told anyone."

"I swear I didn't tell anyone, either," Sophia insisted, taking Nick's hand.

"Maybe it was just a good guess or insurance on their part. They knew you were in love and that Sophia didn't want to marry Michael Mason," I replied.

"So was there a map of some sort in that pouch?" Peter asked.

"I don't know. I never got the chance to open it before I was attacked, but I took it only a couple of days before Sophia was married. Maybe Jeremiah didn't notice it was gone until after that and assumed Sophia took it with her. By the time he realized it was gone she would have been dead."

"And so were you," Sophia added.

I was almost scared to ask the next question. "Is the barn still there?"

Nick and Sophia looked at each other and shrugged. "It's been decades since either of us has been to the old house. I have no idea what remains."

"I guess there's only one way to find out. Who's up for another vacation?" Peter said as he plopped down onto the couch next to Nick.

"You can't be serious," Camille gasped.

"Of course I'm serious. The last thing I want to do is spend my summer sitting around talking. I don't know about you, but I've been having a blast so far." Peter put his arms behind his head and leaned back against the cushions.

"I think *someone* needs to go check, but maybe Nick and I should go again so that you guys aren't in any more danger," Sophia responded.

"You know, humans don't have auras accompanying them everywhere they go. If we send the living ones, it might not tip off the Goodwins as quickly," Nick added.

"But if by some miracle the house and barn are still standing, ghosts can snoop around without alarming the current occupants far better than a living person could," Sophia countered.

"I think we should all go." I couldn't believe the words had come out of my mouth. I must have gone crazy.

"I'm definitely going. How about you, Camille?" Peter prodded.

She was a little more hesitant. "I don't know. I want to go, but what if Jeremiah and Elsa follow us?"

"If we find the map, and the Goodwins come back, then we give it to them. They'll leave us alone," Sophia stated.

"No way am I giving them the map. I thought we were here to get revenge," Nick answered back.

Sophia sighed. "Nick, no matter how badly we want to move on, we can't keep putting others in harm's way."

"We'll cross that bridge when we come to it . . . if we come to it."

"So, how do we get to Virginia?" Peter was definitely the most excited for the trip.

"First we have to get permission to go traipsing off by ourselves. I know that Nick and Sophia have been around for a long time and are much older and wiser than they appear, but my Dad's still not going to agree to this unless we have a really good cover."

"Tell him I invited you to my family's estate in Virginia. It's mostly true. You can do the same thing, Cam," Sophia suggested.

"That sounds fine, but what happens when Dad insists on meeting and discussing it with your parents first?"

"I guess that's when Jack and Rita become useful. They offered to help if they could. It wouldn't be that big of a deal to them to pretend to be my Mommy and Daddy." Sophia perked up. I think she realized there was a good chance our plan would work.

"What about Peter?"

"We just won't tell your Dad that I'm going with you guys," Peter said. "I'm sure he'll automatically assume it's a girls-only trip. My parents aren't going to be home for another week or so. I'll tell them I'm headed to Virginia with a friend. They won't care at all."

"There you go. Problem solved. Any more questions?" Nick asked.

"I have one." I raised my hand. "Will you and Sophia please stay here with me tonight?"

Sophia laughed and came over to hug me. "Of course we'll stay here. I'm not letting my soul saver out of my sight."

The afternoon had faded quickly with all the excitement. Those of us who were living were famished. We made dinner with the groceries we'd picked up and devoured it. Peter and Camille went home, promising to start packing.

Nick, Sophia, and I worked together to get the trunk upstairs to my room. Considering its age, it was in surprisingly good shape. I thought it would look nice at the foot of my antique bed. Someday I would finish going through its contents—if Jeremiah and Elsa didn't decide to come back for their remaining possessions. We made sure to put Dad's den back in order and then returned to the living room. By that time it was dark outside, but I was far from feeling tired.

I spotted the candlesticks and serving platter that we'd pulled from the trunk earlier in the day still sitting on my coffee table. Deciding that then was as good as any time to polish them, I took them to the kitchen and went to work removing years of tarnish. Sophia and Nick watched me work, impressed that I knew so much about antiques.

"My mother owned a silver hair comb. You know, the kind that women leave in their hair as decoration?" Nick reminisced. "I took it with me when I left home and went to work for Jeremiah. I only carried a few things, but since it had been my mother's prized possession, I couldn't part with it. I would love to know where it is now. I also had my father's pocket watch. It didn't work anymore, but it was the only thing of his that I had. He carried it with him all through the Civil War. I have no idea what the crew did with all my stuff after Jeremiah killed me. I hope some of it made its way to a museum somewhere, but more than likely they tossed my entire trunk over the side of the ship along with my body."

It was astounding how much the past still meant to them, even though they'd been living as ghosts for far longer than their short mortal lives. I hoped that I could help them find closure soon.

I slept soundly that night. I trusted Nick and Sophia to keep watch all night and they faithfully reported the next morning that there had been no ghostly activity—other than themselves—around my house all night. I hoped that meant Jeremiah and Elsa were gone for good.

I expected Dad to be home by lunch. Sophia was so sure that he was going to let me go that she'd gone ahead and booked airline tickets for Peter, Camille, and I to fly to Newport News, Virginia, the next day. She and Nick planned to drive to Philadelphia in her car and meet up with us on a connecting flight there. We hoped our plan would throw any unwanted followers off our trail. It would be hard for the Goodwins to follow Nick and Sophia on a six-hour car ride without them noticing. Camille called around eleven to tell me excitedly that she'd gotten permission from her parents to go on the trip. That was a good sign for me. Dad would be more willing to let me go knowing Camille would be along for the journey, too.

Precisely at noon I heard the sound of the garage door being raised. I looked out the living room window and saw him pull into the driveway. I quickly shooed Nick and Sophia away. I wanted to talk to my dad without them there—at least not in their human form. Besides, Dad would have no idea who Nick was or why he was in our house.

"Dad. You're back," I shouted, a little too loudly. I was a really bad actress.

He looked surprised. "I am. You seem pretty happy to see me. Is everything okay?"

"Everything's great. How was Chicago?" My voice was still loud.

"About the same as it always is."

It wasn't my Dad's favorite place to visit and he found himself having to go there for work-related reasons a lot. He walked into the kitchen and parked his luggage at the bottom of the stairs. I saw him look around at everything expectantly. He knew something was up. I'm sure he thought I'd ruined something and was trying to butter him up before I broke the bad news.

"What have you been up to?" he finally asked.

"Oh, you know, the usual. Hanging out with Camille. And Sophia."

"And Peter?"

"A little." I blushed.

"He seems like a nice young man."

I took that to mean that Dad was giving his blessing for me to pursue my relationship with Peter. I didn't know yet if anything would even become of our relationship. So far all of our more intimate moments had been in the rush of panic or when we had made some great find. I didn't know if "we" would happen in the normal world. I'd have to see after Sophia and Nick were gone.

"Dad?"

"Yes, Jamie?"

"I know you've been gone for a few days, and you just got home, but . . . I was kind of hoping I could go on a trip. Sophia invited me to her family's estate in Virginia for a few days and I would *love* to go. Oh, and Cam's already got permission to go, too." I had to throw that last part in.

"Virginia?"

"Yep. That's where she's from."

"I don't know, honey. Sophia is nice enough, but I've never even met her parents. That's a long way to go, isn't it?"

"It is, but it would be a good experience for me. And it would be nice to have something to do that's exciting for a few days."

Dad sighed. "How would you get there? Are her parents driving?"

"No, actually, we would all fly."

"When are they leaving?"

I was beginning to sweat—he wasn't giving in very easily. "Uhh . . . tomorrow morning. I *really* want to go, Dad. Mom's met Rita—I mean Sophia's mom." I hated playing that card. Dad tried so hard to be a good parent and I hated making him feel like Mom had done something more than him.

222

"She has?"

"Yeah. When Mom was here the other day, Sophia's mom stopped by."

"Oh."

"Sooo . . .?"

"Invite her family over for dinner tonight and I will discuss the trip with them. If they're decent people and can assure me that your going won't be a problem for them, then I guess you can go."

"Yes. I love you, Dad. Thank you. Thank you. Thank you." I threw my arms around him and gave him a kiss on his cheek. It totally wasn't like me, but it made him smile and he hugged me back.

I ran up to my room and barged through the door. Sophia sat on my window seat watching the street below while Nick lay on my bed, making himself at home amongst my blankets and pillows. Dad would have freaked out if he knew they were up there. I locked my door behind me.

"Well?" Sophia stood up and crossed the fingers of both her hands.

"If Dad can have dinner with Jack and Rita tonight, and they pass his 'decent people' test, I can go."

"Yay," she squealed.

"Shhhh."

"Right. Sorry," Sophia whispered.

Nick threw a pillow at me and I picked it up and threw it back. Before I knew it the three of us were in a silent pillow fight, trying to smother our giggles. It was nice to feel that at ease again.

Jack, Rita, and Sophia arrived promptly at six. It was a good thing, too, because promptness was one thing that Dad firmly believed defined one's character. Rita wore a retro blue cocktail dress and open-toed pink pumps. It was like a blast from the past. I imagined her in the same outfit at her diner a half century before. I wished I could pull off her look. Sophia looked stunning as always in a gray skirt with a sea foam green blouse. Jack was in a suit, just like

I'd seen him the other day, only he was going without a tie that night and the top button of his cream-colored dress shirt was unbuttoned. The three of them made a gorgeous fake family. All they needed was the handsome Nicholas Trenton to be on the arm of Sophia and the picture would be complete.

After introductions were made all around, Rita wandered through the downstairs complementing Dad on all his choices in antiques. He loved it. The funny thing was that Rita had probably lived when some of the items she pointed out were new. He didn't need to know that, though. We soon retreated to the patio where Dad had hors d'oeuvres—little crab cakes—waiting. It was a good thing he could entertain on the fly since we'd only had a couple of hours to prepare. He wanted to make sure we served something nice, but I knew the food would all taste the same to our ghostly guests. At least Rita would appreciate the *effort* in food choice. Sophia and I whispered at the table while we dined on roast turkey, mashed potatoes, and steamed asparagus—courtesy of a local deli.

"Do you think it's working?"

"I think so. Dad seems impressed by them so far. I just hope he doesn't want to have them over again. It might be kind of awkward to explain where you went when your time comes to go."

Sophia frowned. I felt like our adventure was almost over and I knew she did, too. At first it felt like we were just playing some kind of a game, but the day before, when the Goodwins had held us at gunpoint, the reality of what was eventually going to happen had finally sunk in for all of us. I would seriously miss the girl who had become a sister to me.

When dinner ended and we all pushed back from the table, Rita finally broached the subject. "We really do hope you'll let Jamie come with us tomorrow. She's been so sweet and welcoming to Sophia this summer and we hope we can show her the same hospitality at our home in Virginia. We're right near the water and it should be a lot of fun for the three girls to hang out there for the week. We just need to check on the home and Jack needs to meet with a couple of clients before we come back here."

"I don't see any reason why she can't go. I think it would be a good experience for her." Dad smiled at me.

"Really? Thank you, Dad. I will be on my best behavior, I promise."

Dad laughed. "You're a good kid, Jamie. I'm not worried about you."

I felt a little guilty that every person sitting at that table knew exactly what was actually going to happen in Virginia except for my dad. Oh well, what he didn't know couldn't hurt him. Right?

Chapter 21

"Bye, Dad. See you in a week," I called as he waved from our front porch the next morning. Jack and Rita were loading my luggage into the trunk of their car in the driveway while Sophia and I climbed into the backseat.

"Do you have your phone and did you remember to pack your charger?" he called back.

"Yes and yes. Love you, Dad." I shut the door. I felt sad to be leaving my dad. I was completely deceiving him when he trusted me wholly. I couldn't answer the questions my mind kept asking. *Is it okay to lie if I'm helping someone else out of a tricky situation? How far is too far?*

We drove to Camille's house and loaded her luggage, too. I definitely packed lighter than she did. Jack had to rearrange the trunk twice before he was able to fit everything in. We'd be staying in a hotel in Newport News for a week, but the way Camille packed you'd think we were going to be gone for the entire summer. Jack and Rita drove us back to their home where Nick and Peter were already waiting. Peter got in the car with us and Sophia transferred to her car with Nick. Jack and Rita would drive us to the airport in

Boston while Nick and Sophia headed south for six hours through New York and into Philadelphia where they would hopefully meet up with us at the airport there.

"I'm really glad you got permission to come. It would have been weird if it was only Camille and I going," Peter said when the three of us were nestled in the back of Jack and Rita's car.

"Thanks, Peter. I love you, too," Camille said sarcastically.

Peter turned red. "I didn't mean it like that. I just meant because Jamie's the actual soul saver and all."

"Right, whatever you say."

I was glad it wasn't just the two of them going, too. I didn't want whatever Peter saw in me to be forgotten if he spent time alone with Camille.

The drive to Logan International Airport was uneventful even though I noticed Jack checking his rearview mirror—a lot. He and Rita were easy to talk to and I found myself hoping to still see them once in a while after Sophia and Nick were gone. The adults accompanied us as far as they could to the security checkpoint inside the airport, but couldn't go with us to the actual gate since we'd all opted to fly as unaccompanied minors. They could have vanished and followed us, but that would have been hard to do without drawing attention to ourselves in the busy airport. Jack and Rita already looked suspicious the way they kept looking around in every direction, eyeing every passenger.

"I haven't seen any ghosts since we got here, with the exception of Boston Bob, so I think you're okay," Jack said as we were saying goodbye.

"Boston *who*?" Camille asked

"Boston Bob. Everybody knows about him," Rita said. "He's been a fixture here at the Logan Airport since it was built. He just roams around messing with people's luggage and stuff. He's completely harmless so don't worry about him. I'd ask him to keep an eye out for the Goodwins for you, but the last time I tried to talk to him I ended up being stuck in conversation about absolutely nothing for three hours."

I laughed. "So that's how all the luggage gets lost, huh?"

"Sometimes." Jack laughed, too.

We finally parted ways, with Rita hugging each of us and Jack shaking our hands. I was nervous, but it was time to be alert and completely aware of our surroundings. I had to focus. If the Goodwins were following us, they weren't stupid enough to do it in their human form. Sophia had practiced with me the night before and I was getting pretty good at detecting when the air around me changed and there was a ghost present. It took complete concentration, though, and that was kind of hard in a busy airport where people were jostling each other and moving in all directions.

We still had thirty minutes before we were supposed to board so we grabbed drinks and snacks at one of the food kiosks and found some chairs to camp out in for a while. We didn't talk very much. I think we were all a little anxious. It was crazy that a couple of weeks before I was completely comfortable to be on my own. Now, I felt like I needed a ghostly bodyguard just to go to the bathroom.

Since I'd traveled a lot with Dad, I felt at home in an airport. I knew that Peter had traveled quite extensively, too. He used to miss a lot of school while he traveled with his parents—before he got old enough for them to leave him by himself. Camille's family traveled, too, but they tended to drive everywhere they went. They usually spent a month in a vacation rental near Salem every summer. I'd gone with them a couple of times. I went the summer after fifth grade and the summer after seventh grade. We'd had a blast.

Finally, our seats were announced and we were allowed to board the plane. We'd been lucky enough to get three seats next to each other. Camille grabbed the seat by the window and I sat in the middle between her and Peter. I took a good look at everyone else on the plane. I didn't know if the Goodwins had accomplices. No one looked suspicious and it didn't appear that anyone watched us or even paid particular attention to us. I closed my eyes and concentrated on the surrounding air—nothing felt out of place.

"Are you okay?" Peter asked as he covered my hand with his.

I opened my eyes. "I'm fine. I'm just trying to concentrate."

"Concentrate?"

"Yeah. Last night Sophia tried to teach me how to recognize when ghosts are around. She and Nick would come and go to help me practice."

"Did it work?"

"I could detect when they came in the room about seventy-five percent of the time."

"Do you detect anything here?"

"Nope."

"I guess that's good—unless now is part of the twenty-five percent that you don't sense someone."

I laughed and leaned back against my seat. He did the same thing.

"Can't ghosts fly?" Peter asked, turning his head towards mine.

"Huh?"

"Why don't Sophia and Nick just fly to Virginia by themselves?"

"I don't think they really fly. I think it's more of a floating thing. I think they're only fast when they're in their human form, but I'm not sure."

"Hellooo. Remember me. I'm here, too," Camille complained.

Peter and I turned to look at her.

"You two are boring. I can't even hear your conversation."

"Sorry. What do *you* want to talk about?" I asked.

"Something besides ghosts."

"Global warming?" Peter suggested.

"Nice try. If you weren't here, we'd probably be talking about boys," Camille said smugly.

"Wow. I'm glad I'm here to put a stop to that then."

"What time are we supposed to—" Camille cut off in mid-sentence with a stunned look on her face.

Alarmed, I quickly grabbed her shoulder. "Cam, what's wrong?"

"I . . . uhh . . . nothing," she said sheepishly.

She leaned back in her seat to where Peter could no longer see her, caught my eye, and then nodded toward my lap. I looked down. I'd forgotten Peter's hand was still holding mine—it felt natural there. Embarrassed, I immediately turned red and started to pull my hand away. Peter caught it and entwined his fingers with mine. By that point my face was on fire. I looked up and he smiled back with laughing eyes. Camille stayed back against the seat and covered her mouth with her hands, trying desperately to contain the little giggles that were escaping.

When she finally had herself under control she turned to me again and whispered, "How long has *this* been going on?"

I was still horribly embarrassed. I wasn't used to public displays of affection. "I don't know. A couple of days I guess."

"Are you guys, like, a couple or something now?"

"I don't know. We haven't talked about it," I whispered back, wishing the conversation would just be over.

"What are you guys whispering about over there?" Peter asked as he leaned out from his seat so that he could see both of us at once.

"Boys. I told you we like to talk about boys, remember?" Camille said, but that time she grinned at Peter.

"Maybe I'll just take a nap. That is, unless you need some input from someone who actually *is* a boy."

"Nope. We're good."

The plane took off and we began our trip to the City of Brotherly Love. I wished it was our final destination because I loved Philadelphia. There's so much history there and Dad and I enjoyed visiting it. We'd usually find ourselves there once every year or two. The flight attendant brought around drinks and those little bags of honey mustard pretzels. I was too anxious to eat so I gave mine to Peter, who apparently loved them. I sipped a soda while he and Camille both drank water.

Our plane landed in Philly without any delays. It was a beautiful summer day and I wished I could be outside enjoying it. Our plane taxied to the gate and we gathered our carryon bags, listening to the Captain over the loudspeaker thank us for choosing US Airways and blah, blah, blah, before we exited the plane. We still had a couple of hours before our connecting flight to Newport News was due to depart. Sophia and Nick planned to be in Philadelphia within an hour and a half. I hoped they hadn't met with any unforeseen problems while going through New York. The traffic can get kind of messy there.

I turned my phone on and listened to it ding, telling me I had one new voicemail. I stepped away from the crowds of people and covered one ear with the hand not holding the phone so I could hear.

"Hi, Jamie. We got a little held up in traffic, but I think we can still make the flight. If we aren't there in time, go without us. We'll catch the next flight out and meet you at the hotel later tonight. We've been on the road for about three hours now and haven't seen signs of anyone following us. Anyway, I hope you had a good flight. Text me when you land and get this message. I have big news for you."

Big news? What could possibly have happened in the few hours since I'd seen her? I walked back to Peter and Camille who had staked out a spot on a row of hard plastic chairs.

"Anything?"

"They think they'll make it, but it will be cutting it close. She said she has big news," I said vaguely as I texted her back.

"What do you mean?" Camille asked.

I shrugged. "Dunno. She didn't say."

I waited for a few minutes and then felt the familiar vibration of my phone. I turned the screen on and looked at my messages. There were no words, but Sophia had sent a picture—of her hand.

"What's that supposed to mean?" Camille asked, looking over my shoulder.

"I'm not sure. Is it code for something?"

"Let me see," Peter said as he reached over and took the phone from me. "Yep. It's definitely code for something. I could tell right away. You should be ashamed to call yourselves girls."

I glared at him and took the phone back, enlarging the picture.

"Oh my gosh. Look at her ring finger," Camille squealed.

Sure enough, on her long, slender finger, below her perfectly manicured nail, was a gorgeous diamond ring.

"They're engaged," Camille said excitedly. The people around us turned and stared.

"Okay. The truth is, when Nick picked me up this morning he told me he was going to officially propose to Sophia. I promised I wouldn't tell you guys," Peter said.

"That is so sweet—it's like we're living in a fairytale," Camille said. "I wonder how Nick did it. He better have gotten down on one knee. Do you think he got permission from her father—I mean Jack—first? That would have been funny. If they plan on disappearing soon, how are they going to plan a wedding? Agghhh! Do you think we'll get to be bridesmaids?"

Camille finally stopped jabbering when she realized that Peter and I were about to fall out of our chairs from laughing so hard.

"What?" she whined.

"Maybe you should ask Sophia these questions."

"*Congratulations. We're very happy for you. Camille can't stop squealing, if you know what I mean,*" I texted back, hiding the screen from Camille's view.

We figured we had a long wait so we found a deli and ordered sandwiches. I got ham and turkey with all the veggies—my usual. Camille skipped the bread and went for the veggies in the form of a salad, and Peter ordered a footlong double-meat sandwich. I could never understand how the teenage boys at our school could stay so skinny with the way they all ate.

The time ticked away faster than I expected and before we knew it they were beginning to board our flight.

Camille freaked out. "They're not here. What are we supposed to do?"

"Cam, it's okay. I have all the hotel info with me. If they don't get here in time, we can grab a taxi at the airport and wait at the hotel for them. It's not a big deal." I loved being able to take charge. My relationship with Camille was finally evolving.

Sure enough, our seats were called and there was still no sign of Sophia or Nick. The second plane was a lot smaller than the first one had been and there were far fewer seats. Peter and I sat in a row of two chairs and Camille sat across the aisle from us. We watched the aisle carefully, waiting for the newly engaged couple to rush onto the plane, but there was no sign of them. I tried to text Sophia again, but she didn't respond and we were being told to turn off our phones. Finally, the flight attendant closed the door and the plane moved away from the gate.

"I guess it's just us," Peter said quietly.

"Yeah. I'm sure they'll meet up with us soon," I replied somberly.

I wanted to be strong for Camille's sake. She wasn't happy that our carefully laid plan had failed. As soon as we were in the air, she turned toward the window and curled her legs up to take a nap.

Peter looked at her. "That's a good idea. I'm going to do the same thing." He grabbed one of the little airplane pillows and put it behind his head, slipped off his shoes, and closed his eyes.

I wished I could sleep, but I felt like one of us needed to stay awake. It was quiet around me and I quickly became bored and found that my own eyes were starting to droop. I tried to fight off the sleep, but it was a struggle. Finally, I gave in and let my eyes close. I don't know how long I'd been like that before I felt it, but I don't think it had been very long. At first, I didn't know what had happened. Something had gotten my attention. I sat, not moving, my eyes still closed and breathed deeply in and out.

There it was again. The air around me had moved slightly and there was a subtle change in the temperature. The hair on my arms began to stand up and my heart raced. Something was definitely present—something that wasn't alive. I slowly reached over and squeezed Peter's arm, still not opening my eyes. I wished my heart would stop beating so hard. I couldn't hear anything over its hammering.

Peter opened his eyes and squeezed me back. I opened my eyes and mouthed the word "ghost" toward him. He sat forward and looked around frantically. I closed my eyes again and felt a prodding sensation, as if someone or something had tapped me gently. All of a sudden realization hit and relief flooded me. I laughed out loud.

"What?"

"It's Sophia. I recognize the feel of her. *Sophia?*" I whispered into the air.

I felt the prodding again. It was definitely Sophia. I turned the other way and looked at Camille. She slept peacefully so I decided to wait until we landed to give her the news. It wasn't a very long flight and we could wait.

When the plane landed a short time later we gathered our luggage for the last time and headed for the exit. I wasn't sure when Sophia and Nick were going to reappear. They couldn't exactly do it in the middle of a crowd. I wondered if they'd have to wait until we were at the hotel, but then a thought occurred to me.

"Hey, Cam. I think we need to use the bathroom. You probably should too, Peter."

"I'm fine. I can wait until we get to the hotel. Airport bathrooms are disgusting. Think of how many gross people go in and out of those every day," Camille said.

"Just come with me. You don't have to touch anything."

Camille rolled her eyes but dutifully followed. We stood at the long mirror and touched up our makeup.

"Are we in here for a reason?" Camille asked.

"She's waiting for me." Sophia emerged from one of the bathroom stalls, completely in human form and looking much better than Cam and I who had just spent the day in airports and on airplanes.

Camille whirled around. "Sophia. You made it. Let me see your hand."

Sophia beamed as she held her hand up for inspection. The diamond sparkled under the vanity lights.

"Tell us all about it." Camille bounced up and down.

"Well, after we left you we headed out of town just as planned. Right before we got to Providence, Nick pulled off the interstate and stopped at one of those scenic overlooks. I was really confused, but he made me get out of the car and we walked to the lookout area. He got down on one knee—"

"Awwww." Camille couldn't contain herself.

"—and popped the question. It was really sweet. I had *no* idea he was going to do that."

"What do you plan to do then?" I didn't want to be a pessimist, but Sophia could finish her business any day and that would be the end of any wedding plans.

"Nick and I talked about it on the way here. We've been waiting *forever* to get married. If you guys are willing, we want to forget everything about the Goodwins and strange maps and our old life for one day and get married tomorrow."

"Agghh! Yes we're okay with that," Camille answered immediately. I nodded in agreement.

"Good. It's settled then. I'm getting married tomorrow."

The three of us hugged and with our "girl moment" finished we left the bathroom. Peter had found Nick and the two of them resided on a couple of the uncomfortable chairs. They could almost be brothers the way they both lounged. We retrieved the luggage we'd checked—Sophia and Nick had sent their bags with us back in Boston so that they'd have clothes even if they didn't catch the connecting flight—and headed to the rental car counter. Nick figured the oldest he could ever pass himself off as was 22, which is what his fake ID said. Car rental companies usually won't rent to people under the age of 25 unless you pay extra. If they only knew his real age . . . Once the paperwork was finally finished we loaded the luggage into the rental car and headed for the hotel.

Sophia and Nick sprung for an upper class hotel. They were both so sure that they were about to finish their business that they felt like they should start spending some of the money they'd been saving and investing, not knowing how long they would be living as humans. Camille and I had a suite with two beds in one room and a living area and kitchenette in the other room. I assumed the boys' room was similar. Sophia would most likely not be sleeping, but she stashed her bags in our room anyway.

"So what's the plan for tomorrow?" I asked when we were all seated around a table at a café in the lobby that night.

"Well, in the morning, the girls are going to go dress shopping while the guys try to find something appropriate to wear. Apparently Mr. Secretive over here has already called ahead and found someone to officiate. I guess it's a good thing I said yes," she nudged Nick. "The officiator typically performs ceremonies for people who want to renew their vows. We don't have time to get a marriage license and all that so we're just going to have a commitment ceremony of sorts. It's good enough for us. We're told there's a beautiful park overlooking the water near the hotel and we're going to meet the officiator there tomorrow evening—just before sunset."

"It sounds perfect. I'm so happy for you two." I really meant it.

The next morning was another beautiful summer day. Camille and I grabbed some fruit from the little market in the lobby of our hotel for breakfast before we headed out with Sophia in search of a wedding dress.

"There's no way I'm going to find a traditional dress and still have time for alterations before this evening. I think we need to stick to department stores so we can buy something off the rack," Sophia said as we rode in a taxi to the nearest mall. Peter and Nick had taken the rental car.

After not finding anything interesting in the three department stores anchoring the Patrick Henry Mall, we grabbed another taxi and headed for the nearest Nordstrom's twenty-five miles away. Sophia chose a couple of white cocktail dresses and headed for the dressing room. She emerged looking absolutely radiant in a dress with a lace covered bodice and a skirt that flared slightly at her knees. There was a dainty white bow at her waist. We knew immediately that it was the one.

"Oh. I'm going to cry. That's definitely the dress." Camille beamed.

"You think so?" Sophia asked as she twirled in front of the three-way mirror.

"I agree with, Cam. It's definitely the one." I added.

"Great. That was easy. Let's find something for you two. I saw a lavender dress on the other side of the store that I liked. Let's go back and see if it will work."

That time Camille and I were the ones to be oohed and aahed. I had to try on a couple of sizes before I found the perfect fit, but I agreed that the little lavender dresses with spaghetti straps and mini ruffles at the hem were cute. I didn't usually feel very feminine and I blushed when I thought of Peter seeing me in it.

We made our way back to the hotel where Sophia proceeded to give us makeovers. She was subtle with the makeup she put on me. It was as if she'd known me my entire life. She pulled our hair up into curly twists on the backs of our heads and then went to work on herself. She looked amazing when she was finished, with her hair cascading down her back in soft golden curls. Instead of a veil she tied a white ribbon in her hair. A pair of simple pearl earrings was the only accessory she needed.

Camille excused herself to the restroom and I had Sophia all to myself for the first time in a long while.

"Sophia?"

"Yeah?"

"Are you having any second thoughts?"

"About marrying Nick?"

"No. About finishing your business. Jack and Rita don't want to finish their business now that they've found each other. You and Nick have had so little time together, I just wondered if you were still as excited to go."

She was quiet for a long time. "Honestly? The thought has definitely crossed my mind, but Jamie, I have faith that it will all work out. I don't think we would have remained on earth to find each other again if we were just going to be separated once we got to heaven."

"So you believe in heaven then?"

"I do. I believe Nick and I will be together there and I will finally be able to see my real family again. Nick will be with his mother and his sister, too. It will be a great reunion, Jamie. Besides, if we don't go know, when we have the chance, we might never be able to leave. I'm not sure I want to stay around forever, watching the world at war and witnessing tragedy after tragedy. Do you realize that I've been here for both World Wars, the Great Depression, the Korean conflict, the so-called Cold War, the Vietnam War, the Gulf War, the tragedies of 9/11, and everything that's happened since then?"

I nodded. I couldn't imagine witnessing all of that. My parents had never taken me to church and I didn't know whether I believed in God and heaven or not. I wanted to, but I didn't think I'd ever seen any proof that either thing existed. Maybe Sophia was my proof. She'd lived a rotten life, but remained true to her values, and things were looking up for her. The Goodwins had led a life of crime and they still weren't happy in their afterlife. Maybe there was some truth to everything churchgoers believed. It was something I was going to give deeper thought to in the future.

Camille came out of the bathroom and we slipped into our shoes before heading for the lobby. I was kind of nervous about walking in heels in the grass at the park. I'd only worn heels a couple of times before.

Sophia had called in a flower order earlier in the day and they were waiting at the hotel desk for us. She handed Camille and I each a single white daisy and then tied the remaining ones with a purple ribbon to make an impromptu bouquet. It couldn't have been more perfect.

"Nick and Peter have already left and are just arriving at the park now," she said as she read a text.

We emerged from the hotel and turned right. The park was supposedly only a block or two away and sure enough, there was a large green space with big shady trees just down the road.

Peter and Nick were standing in their tuxedos, talking with a man who I assumed was the officiant, when we came up behind them. The look on Nick's face when he turned and saw Sophia was priceless. It was a look of true love.

The ceremony was short and sweet. Nick and Sophia faced each other, holding hands under a leafy tree. The three of us who were attending stood behind them—there were no seats. Camille snapped about a million pictures with her phone in between wiping tears from the corners of her eyes. They exchanged vows they'd written themselves and the officiant pronounced them joined. They didn't need an official paper and no witnesses needed to sign anything. It was just a sweet and magical moment where two people pledged their love to each other.

When the mini ceremony was over, Nick and Sophia kissed and he picked her up and twirled her around. She laughed and threw her head back. Camille had tears streaming down her face by that point. I looked away so the tears threatening to fall from *my* eyes wouldn't be noticed. After congratulations and well wishes from the man performing the ceremony, he left and we were alone in the park. Sophia threw her bouquet and Camille grabbed it. She was ecstatic.

Peter offered to crash on the couch in the girls' hotel room so that Nick and Sophia could be alone that night. The three of us stayed up watching late night comedy and eating junk we bought from the convenience store in the lobby. I wondered what Dad would think if he could see me then. I needed to break the junk food habit or I'd look like a blimp for my sophomore year. The next day would be business as usual and we were all keenly aware that it might be the last night all of us were still around.

Chapter 22

"G ood morning, sleepyhead." I woke with a start and found myself staring into Sophia's big blue eyes. She was laying on her stomach on the other half of my bed, propped up on her elbows, her face just inches from mine.

"*Sophia*. You promised not to do that anymore."

"I'm sorry, but I might not be a ghost for much longer and I've got to get my fill of scaring people while I still can."

Suddenly realizing that Nick was a ghost and could very well be in the room too, I covered my head with my pillow. I was sure I *looked* scary that morning.

Embarrassed, I mumbled from beneath the pillow, "Is Nick in here?"

"He went to get some food for you guys. Why are you all still in bed?"

I pulled the pillow off my head, rubbed my eyes, and looked at the clock sitting on the bedside table. It was ten o'clock.

I groaned. "Sorry. I guess we stayed up too late last night. Cam!" I yelled and tossed a pillow at the sleeping body in the other bed. She pulled the covers over her head and rolled over.

"I guess I'll shower first. Maybe she'll be awake by the time I get out," I told Sophia as I swung my legs over the edge of the bed and sat up.

"Okay, but before you get too far, I should warn you that Peter's already in your shower."

Crap. I'd forgotten he was still there. I looked in the mirror hanging over the dresser. My hair looked like a rat had made a nest in it. The curls Sophia had so carefully created the day before didn't look so good on day two. I grabbed a hoodie, pulled the hood over my head, and sat back on the bed to wait.

"How was your night?" It was an awkward question to ask someone that was technically on their honeymoon and it slipped out before I could stop it.

She laughed. "It was nice. We talked all night and we're definitely on the same page about finishing our business. I know you were worried about that."

"Good. I wouldn't want to waste a perfectly good trip to find a mysterious missing map."

I heard the bathroom door squeak outside the bedroom door and footsteps retreat towards the living area of our suite. I waited a moment longer and, not hearing anything, opened the door a crack. I didn't see anyone so I quickly ran across the hall to the bathroom, pushed the door open, and then slammed it shut behind me.

"Uhh . . . good morning."

I looked up to see Peter still standing in the bathroom in front of the mirror.

"Oh my gosh. I'm so sorry. I thought you'd left." Mortified, I kept my head down and pulled the strings of my hoodie even tighter.

Peter laughed. "I did leave, but then I came back. I forgot something and had to go get it out of my suitcase." He stepped toward me with his hand out and I jumped back.

"Calm down—I'm just reaching for the doorknob. The bathroom's all yours now."

I locked the door behind Peter and sat on the floor with my back to the door, the hood of my jacket still covering my head. I wished I could crawl down the shower drain and never come out. I guess I had a new "most embarrassing moment" to share the next time the subject came up. I took a long shower letting the warm water wash away the sleepiness I still felt. It wasn't until the water started to turn cold and I realized Camille would kill me that I shut it off. I dressed quickly, ran a comb through my hair, and then darted back across the hall. I could finish my morning primping in the bedroom and let Cam have a turn in the bathroom—if she was even awake.

"Is there any water left?" She was sitting cross-legged on her bed staring at the wall.

"There's definitely water left, I just can't guarantee it will be the temperature you're used to."

She rolled her eyes and crawled off the front of her bed to rummage through her suitcase for clothes.

"Where'd Sophia go?" I asked.

"I dunno."

"She didn't say where she was going?"

"I haven't even seen her yet this morning. I think I heard voices in the living room a minute ago, but it might just be Peter watching TV."

"Oh."

She continued to sit on the floor in front of the suitcase, staring at me while I applied my makeup.

"What?" I snapped without thinking.

"Nothing," she said defensively. "I just find it amusing that you're suddenly so interested in your appearance. I've been trying for years to get you to care. Sophia comes along and all of a sudden you look like a prom queen."

"What are you saying? You don't think I look better?" I frowned into the mirror.

"That's not it. You look great. I'm just surprised, that's all. Was it Sophia that made you change, or Peter?"

I looked at her behind me through the mirror, but didn't answer.

She smiled. "Are you guys together, then?"

"No. I mean, I don't know. We haven't talked about it." It was hard to explain something that I didn't completely know the answer to.

"I think you guys would make a cute couple if that helps."

I turned and smiled at her. "Thanks. That means a lot coming from someone who can always find a date."

She shrugged and left the room.

"I agree. You guys *are* really cute together."

"*Sophia.* Stop doing that. I'm not going to be much help as a soul saver if you give me a heart attack before I can finish the job." I looked in the mirror as Sophia reappeared. She was still lounging on my bed, right where she'd been when I'd first left for the bathroom.

"Have you been in here the whole time?" I asked.

"Yeah, pretty much."

"Why didn't you talk to Cam?"

"She looked like a zombie sitting on her bed and staring at the wall. I didn't know if she was really awake or just on the verge of sleep walking so I decided to ignore her. Did you walk in on Peter a little while ago?"

"Maybe."

She started laughing. "I thought I heard his voice in there after you slammed the door shut. You need to loosen up, sister. I'm going to go see if Nick's back." She left the room and I was finally alone.

Loosen up? What is that supposed to mean? I finished getting ready and opened the bedroom door. I would have to face Peter at some point and I figured I should just get it over with.

The three of them—two ghosts and one living soul—were sitting in the living area looking totally relaxed. Sophia and Nick were next to each other on the couch and Peter was in a chair. Thankfully, he just smiled and nodded when I came out. I was grateful that he wasn't going to make me relive my embarrassment.

Nick had bought a variety of doughnuts and juices. I grabbed a maple bar and an orange juice.

"I only had doughnuts a couple of times before I died, but I really miss them. I keep eating them, hoping I can remember the taste, but they just taste like everything else," Nick commented as he took another bite of a chocolate and sprinkle covered doughnut.

"I'll just have to eat them for you then, bro," Peter said as he grabbed another one from the box and took a bite. Mmm . . . that's good."

Nick threw his half-eaten doughnut at Peter who stuck his arm out to deflect it. It ended up hitting me in the cheek.

I rolled my eyes and reached for a napkin. "What are we doing today?" I felt like I'd been asking that question a lot.

"Well, we thought we should try to find my old home and see if any of it still remains. Chances are it doesn't, but we should check. I'm hoping that even if the structure of the old barn is gone we can still dig around in the dirt and see if anything is buried out there," Sophia responded.

"What if something is built on top of the old site?" I asked.

"That's a real possibility, but I've got to check. I can't just wonder forever."

"Does the city look anything like it did when you were here before?" Peter asked.

"Only geographically," Nick answered. "We should be able to navigate fairly well just because the landmarks have stayed the same. It's a good thing Jeremiah and Elsa lived so close to the waterfront. That will make it easier, too."

"There are a lot of nice homes built near the water now. I hope you guys can get close enough to see anything without getting caught trespassing," Sophia added.

"What do you mean by 'you guys'? Won't you be there?"

Nick and Sophia exchanged looks. They did that a lot.

"Umm," Sophia began, "we think it would probably be best if you three did the actual searching—after it gets dark tonight. Nick and I can watch from the edges of the property for anything—or anyone—that appears out of place."

"That makes sense," Peter said.

"Maybe I should watch from the shadows, too. I don't have an aura like you two. Or maybe I should wait with the car. Someone should definitely wait with the car," Camille said as she came into the room with a towel wrapped around her hair. She plopped onto the couch with Nick and Sophia.

"*If* we find a place to search, we'll park the car far away, Cam. I don't think you'd want to sit in it. If you're nervous, you can always stay back here at the hotel. We're fine with that."

Camille crossed her arms over her chest and stuck out her chin. "I'm not nervous. I just don't think three of us should be poking around someone's property at night."

Peter rolled his eyes. "We can't exactly poke around someone's property during the day, Camille."

"Let's just check everything out before we decide what we're doing. For all we know there's a prison or a school or a grocery store built where the barn used to be. We can't make any definite plans until we see what's out there," Nick said.

We continued eating the doughnuts and juice while waiting for Camille to finish getting ready. By the time we left the hotel it wasn't even morning anymore. We climbed into the car with a map of the city we'd gotten from the concierge at the hotel. Sophia and Nick stared at it for a while, pointing and talking quietly. Finally, Sophia turned to the three of us in the backseat.

"Okay. We can tell on the map where the main part of Newport News is. I assume that's the part of town that was just starting to boom when I was alive. I lived south of the town so we're going to

246

take a road down that way. Hopefully we can see the water from this road," she said, pointing to a squiggly black line on the map.

"Sounds good. We have no idea what to watch for so we'll just be along for the ride. I trust you to navigate," I said.

Nick pulled out of the hotel's parking garage and into a bright June afternoon. The sky was blue except for a few gathering clouds off in the distance. He navigated through town by listening to Sophia's instructions and within a few minutes we were on the road they hoped would take us to Sophia's former home. We were all pretty quiet on the drive. Sometimes someone would make a comment about this or that, but for the most part, conversation didn't exist. We drove around for half an hour—turning onto side roads, making U-turns on roads that ended in nothing, and basically not finding much.

"Wait," Sophia suddenly yelled as Nick was about to turn off a road he'd been on. "Drive to that ridge over there. I know where we are."

Chapter 23

"You know where we are?" Camille asked excitedly.

"Yeah. There's a cemetery on that rise. That's where I'm buried."

We were all silent as Nick followed a winding road that took us to the top of the ridge. Sure enough, amongst the tall old trees was a scattering of headstones. A weathered wooden sign that looked as if it had been broken for many years leaned against a tree: Old Plantation Cemetery.

"I never did like hanging around here much. I guess I'm an odd ghost in that way. Maybe it was because there weren't any other ghosts around to talk to," Sophia thought out loud. "In the years I hung around Newport News, I only saw one up here. It was an old lady and she was only here for a few days before she finished her business and was gone. I haven't been back here since I learned how to make myself look human."

Nick shifted the car into park and Sophia opened the door. She didn't turn around or look as if she were waiting for us to follow so we all stayed in the car. Nick eventually got out and stood next to his door, but didn't go after her. We watched as she shuffled through piles of dead leaves and knee-high weeds to where she knelt in front of a small stone that had been knocked over. She picked the stone up and brushed it off, carefully placing it back on its base. She sat there for a few more minutes, with her back to us, and then got up and came back to the car. Nobody said anything until we'd driven back down the hill and reached the main road again.

"The cemetery was just off the main road into the village when I was alive. If you keep following this road, I think it will come to my old home." Sophia finally broke the silence.

"That's how I remember it." Nick reached over and held Sophia's hand.

We drove about a mile further until the road suddenly forked.

"I don't remember the road being like this, honey," Nick said.

"It wasn't, but that's the old Mason farm over there," Sophia pointed to the land just beyond the fork on the left. "The home isn't the same one that was there, but it's in the same spot and that grove of trees is the same—only the trees are a whole lot bigger."

The reality of our situation started to sink in. We'd gone there hoping to find something, but the pessimist in me had assumed we were on a wild goose chase. As I watched Sophia point at the farm where she'd died, I realized just how deep into the situation we were.

"If the Mason's farm is over there, we need to take the fork on the right, correct?" Nick asked.

"I think so. It doesn't look like much has been built up around here. I guess that's a good thing. Our chances of not finding a mini-mart built over top of the old barn are better," Sophia said.

We continued to follow the road until Sophia suddenly yelled, "Stop!"

Nick braked hard and we all lurched forward in our seats.

"This is it. I recognize it all. This new road circles around to what used to be the back part of the property."

"And that's where we used to dock the little rowboat when we came in from working on the *Mist Seeker*," Nick said excitedly as he pointed out the window toward the wide James River.

"Was *that* your home?" Camille asked in awe as she looked at the massive home built at the top of the slope.

"I wish, but no. That is definitely new. I'm sure whoever built it wanted to have a view of the water. From our home site the water wasn't visible. You had to walk down to the well before you had the best views. If the old well is still there, it will be back there at the edge of those trees." Sophia pointed to a spot beyond the home.

"Can you tell if any part of the old home or barn is still here?" Peter asked.

"Not from here. We'd have to be higher to see."

"You should pull into the driveway, Nick," I said.

"What if someone looks out the window and sees us?"

"I'll pretend like we're lost and looking for directions while Sophia disappears and sneaks around back to see if anything is there."

"Nice. Good plan, Jamie. I knew I brought you for a reason." Sophia winked at me.

Our tires crunched as we drove up the little gravel hill and parked on the circular drive in front of the house. Peter and I got out and stretched our legs before walking up to the front porch. Sophia "vanished" before we even got to the door and I hoped that she was well on her way. The view from there was spectacular and I wondered why the original landowners hadn't built on that spot.

"Do you want to do the talking or do you want me to?" Peter asked.

"Go ahead. I want to see if a man can actually ask for directions."

"Ha. Ha. Ha," he said as he pushed the button for the doorbell. We waited silently for a minute before we heard the tap, tap, tap of someone's shoes on the entryway tile. A tall, thin lady with graying hair pulled up in a tight bun opened the door.

"May I help you?"

"Yes, ma'am. We're trying to locate the Smith property and hoped you could help us," Peter answered.

"The Smiths you say? I'm afraid I don't know any Smiths out here. They might live in that new subdivision that's going in just off of Fillmore Street. What's the address, dear?"

"Uhh . . . I think I left it in the car." Peter looked like a deer caught in the headlights.

"You have a beautiful home, ma'am. Have you lived here long?" I jumped in.

"Thank you. I've lived here my whole life. I lived with my parents in an old home at the back of our property as a child, but my husband and I built this home out here in the early 70s. We liked the view much better from here."

"I love old homes. Is your other home still there?" I continued.

"Not really. The main structure burned down years ago so there's just a pile of rubble out there. There was an old barn, too, but it collapsed in on itself a couple of years ago. I keep telling my husband we need to just tear everything out since it's probably such a hazard out there, but we never get around to it." She chuckled.

I was so excited I could barely contain myself. I felt Sophia's presence next to me and quickly ended my conversation with the woman. "Thank you for your time, ma'am. I hope you have a great day," I said and pulled Peter down the porch with me.

"Did you hear that?" I whispered loudly as we walked back to the car.

"I did." Sophia's voice whispered back.

Peter looked surprised and glanced around. "How did you know she was there?"

"I told you I'm getting good at it."

Our car again crunched down the drive as we left. Camille rolled down her window and began snapping pictures with her phone.

"What are you doing? If she's looking out her window she might call the cops," I hissed.

"What's so illegal about taking pictures? I need to have something to show my parents and Allison when I get back or they aren't going to believe I really came to Virginia." She turned and started taking pictures on the water side of the car. She had a good point. We needed to remember to take some pictures with us in them, too.

When we were safely on the road back to Newport News Sophia reappeared. "I saw the barn. It's still there, sort of. The lady was right when she said it collapsed, but I bet we can get inside it. Since the road doesn't cut through there anymore we should be able to move around without anyone seeing us. This is even better than I imagined."

We filled Nick and Camille in on what we'd learned and a plan began to emerge.

"We need to find a hardware store and buy flashlights, gloves, and maybe a small shovel in case we have to dig," I said, taking command.

Peter suggested we buy black ski masks, too, but since I didn't know if he was being serious or just making a joke, I ignored the comment and continued on.

"We can park the car at the public beach access we passed just before the road forked. I didn't see any signs saying the parking lot closed at a certain time so I think that should be okay. Peter, Cam, and I will walk to where the road forks and go cross-country through the back of everyone's property until we get to the old house and barn. Nick and Sophia, one of you can trail us just until you have the barn in site, and then stop. The other one of you can go down to the new home and watch to make sure no one is alerted to our presence. We'll wait until nine thirty or ten to go because then it will be dark enough, but not so late as to attract attention if anyone sees us while we're parking at the beach."

Peter began to clap. "Well done, Ms. Peters, well done."

I rolled my eyes at him.

"It sounds like a great plan to me," Nick said.

We began our search for a hardware store as soon as we were back in the main part of the city. We also needed to find a place to eat since Peter's stomach was endlessly growling already.

"Hey, there's a hamburger place with a hardware store across the street over there. Turn right," Peter instructed.

While those of us with taste buds ate lunch—at four 'o-clock in the afternoon—Sophia and Nick crossed the street to the hardware store.

"Do you think we'll actually find anything tonight?" Camille asked.

"I don't know. Maybe I should have asked the lady who lives there now if she ever found a treasure map when she was playing in the barn as a child," I joked.

"She would have called the mental hospital." Peter twirled his finger next to his head as if to say I was crazy.

My phone rang and I pulled it out of my pocket and looked at the screen. "It's my dad. Whatever you do, stay quiet, Peter."

"Dad? Hi," I answered.

"How's Virginia?"

"It's beautiful. Sophia's home is amazing and it sits right over the James River. I don't know why they want to get a summer home in Massachusetts if they've got this kind of a home to live in."

I continued talking to him, describing the home that now sat on the old Goodwin property. I didn't know what it was like inside so I had to use my imagination.

"I'm glad you're having a good time. Remember to be polite to your host and hostess."

"I know, Dad. I will." I kicked Peter under the table. He was making faces at me in an attempt to get me to laugh.

"I'll see you in a few days."

We ended the call and I glared at Peter.

"What?" he asked, feigning innocence.

My cell phone rang again and I wondered what Dad had forgotten to tell me. I answered it, but it wasn't my dad.

"Jamie? The Goodwins are here." It was Sophia.

"Are you kidding me?" I asked fearfully.

"No. Nick and I just saw them go into a store next to where we are. I don't know if they're following us or if they came here on their own. They weren't looking our way." Sophia spoke in a half-whisper.

"What do we do?" I was panicking. Peter and Camille were both trying to get my attention to see what was wrong, but I waved them away and covered my other ear with my hand.

"I think we need to split up. We'll follow them when they come back out of the store. You guys need to call a cab and get back to the hotel. Go up to our rooms and don't open the door for anyone."

"Maybe we should just walk to the hotel. It's only a couple of blocks."

"I don't want to risk you being seen."

"Okay. I get it. Keep in touch, please."

"I will. Be careful." Sophia hung up her phone and I turned back to Peter and Camille who were looking at me expectantly.

"Well?" Camille asked.

"Jeremiah and Elsa are across the street."

"*What*?" Camille whimpered and Peter ducked down in the booth.

"How did they find us? We were so *careful*." Peter was angry.

"I don't know. Sophia said they didn't look like they were following us. She's wondering if they came to look for the map and we just *happened* to cross paths."

"I knew I should have stayed home. Why did I agree to this? I have seriously gone crazy. Who in their right mind would fly to an entirely different state to try to help ghosts of all people? I thought this would be a fun trip, but now I'm having second thoughts." Camille was on the verge of tears again. I put my arm around her and she laid her head on my shoulder.

"It'll be fine. Nick and Sophia aren't going to let them out of their sight."

For what felt like the millionth time in the last few days, we called a cab. We instructed the driver to pull around to a back entrance, away from any roads. After paying him, we jumped from the car and ran for the door. I was nervous even being in the elevator. I fumbled for my room card and finally got our door open. We locked the door and the deadbolt out of habit, not that it would have actually helped.

"*Any news?*" I texted Sophia.

My phone rang a minute later. "Hey, are you back at the hotel?" Nick rushed.

"Yes. We just got here."

"Good. Stay there."

"What's going on?"

"We followed the Goodwins when they came out of the store. They hailed a cab and came to a hotel about three miles from where you are. They didn't look around at all. We think they're here on their own and haven't yet realized that we're here, too."

"That's good, right?"

"Yeah, except that we're going to have to follow them everywhere they go. Sophia's driving to our hotel right now. She's going to give you all the stuff we bought and then come back here. Jamie, you guys are going to have to go to the old barn by yourselves tonight."

My heart thumped. "Okay. Don't worry about us. We can do it, Nick."

"I know. I trust my soul saver."

Sophia tapped on the door soon after I ended the call.

"Here's all the gear we bought. I can't stay long because I need to get the car back to Nick in case the Goodwins leave their hotel. I don't think he can keep up with a car if he's on foot."

Peter took the bags from Sophia and set them on the little table in our room.

"Good luck tonight." Sophia hugged each of us and then vanished.

"And just like that, we're on our own again," Peter said.

"I'm scared. Traipsing through an old barn was one thing, doing it at night was another, but doing it without Nick and Sophia as bodyguards is downright freaky, especially knowing that the Goodwins are out there somewhere." Camille frowned.

"Cam, if that's how you feel you can stay behind. I think it would be a good idea to have a middleman anyway. You're okay with that, right Peter?"

He nodded.

"I don't want you to be out there if you think you might freak out. That will just make things worse. Besides, someone should stay behind to explain what happened when everyone else turns up missing."

"*Please* don't go missing. I just don't think I was cut out for this dangerous stuff."

The evening dragged as we paced the hotel room, anxious for what we were about to do. Finally, it was time to get ready to go. Peter and I searched our suitcases along with Sophia's and Nick's for the darkest clothing we could find. The clouds that had been gathering earlier in the afternoon covered the skies and threatened to release their rain. In my nervousness, I yanked on the shoelace of my tennis shoe so hard it tore off.

"Dang it," I cursed. "I'm going to the lobby to see if they sell shoelaces in the little store. I'll be right back," I yelled as I slammed our door behind me.

There were a lot of people roaming around the lobby and I suddenly became self-conscious. *What if Nick and Sophia lost track of the Goodwins? What if the Goodwins have other ghosts working with them and they're following us? Any one of these people could be a ghost and I wouldn't even know it.* I closed my eyes and concentrated, trying to see if I could sense anything.

"Is everything okay? Can I help you find anything?" I opened my eyes to find the clerk tapping me on my shoulder.

"Umm . . . shoelaces. I need shoelaces," I said, embarrassed.

"We have some right over here," she said as she led me to a box in the back. I chose a pair and paid for them before grabbing a couple of matchbooks with the hotel's logo out of a basket by the cash register on my way out. I figured I needed a souvenir of our little adventure.

At nine o'clock, I called Sophia. "We're ready to leave. Are the Goodwins still in their hotel?"

"I hope so. They're staying in a place where all the doors open to the outside and we haven't seen any auras or people come out yet, but it's hard to watch all the doors at once."

"Good. We'll try to hurry and we'll call you if we find something."

"I can't wait until I have my license. This sucks," Peter said as we waited for yet another cab to take us out to the beach.

"I know. We're so close, yet so far away." Peter and I both had birthdays in the fall and had less than six months until we could get our permits. It couldn't come soon enough.

We gave instructions to our driver on where we wanted to go. "Are you sure you want to go there in the rain?" he asked in a thick accent.

"We're sure," Peter answered.

The driver muttered something under his breath about stupid teenagers, but obediently drove us where we asked. I can only imagine what he thought we were going to do there. By the time we pulled into the beach access parking lot, the skies had started to release their cargo and giant raindrops were landing on the windshield. The driver didn't say anything else to us as we paid him and jumped out. Peter grabbed my hand and started walking toward a rocky outcropping.

"He thinks we're up to something," I said, nodding toward the cab that slowly turned around.

"If he thinks we're here to do something, we might as well give him a show," he said and pulled me in for a hug.

"*Peter.*" I punched him in the chest.

"I'm just kidding, Jamie." He laughed at me.

"I know. I'm just tense."

"Yeah, I can tell."

He grabbed my hand again and we continued walking in the dark. As soon as the taillights of the cab were out of sight we reversed our direction and headed back to the road on which we'd just arrived. Making sure there were no cars in sight we darted across the road. Following a barbed wire fence, we stayed close to the highway until we got to the place where it forked. At one point a car came toward us and we crouched down with our hoods covering our faces. I felt like a criminal. I was about to trespass on private property, so I guess I was.

At the fork, we left the main road and I crawled through the fence to the field on the other side. My hair got caught in some of the barbs on the way through and Peter had to help me untangle it. I had to hold the barbs up for him since he was a lot bigger, but he managed to shimmy through with only a couple of scratches.

The rain had turned from an occasional drip to a full downpour and the ground was getting slippery. I lost my footing as we ran through a field and started to fall. Peter caught me just before I hit the ground and held me up. Hand in hand we made it to the first set of trees and stopped to get our bearings. I put my hands on my knees, panting—partly from our dash through the field and partly from anxiety. I desperately wanted to turn on a flashlight, but that would be stupid. I didn't know how many homes were out there, but I could see a few lights off in the distance. We didn't want someone coming to investigate.

We continued running through the trees, our clothes dripping wet and our feet sloshing until a clearing came in to view. "Peter, I think that's the old well Sophia told us about," I said.

We could see a crumbling rock structure just past the line of trees, and beyond that the lights of the new home that had been built on the Goodwin property.

"You're right. It's exactly where Sophia told us it would be. Why do they still have so many lights on over there at the house? It's ten o'clock. I thought old people went to bed early."

"With our luck, they're probably having a party tonight."

We watched the house for a little while to make sure no one was staring out any windows or on the back porch or upstairs balcony before we quietly stepped out from the trees and over to the well.

"So much of Sophia and Nick's history surrounds this place," I said as I ran my hands along the top of it. I peered over the edge, but it was too dark to see anything. An old wooden bucket was still attached to a rope hanging from the top cover of the well. I wondered if it was the same one Sophia would send down to retrieve water every morning when she was alive.

"Hey, Jamie, look at this. I think the path to the old house is right here." Peter had crouched down and turned a flashlight on, aiming it at the ground with his back toward the house to help block the light.

I followed behind him, stepping where he stepped as we did our best to follow the overgrown ruts up the sloping land in the rain. A few minutes later we found ourselves standing at the burned out shell of Sophia's former home. An overwhelming urge to cry suddenly came over me and I had to grab onto a piece of the charred wood to keep my balance. My chest burned and every part of my body screamed, *This is it.*

"Jamie? Are you okay?" Peter asked.

"Yeah, I think so. I feel weird. I think it's my connection to Nick and Sophia. I feel like I'm on the right path and I'm being urged on."

He didn't say anything. It was a strange feeling to try to describe and I'm sure the only thing he understood was that he couldn't understand. We walked around the structure for a minute, trying to see if anything stood out. Nothing did. The home was a complete loss and barely even looked like a home. If I didn't know better, I would have thought it was nothing more than the remnants of a huge bonfire. With the strange feeling still urging me on, I told Peter we needed to move to the barn. From where we were we could only see the upper floor of the new home and we watched as one by one the lights went out. *Good—they've finally gone to bed.*

The rain slowed, but we were already soaked through and both of us were shivering. Peter kept his arm around my shoulder, trying to warm me up as we crossed to the old barn. The lady of the house was right—it *had* collapsed in on itself, but it wasn't nearly as bad as I'd imagined. Instead of a pile of rubble, a dreadfully dilapidated building loomed in front of us.

"Nick and Sophia said there were two entrances to the barn with a walkway between them and stalls on either side," I reminded Peter as we approached. "Nick said we should go in the back entrance if possible."

We circled around the building and stared at the rotting wood. The doorway no longer existed. In its place were giant pieces of wood, splintered like matchsticks.

"This doesn't look safe. I think you should stay out here while I go in," Peter volunteered.

"No way. I'm going in, too. I didn't come all this way to just watch."

"You definitely aren't as much like Camille as I thought you were."

"Is that a bad thing?"

"Not at all. I like this side of you."

We examined the pile again and shook a few of the bigger pieces of wood to see how sturdy they were. Nothing moved and the jumble seemed to hold up. Peter climbed onto the pile and jumped up and down a couple of times. Still nothing.

"Okay. Let's do this." He reached down and pulled me up next to him.

A cracking sound in the trees behind the barn stopped us. We both crouched down, not daring to move. I don't think I even breathed. *There it is again*. It sounded as if someone were stepping on tiny twigs. My legs wobbled from crouching on the pile of wood, and I was getting lightheaded from holding my breath. Suddenly, a figure emerged from the trees.

Chapter *24*

P eter nudged me and tilted his head toward the figure that had just stepped from the trees. "Do you see it?" he whispered.

I nodded, terrified. "Who is it?"

He snickered. "Jamie, it's a deer."

I looked closer and sure enough, the figure stood on four legs, looking our way with its ears alert and listening. Peter tossed a stick to the ground and the deer bounded away back into the trees.

"I thought for sure it was going to be Jeremiah," I finally breathed.

"I have a feeling that if Jeremiah were to come, he'd be a lot quieter."

"Thanks, but that's not reassuring at all."

"It wasn't supposed to be."

We continued to scramble up the pile until we found an opening big enough for us to slip through. Peter turned on his flashlight and shined it down into the hole. Debris littered the floor below us, but for the most part it was open space. The main part of the barn had been preserved when the walls started to crumble.

"Let me help you go down first," he said.

"Okay." I slid through the hole on my stomach as far as I could and then Peter took both my hands and lowered me down. I let go of him and dropped the last two feet to the floor. The thud of my feet hitting the ground echoed through the room. I flipped on my light and shined it around, turning in every direction. A mouse scurried across the floor in front of me and I shivered.

"Is it clear?" Peter called through the hole.

"Yeah. Come down."

He dropped through the hole and landed gracefully on his feet. For some reason I began to laugh.

"What's so funny?"

"All of this. Last month I was making plans to spend my summer at the library and now I'm trespassing in an old barn, in a different state, while looking for a treasure map. I keep expecting to wake up from a really long dream."

"Would you rather be at the library than doing this?"

I didn't even have to think about it. "Absolutely not."

"Nick said he put Jeremiah's pouch under a floorboard just outside the second stall from the back on the right, correct?" Peter asked.

"That's how I remember it."

We both dropped to our knees and began to brush dirt and debris away with our gloved hands. None of the boards were the slightest bit loose.

"Look at these nails," Peter said as he aimed the light close to the floor, "they've definitely been added since the barn was built. They're modern."

My heart fell. "Do you think the whole floor has been replaced? If so, whoever tore it out would have found the pouch for sure."

Peter slowly walked forward, still bending down with his light close to the floor.

"Look over here, Jamie. Do you see the difference between the nails over there and the ones here?"

I walked to him and crouched down. "The nail heads are a different shape," I said.

"Exactly. I would bet money that the ones over here are from the 1800s. I don't think the floor has been completely replaced. They probably just nailed down the loose boards at some point."

"Is that something you learned from your parents?"

He grinned. "Sometimes it pays to live with a couple of archaeologists."

We crawled back to the spot where we thought the pouch should be and began to pull on the boards. It was a tight fit and I could barely fit my fingers into the cracks between the boards. I removed my gloves and pulled.

"Stand back, I'm going to see if I can pry a board up," Peter said. I obeyed and turned to see him holding an old pitchfork.

He wedged the tines under a board and started prying. I helped push back on the pitchfork's handle with him, but nothing budged. I stood in front of the pitchfork and we kept pushing, putting all our weight into it, until the handle snapped and we both flew backward. I hit my head on one of the old stalls and immediately felt a trickle of blood run down my forehead. I pulled my hood tighter around my face in hopes that Peter wouldn't notice.

"You okay?"

"Yeah. I'm fine," I lied.

I crawled back to the board we'd been working on. "Peter, we got it loose." I yanked and pulled on the board until it broke off with a thunderous cracking sound. Peter moved quickly to my side and shined his flashlight at the dirt below the board I'd just removed. There was nothing but empty space.

"Pull up another board." Now that we had a way to get at the boards we could pry them up fairly easy with our hands and the little shovels we'd brought. My bare hands were full of slivers and started to bleed. I should have put my gloves back on, but I didn't even care.

Underneath the seventh board sat the old, brown, leather pouch. The burning sensation in my chest deepened and I again felt lightheaded.

"We found it," I whispered in amazement.

"You do the honors," Peter said as he shone the light at the pouch.

I reached down and lifted it from the hole. It was covered in dust, but not wet—which was a good thing considering where it was found. I sat on the floor, cross-legged, and unwound the string holding it closed. Peter sat next to me, his head close to mine.

The papers inside were brittle and I touched them gingerly, afraid they would fall apart in my hands. I slowly turned each sheet over. Most of them seemed to be financial records—contracts, and things like that. Finally, near the bottom of the pile was a page with squiggles, symbols and weird markings. At the top of the page was a large 'H' written just the same as the signature on the letter to the mysterious Catherine we'd found back home in my attic.

Peter and I looked at each other. *This is it. This is what we came all this way to find.* Suddenly we both laughed.

Peter reached over, put his hands on my shoulders, and kissed me right on the lips. I felt the familiar tingle run through my spine and up through my body, warming me all over. Again, he pulled away after just a few seconds. Our moment was interrupted by the ringing of my phone. The sound of such a modern device in that cave of antiquity was horribly out of place as the noise bounced from wall to wall.

"It's Sophia," I whispered before putting the phone to my ear and saying, "Hello?"

"Jam . . . I . . . sorry . . . Goodwins . . ."

"Sophia, you're breaking up. I can't tell what you're saying."

"Goodwi . . . gone . . . can't . . . find . . . hide . . ." The phone beeped, alerting me that the call had been dropped.

"Crap, Peter, I think she said they lost the Goodwins. We've got to get out of here. I'm sure their old home site is one of the first places they'll go."

We scrambled to put the remaining pages back in the pouch and Peter slipped it inside his jacket. I carefully folded the map and tucked it down inside my shirt. Going back out the way we came in would be difficult and it would take a long time. We decided to try the front entrance to the barn instead. We wouldn't have to climb, but we'd have to move some of the boards apart. It probably wasn't the safest idea, but we were left with no other choice. I wanted to get as far from there as we could get—and fast.

"Pull on that board," Peter commanded as he pushed on another. He used the broken pitchfork as a wedge to make an opening just big enough for me to crawl through to the cold air outside.

The rain had completely stopped by that point and the earth smelled musty in the darkness. I held the boards I'd just slipped between as Peter tried to climb out after me. Since he was bigger, the opening had to be pried open even farther. I pulled as hard as I could, but just as I managed to open up a space big enough for him to slip through, the boards above shifted and the barn began to groan as boards snapped and pieces fell.

"*Peter*," I screamed as the wall he was climbing through completely collapsed. Flying debris knocked me to the ground, but I quickly jumped back up on my hands and knees and crawled to where I'd last seen Peter.

"Jamie. Jamie!" he yelled from somewhere under the rubble.

"I'm here, Peter."

"Are you okay?"

"I'm fine, but what about you?" A sob escaped my throat as I pulled at the boards holding him down.

"I'm okay. They mostly fell around me. My foot is stuck, though. I can't get it out."

I continued to pull on the boards, but every time I did the pile shifted. I was terrified that if I pulled on the wrong board the entire structure would collapse, crushing Peter beneath it.

"Peter, I can't do this without help." I fumbled for the phone in my pocket, grateful that Camille had stayed back at the hotel—she could get Sophia and Nick to come help. I turned it on and began to dial before I realized that I still didn't have any reception.

"Peter?"

"I'm still here."

"Are you sure you're okay?"

"I think so."

"I can't get any reception on my phone. I'm going to go find a place where I can call Camille. Will you be all right until I get back?"

From under the pile of wood I heard him laugh. "I'll be fine, Jamie. It's not like I'm going anywhere anytime soon. *Please* be careful."

"I will." I stood to leave and turned around.

"I can help."

I screamed again, breaking the silence of the still night air. Birds in the nearby trees fluttered away, rattling the leaves as they went. And there, right in front of me, appeared Jeremiah Goodwin.

"What're ya doing in the old barn?" he asked in a mocking tone.

I didn't say anything.

"You wouldn't be looking for something would you?"

I remained silent.

He snickered. "After we talked to you the last time, it occurred to us that we'd been tracking the wrong person all these years. Sophia was too dumb to steal the map. She couldn't possibly have come up with the idea on her own. And then it hit us like a ton of bricks—I killed Nicholas Trenton the same time Sophia died. He knew where I kept things in my house, and he wasn't as stupid as Sophia had been. We decided to confront him about it and guess what? He was nowhere to be found."

267

I involuntarily shuddered as his tone became angrier and he took a step toward me. I took a step back.

"Don't worry. Our friendly little librarian here paid a visit to your father to find out where you were and why you hadn't returned your overdue books." Elsa appeared out of the shadows behind him. "Imagine our surprise when he told her that you'd gone to Virginia of all places."

They've been to my house? They talked to my dad? My mind raced. I had to get out of there, but how? I didn't want to leave Peter, but there was no way I could pull him from his trap by myself. I didn't know where Sophia and Nick were and I had no way of contacting Camille. I bit my lip to keep myself from crying. I had to stay strong if I was going to get out of the situation.

Jeremiah was done pretending to be nice. "*Give me the map,*" he bellowed as he lunged toward me.

"Jamie, *run.*" Peter broke his silence and yelled from beneath the rubble.

I didn't hesitate, but turned on my heel and bolted down the path we'd come in on, back toward the old well. I stumbled, but caught myself and continued in a full-on sprint, hoping there was nothing on the dark path ahead of me. At first I heard the yells and footfalls of the Goodwins behind me, but I soon realized they'd stopped.

I dared to sneak a peek behind me, but I couldn't see anything. My eyes darted in every direction. They had to have vanished. I knew that I couldn't outrun a ghost and at any moment they might reappear in front of me and I would be caught.

I made it all the way to the well and stopped, my chest heaving from the run I'd just made. I gripped the edge of the well as I tried to catch my breath.

The lights of the new house were still turned off. I thought about screaming in an attempt to alert the owners, but I was afraid the

Goodwins would just harm them right along with the rest of us. They had no respect for human life.

I was still searching the shadows, waiting for the Goodwins to reappear when I realized my mistake. I'd left Peter alone. That had to have been why my pursuers stopped.

I didn't know what to do. *Should I go back for him? Should I try to call Sophia or Nick again? Should I pray?* Sophia had told me that the only way to beat Jeremiah and Elsa was to con them, but I didn't know how to do that.

I didn't have long to think about it because only a moment later I heard them coming up the path I'd just run in on. I could tell by the noises being made that the Goodwins had Peter with them, and he was fighting to be free.

"Get your hands off me," he yelled.

I heard a thump and Peter moaned. Jeremiah had definitely done something to him. I stepped out from behind the well.

"Let him go," I yelled boldly.

"Give me what I want first," Jeremiah answered. He held up a battered Peter with one hand as the other hand held a gun to Peter's head.

I'd come so close to getting what I thought was the key to Sophia and Nick's extrication, yet I was so far. I hesitated for a minute and then reached down inside my shirt and pulled out the sheet of paper.

"Is this what you want?" I held up the paper, not yet ready to give it up.

"It's the map," Elsa squeaked. I could feel the evil of the people around me as thick as the mist that was gathering after the rain.

"Give it to me," Elsa snapped.

"Not until you let him go." I held the paper up with both hands as if I was going to tear it in half.

"Well I guess we have a problem then—because we're not letting him go until I have that map in my hand," she hissed back.

I had to stall until I could think of a plan. "If I give you the map, you'll just shoot him anyway. In fact, you'll probably just shoot me, too."

Jeremiah laughed. "That sounds like a great idea. No one can pin anything on us—since we're dead—and I haven't killed anyone for a while. I was kind of starting to miss it. I wonder if we can make it look like a tragic murder-suicide of two teenage lovers."

Tears again threatened to spill from my eyes to my cheeks. That time they weren't so much tears of sadness or fear as they were tears of anger. Anger for the lives the Goodwins had ruined in the past, and anger at myself for getting Peter involved in the stupid affair. I stuck my hand in my pocket. I thought if I could feel the right buttons, I could dial Camille's number on my phone—if I had reception. She might not be able to do anything to save us, but maybe she could at least hear what happened to us so she wouldn't have to live with the mystery of how her best friends were killed.

When I reached into my pocket, my hand brushed against something small and square next to my phone. I felt it again. Even though every part of me was still damp from all the rain, that thing was miraculously still dry. My heart thumped. I knew I had to do it. It might mean that I was sacrificing my life and Peters, but I was compelled to do it to save the souls of Nick and Sophia.

"Enough games, hand it over," Jeremiah growled.

A split-second of hesitation was all I still needed before I yanked the hotel matchbook out of my pocket and tore a little cardboard match from the row. I rubbed it along the coarse back of the wrapper, praying that it would light. It started immediately, a little orange glow breaking up the darkness of the night.

"What're you doing?" Elsa demanded.

"I'm getting revenge. For Sophia . . . for Nick . . . and for everyone that was on the *Mary Celeste*," I said. I lifted the brittle paper to the match and it began to burn, engulfing the aged paper immediately.

"Noooooo. You *witch!*" Elsa screamed and lunged for the burning paper.

I stuck my hand out over the top of the well and let go. Jeremiah shoved Peter to the ground and jumped to the well. He vanished immediately and I felt a brush of air pass me as he raced into the well after the burning paper. The screams of horror coming from inside the well echoed up at me and I stepped back, trembling.

"I'm going to kill you." Elsa's eyes had become wild and she loomed large as she bent to retrieve the gun Jeremiah had dropped as he jumped into the well.

I backed away slowly. I knew there was no outrunning them that time. They had no cards left to play—nor did I. Elsa lifted the gun as Jeremiah reappeared at the edge of the well, shaking with rage. I closed my eyes and covered my face, waiting for the sound or the pain, whichever came first. But instead of a gunshot, I heard a scream and a thump. I opened my eyes to see Nick standing over a lifeless Elsa, holding one of the shovels we'd left at the barn. Sophia was right beside Nick, staring down Jeremiah, posed for a fight.

Elsa recovered quickly and tried to sit up, but in the faint glow of the moonlight I saw a look of pure terror spread over her face. Confused, I looked at Jeremiah. He had the same terrified expression, staring at his wife.

"Nooo . . ." Elsa moaned quietly. "Not *now.*" She tried to crawl toward Jeremiah as the rest of us gawked in wonder. But just before their outstretched hands touched, their bodies slowly disappeared. Nothing remained except for a pile of clothes and the pistol that had threatened to end my life.

Peter picked himself up from the ground and limped toward me. I whipped my head around, trying to figure out where the Goodwins had vanished to. Sophia sat on the ground where she was and sobbed—huge, body shaking sobs. Nick hunched over her, his arms wrapped tightly around her heaving shoulders.

"Where are they?" My voice trembled in fear.

"They're gone," Nick said.

"I know they're gone, but where did they go?" My body still pumped adrenaline and I couldn't calm down.

Sophia lifted her head and instead of the fear I expected to see, I saw the smile I loved so much. They were tears of joy.

"They're gone, Jamie. Forever. You finished their business for them. That's why when they vanished this time their clothes were left behind. Their auras disappeared with them. They're not *ever* coming back." She sobbed again.

I was so overwhelmed and relieved that I had to sit down, too. I stepped back against the rock well and slid down until I was sitting on the ground. Peter sat next to me and put his arm around my shoulders.

"You got our revenge for us, Jamie. You took away the thing that was most important to them, just like they took away the things that were most important to us when we were alive," Nick said quietly.

A light came on at the back of the new house. "Hello? Is someone out there?" a male voice called from the balcony.

"We've got to get out of here," Peter whispered. "We can't just disappear like you two."

We quickly gathered the Goodwins clothing and, removing their wallets first, dropped the pile and the gun into the old well. We listened until we heard a faint thud and knew the items had reached the bottom. It would be a long time, if ever, before they were found again.

Peter stuffed the wallets into his jacket with the leather pouch, took my hand, and we all ran into the trees beyond the well, back to where our wild night had started.

We didn't get very far into the grove before Sophia yelled for Peter and me to wait. I turned to see that she and Nick had stopped a few paces back. They weren't moving.

"What's wrong?" I whispered loudly.

"Jamie . . ." From the tone of her voice, I knew immediately what was wrong.

They'd finished their business, too.

"I can feel the pulling sensation everyone talks about—it . . . it's . . . time for us to go."

A lump worked its way up my throat. I couldn't speak. I wanted to say so much, but I couldn't form my thoughts and feelings into sentences. Sophia let go of Nick and walked slowly toward me, concentrating hard on every step she took. She put her arms around me and we hugged, both of us crying into each other's shoulder.

"Thank you," she managed to whisper.

I still couldn't say anything but I hugged her tighter, desperate not let go of the one person I'd ever felt was truly like a sister.

"Sophia . . . it's time," Nick said quietly from where he stood.

Sophia unwound herself from my arms as another sob escaped my throat. She walked back toward Nick and Peter took over the place she'd just vacated, holding me tight in his strong arms.

"Jamie . . . I should . . . warn you." Sophia stopped to catch her breath. "Once someone . . . becomes a soul saver . . . they're more likely . . . to become one . . . again."

"What did you say?" I lifted my head to look at her, but it was too late. She and Nick were gone—and their clothes lay entwined on the muddy ground of the forest floor.

Chapter *25*

Morning came with a vengeance the next day. The sun had returned and mocked us with its presence. I would have preferred to go to sleep and not wake up for a month. After Nick and Sophia had extricated the night before, Peter and I gathered their things and went in search of their rental car. We found it parked at the fork in the road at the spot where Peter and I had climbed through the barbed wire fence hours earlier.

We found the car keys in the pocket of Nick's jeans and Peter insisted he could drive. I climbed into the passenger seat. That was the least crazy thing we'd done all night.

We drove back to Newport News and into the parking garage of our hotel in silence. Everything we did seemed to be done in a blur. I didn't want to explain everything to Camille. All I wanted to do was take a bath and pull the covers over my head, but Camille met us at the door, gasping in shock when she saw the way we looked.

"What happened to you? Where's Nick and Sophia?" she said.

I still couldn't speak so I just walked past her and closed the bathroom door behind me, stripping down to nothing and climbing into the tub before it was even full. I sunk down into the water with nothing but my mouth and nose showing. When I finally emerged an hour later, Camille was sitting on the floor outside the bathroom door, holding my pajamas for me.

"Peter told me what happened."

I took one look at her and tears started streaming again. The two of us sat in the hall and cried for a long time. Peter had gone back to the other hotel room by then and it was just the two of us. Eventually I crawled into bed and stayed there until noon the next day.

We had three more days on our hotel reservation and before our round-trip airline tickets would work. We weren't really sure what to do with ourselves. We didn't dare risk driving the rental car again. We took some time going through Sophia and Nick's luggage—keeping some things and discarding others. Camille was devastated that she hadn't gotten to say goodbye to Sophia and Nick, but she was ecstatic to claim most of Sophia's clothing. I didn't think I could ever bring myself to wear any of it. The memories were too close.

I did take the flowers Sophia had carried during her wedding and pressed them between the pages of a book. I would do something with them later—when I was ready.

We took a wad of cash we found in Jeremiah's wallet and ordered a simple headstone for Sophia's grave. "Nicholas and Sophia Briggs Trenton—Together At Last, Never To Be Forgotten" was the inscription we chose. We thought it was much better than the crudely etched stone currently at her grave that only said, "Sophia Mason." We cleared the dead leaves and weeds from her grave and covered the site with flowers, hoping Nick and Sophia were somewhere watching—knowing we had not forgotten them. The rare visitor to the Old Plantation Cemetery would never know the true identity of the person buried there, but maybe wherever she was, she could watch and appreciate our gesture. The three of us sat under the tree next to her grave for a long time that day.

"Do you wonder where the map would have led? I mean, if you hadn't set it on fire, do you think we could have figured it out?" Peter asked.

"I know I've been wondering about it. What if there was *actual* buried treasure somewhere?" Camille added.

I looked at Peter and then looked back at the ground. "I didn't burn the map."

"What?"

"I didn't burn the map."

"What are you talking about, Jamie?"

"When we were getting ready to leave the barn I saw another piece of paper lying in the dirt. Out of curiosity I picked it up. It was just an old bill of sale for some horses, but I stuffed it in my shirt with the map anyway. That's the paper I lit on fire."

"Are you being serious right now? Why didn't you tell us before now?"

I shrugged. "After the Goodwins disappeared, I was scared to say anything because I didn't want them to come back."

"Jamie, do you realize you conned the con man?" Peter asked incredulously.

I nodded.

"Ooo! We're going on a treasure hunt," Camille squealed.

"Not now," I said. "Someday we will, but not now. That adventure can wait."

AUTHOR'S NOTE

Shadow of a Life is a work of fiction. But not entirely. In November of 1872, Captain Benjamin Briggs really did board the *Mary Celeste* with his wife Mary and daughter Sophia. Captain Briggs was a seasoned mariner and sailing had been a part of his family for generations.

In early December, the ship was spotted by Captain David Morehouse's ship, the *Dei Gratia,* in the middle of the Atlantic Ocean. Morehouse was an acquaintance of Captain Briggs. As the *Dei Gratia* approached the *Mary Celeste* it became apparent that something was not right. After boarding the ship, the crew of the *Dei Gratia* found that no one remained aboard. The *Mary Celeste* had become a ghost ship, seeming to sail itself.

Although theory after theory has been given for what happened on that fateful trip, no one will ever be able to say for sure what really occurred. And no one will ever know what *really* happened to little Sophia Matilda Briggs.

Special thanks to Brian Hicks. I found "Ghost Ship: The Mysterious True Story of the Mary Celeste and Her Missing Crew" by Brian Hicks to be an extremely important research tool.

Haven Waiting

Soul Saver: Book Two

Turn the page for an excerpt.

She rose to her feet, brushing the dirt from her clothes, and stuck her hand out for me to shake. "I don't think I've introduced myself properly. I'm Haven Mills."

My mouth dropped and I stared at her. *Haven? With an H? Could this be the ghost of the person who made the map?* My mind screamed and every part of my body felt as if electricity was running through it. I'd felt that feeling before—right before we found the map in the barn in Virginia.

Haven still held her hand out to me and I forced myself to reach one of my own trembling hands out to shake hers. It felt as if a shock went through my body the moment our skin touched. I knew Haven felt it, too. We continued to stare at each other for a long moment, not breaking the grip of our hands. I forgot that Peter and Camille were even there.

Finally, she whispered, "How do you know about ghosts?"

My voice caught in my throat, but I managed to choke out, "I'm a soul saver."

About the Author

Tifani Clark grew up on a farm in southeastern Idaho (yes, that's where they grow all the potatoes) as the middle of five children. She had a lot of space to imagine and daydream and often pictured herself as a character in one of the many books she read. She was habitually found pretending to be Scarlet O'Hara. Tifani loves mystery and hates it when one goes unsolved. She is married to the love of her life and is the mother to four fabulous children. When not writing, she enjoys playing the violin and piano and traveling to new places. She especially enjoys visits to national parks and places of historical significance.